"Shed your garments and join me beneath the blanket."

Sara shook her finger at him. "There'll be no joining tonight."

"I agree, not tonight."

Why didn't she believe him?

She decided she couldn't be a coward and besides she didn't want him thinking he was in command, so she shed her skirt and blouse, glad she had donned a shift before leaving the abbey.

It was plain white linen and hung like a sack on her.

Cullen shook his head. "That is an ugly shift. Take it off."

"I will not."

"Afraid to stand naked in front of your husband?"

Again a challenge she wasn't certain she could match.

He threw the blankets off him. "I have no trouble baring all in front of you."

Other AVON ROMANCES

A Dangerous Beauty *by Sophia Nash*
The Devil's Temptation *by Kimberly Logan*
Mistress of Scandal *by Sara Bennett*
The Templar's Seduction *by Mary Reed McCall*
A Warrior's Taking *by Margo Maguire*
When Seducing a Spy *by Sari Robins*
Wild Sweet Love *by Beverly Jenkins*

Coming Soon

Tempted at Every Turn *by Robyn DeHart*
What Isabella Desires *by Anne Mallory*

And Don't Miss These
Avon Romantic Treasures
From Avon Books

Bewitching the Highlander *by Lois Greiman*
How to Engage an Earl *by Kathryn Caskie*
The Viscount in Her Bedroom *by Gayle Callen*

DONNA FLETCHER

The Highlander's Bride

AVON BOOKS
An Imprint of HarperCollinsPublishers

AVON BOOKS
An Imprint of HarperCollins*Publishers*
10 East 53rd Street
New York, New York 10022-5299

Copyright © 2007 by Donna Fletcher
ISBN: 978-0-06-113626-9
ISBN-10: 0-06-113626-3
www.avonromance.com

First Avon Books paperback printing: July 2007

Avon Trademark Reg. U.S. Pat. Off. and in Other Countries,
Marca Registrada, Hecho en U.S.A.
HarperCollins® is a registered trademark of HarperCollins Publishers.

Printed in the U.S.A.

10 9 8 7 6 5 4 3 2 1

The Highlander's Bride

Chapter 1

"**L**ord, please send me a husband."

Sara was desperate. Otherwise, she wouldn't have been kneeling on the hard stone floor in the chapel of Stilmere Abbey for near an hour, praying.

The good Lord certainly had to have heard her by now, she thought, and realized she required immediate attention.

"I need a husband now, Lord, this very moment. My father isn't going to wait any longer. You must send me a husband today."

Sara expelled a heavy breath and got off her knees, stretching the ache out of her back. She paced in front of the small wooden altar draped in fine white linens, a gold cross gracing the center.

All she had to do was obey her father's edict and marry the man of his choosing.

Donald McHern was a large man built as solid as a tree trunk and his width almost equal to one. His craggy narrow face was beset with a mane of fiery red hair that clansmen swore looked as if it were set aflame

1

when he lost his temper, and his height towered over all in the clan. The soft blue-green color of his eyes was the only thing that attested to the man having a spark of kindness. But his people considered him a fair laird, would attest to his attributes and often sang his praise. He provided well for the clan and kept them free of senseless feuds, though he took up his sword whenever necessary.

The clan had remarked on their chieftain's fairness when her father had issued the same edict to Sara as he had to his older daughter Teresa: "Find a husband or I'll find one for you."

Luckily, Teresa had already fallen in love with Shamus, a clansmen her father favored, and he had been quick to approve her choice.

Unfortunately, Sara had inherited much of her father's outspoken, authoritative nature, not to mention his fiery red hair, blue-green eyes, and height. She had stood eye-to-eye with her six-foot father and claimed she couldn't find a husband worthy of her.

Donald McHern had pointed out, with a shout, that it was her blunt nature and refusal to obey a man that kept her from finding a husband. No decent man wanted to put up with the likes of her; he'd forever have to battle her willful nature.

So her father did what he felt was his duty and found her a husband.

Sara shivered at the mere thought of Harken McWilliams. He belonged to a nearby clan but harbored aspirations of joining forces with the mighty McHerns.

And what better way than wedding the chieftain's daughter?

Harken wasn't a bad-looking man, but he was a filthy one, with the stench to prove it. Throw in teeth that were crooked and half rotted, and as she told her father right in front of Harken . . .

"There's no way in hell I'd let the putrid man kiss me, let alone touch me."

Harken had stepped forward with a rush to intimidate her, though how he had expected to do that when his height paled hers by several inches, she never understood. She had moved with her own speed and informed him quite bluntly, with her hand on the hilt of the dagger tucked at her waist, that she'd cut his balls off if he laid a hand on her.

He had jumped back, startled and shaken, to stand directly behind her father.

Her father's face had burned bright red, and there and then he ordered her to Stilmere Abbey to reside with the nuns until she came to her senses. That had been two years ago.

Now, at twenty and two, she had yet to come to her senses, and so her father sent a message to the Abbess informing Sara that she had two choices. Marry Harken McWilliams, who agreed to still honor the marriage arrangement despite her disrespectful remarks, or take her vows and remain in the abbey the rest of her life.

Neither option appealed to Sara, so her only choice was to ask the good Lord for help. After all, no higher authority existed that she could seek help from, and certainly no higher authority that could perform the miracle she needed.

Now, she sank to her knees in front of the cross and once again clasped her hands together in prayer. Her voice was soft and reverent, though touched with desperation. "No disrespect, Lord, but I just can't stay here. It's too barren of a life for me, and while I've learned some skills, I can't stand the confinement. This life is not for me. So, please, please, please send me a husband. I won't be fussy. I'll take whoever you send me, though I ask that he doesn't stink." She sighed. "But if that's all you've got available, I'll take him and throw him in the first river or loch we pass and wash the stench off him. Please just send me a man. I'll do the rest."

Sara continued to pray. It seemed to her that prayer was all she had left. If the good Lord didn't see fit to take pity on her and offer a helping hand, she didn't know what she was going to do. The two options open to her were simply not acceptable. She could never wed the foul-smelling Harken. And—Lord forgive her—she could never take the vows of a nun and remain forever confined to the abbey.

She muttered prayer after prayer, while reminding the heavens of the urgency of her intolerable situation.

A gentle tap on her shoulder startled her to her feet and sent her stumbling, though she was quick to right herself.

"I did not mean to alarm you or intrude on your prayer time," Sister Mary said in a respectful hush for her surrounding. "The Abbess wishes to speak with you immediately."

Sara burdened her mind with the last few days' activities, wondering what she had done now to annoy or upset the Abbess. Try as she might, she always managed to get herself into some type of quandary. It just served to prove that she was not at all suited to becoming a nun.

She draped her heavy blue wool shawl over her head and around her shoulders as they left the chapel and the last stirrings of a winter wind stung her cheeks red. "Do you know what it is she wants of me?" she asked.

Sister Mary shook her head. "The Abbess did not say, though I think it has something to do with the man who waits with her."

Sara froze abruptly in her tracks. Had she heard the sister correctly? *A man!*

Sister Mary halted her own tracks once she realized Sara was not keeping pace with her. "Are you all right?"

"I am wonderful," Sara said, startling the sister by rushing up to her, taking hold of her arm and practically dragging her along. "Miracles, Sister Mary. Today is a day of miracles."

Chapter 2

Cullen's broken heart shattered completely. His search couldn't end like this. He had traveled miles alone, purposely avoiding people when possible. It couldn't be known that Cullen Longton remained in Scotland. The king's soldiers would be on his trail in no time, though he would battle them and heaven and hell to keep his promise to his beloved Alaina. He had lost her; he couldn't lose their son.

"I am so sorry for your loss, Mr. Longton," the Abbess said. "At least you have the solace of knowing your son received a proper Christian burial."

The woman was wrong; she had to be wrong, he thought. Alaina had fought with her dying breath to tell him of the son she had birthed. She had told him of how loudly the babe wailed upon entering the world, how his son had been forcefully taken from her alive and well, and that she had never seen him again.

With her final breath, Alaina begged him to find their son and keep him safe. He had relived those last few moments of her life every day since it happened over five months ago. And his tireless search had brought him here to Stilmere Abbey. He had planned to find his son and then settle his debt with Alaina's father, the Earl of Balford, the man responsible for her untimely death.

Cullen stared at the Abbess, tall and regal in her white robe, a large gold cross resting against her chest. She was a woman of God and yet he didn't believe her. He couldn't believe her. "My son can't be dead."

"I'm afraid he is," the Abbess said gently. "He took but a few breaths, then perished quietly. His grave rests here in the abbey's cemetery, on sacred ground."

"I want to see it," Cullen demanded sharply.

"Of course," the Abbess agreed. "You will want to offer your own prayers for his soul."

Cullen followed the woman out of the room and down a long corridor. His heavy footfalls caused an eerie echo against the stone pathway. He had shed his worn sandals, soiled kilt, and threadbare shirt for fresh ones as soon as he left his half brother Burke's ship at St. Andrew harbor.

He hadn't known he had a half brother from America, and if it hadn't been for Burke and Storm, the once infamous outlaw angel of the wrongly accused, he would have rotted in prison. They had rescued him and reunited him with Alaina, with plans for all of them to sail to America and start a new life in the Dakota Territory. It seemed to Cullen that his father had provided more than well for his family, for he now had more wealth than he knew what to do with.

Burke had provided him with enough coins and the promise of more if needed. Burke even offered to remain with him and help him search for his son. Cullen had preferred to go it alone. This was for him to do—to find his son.

If his presence in Scotland were known, there would be a bounty on his head. Soldiers would search tirelessly for him, though they would look for a man far removed from his renewed appearance. Freshly bathed, his long brown hair shining from its recent washing with single braids at the sides, and a tartan of bold red, black, and yellow over a pale yellow linen shirt, all announced him a man of stature and means.

The Abbess, upon meeting him, had addressed him respectfully, though after his initial inquiry into his son, she appeared to grow uneasy, though kept her calm. That he had disturbed her made him think that perhaps the Abbess hadn't been completely honest with him.

He intended to make certain he got the truth, no matter what it took to get it.

Cullen followed the Abbess into a small courtyard that ran parallel with stone arches framing the east side of the abbey's main building. He realized soon enough it was a cemetery with a mixture of headstones and wooden crosses marking the gravesites. The woman kept to the trodden dirt pathways, walking to the rear right corner, where she stopped.

"Your son," she said softly and stepped aside.

A small white, tilted wooden cross with the name Alexander carved into it marked the grave. Cullen stared at the name haphazardly sprawled across the wood as if the carver had no patience or want to do the deed. It was as if his son had been discarded without thought or care. His heart pounded in his chest, the thump so viciously strong that it resonated in his ears and stole his breath.

He wanted to scream out at the pain that ripped violently at his heart and cry for a son he had not been there to protect, or to hold and welcome into the world, and for the woman he loved who had to face this tragedy alone. His eyes, however, remained dry as he bowed his head and silently prayed for the tiny lad he'd never get to know.

Find him, Cullen. Promise me you'll find our son.

Alaina's dying words intruded on his grief and grew more forceful until they consumed him and he could hear nothing else but her insistent voice begging him to find their son.

He looked to the Abbess, who kept her head bent as if in prayer. But was she praying, or afraid to meet his eyes? Was there something she hadn't told him? Hadn't wanted him to know?

"You attended the burial?" he asked.

"I—I—I didn't—"

"You didn't actually see my son buried," he finished bluntly.

"I assure you, he was given a Christian burial."

"So you have said." Cullen glanced again at the cross that carelessly bore his son's name. "I want to see my son."

The Abbess pointed to the wooden marker. "You are seeing your son."

Cullen shook his head slowly. "No. I see a grave, not my son. Until I hold his body in my hands—"

"You cannot mean to sullen his final resting place?" the Abbess asked, shocked.

"I mean to hold my son in my arms," Cullen said firmly.

The Abbess drew her shoulders back. "I will not permit it."

He settled a cold hard stare on her. "How will you stop me?"

The Abbess sputtered and choked, unable to respond.

"I'll need a shovel."

The Abbess found her voice. "I will not aid you in defiling a grave."

Cullen walked over to the woman whose head barely reached his shoulder, but then his height of six feet four inches usually thwarted and intimidated most women and men.

"I will use my bare hands to dig if need be. One way or another I *will* hold my son."

The Abbess remained defiant. "I will not defile sacred ground."

Cullen stared at her a moment, then cast his glance around the small plot of land, his eyes connecting with what he needed.

The Abbess followed his glance and hurried past him in a rush to beat him to the hoe that lay against the lone tree in the cemetery.

Cullen let her take the lead, but she no sooner grasped hold of the hoe than he swiped it out of her hands. Then he turned and headed back to his son's grave.

"You cannot do this," she implored, rushing after him. "You will disturb his soul."

A blustery winter wind rushed across the land when Cullen struck the grave with the hoe. "It will disturb my soul even more if I do not make certain that my son lies buried here."

The Abbess gasped. "You think I lie to you?"

The hoe struck the ground again. "We will soon find out."

Several nuns had gathered at the edge of the cemetery beneath the stone arches of the abbey, grasping hold of the rosary beads that hung at their waists and praying feverishly.

The Abbess grabbed the cross at her chest. "I will pray for you both."

Cullen swallowed his response and dug until the hoe unearthed more than dirt. He threw the tool aside, hunched down over the grave and stared at the small bundle huddled in the earth. He reached out slowly, fearful of what he would find yet fearful not to find out. Gently, he brushed the dirt off the blue blanket and choked back his pain.

The bundle was so tiny and his hands trembled when he reached down and lifted it gently. He stilled. Something didn't feel right. With anxious hands he ripped the blanket off to uncover a sack.

He turned to the Abbess. She looked stunned, and he

quickly opened the sack to look inside, his eyes shutting tight for a moment, uncertain at what he'd find. Then they sprang wide open and he turned the sack upside down, sand spilling out.

"Where's my son?" he demanded.

"I—I—I have—"

"Who buried my son?"

The Abbess's eyes turned wide.

Cullen dropped the sack to the ground and stood, brushing the dirt from his hands. "Bring him to me now."

"I—"

"Now!" he bellowed, then tempered the anger boiling within him while renewed hope took hold.

His son was alive.

Chapter 3

Sara left Sister Mary at the arches with the other nuns who were clutching their rosary beads like weapons. Prayers were their protectors and their solutions. Whenever the abbey was faced with a problem, the nuns would take to a prayer vigil in the chapel. This scene, however, with nearly the entire inhabitants of the abbey congregating beneath the arches, rosaries in hands, reminded her of soldiers prepared to battle.

The enemy?

She slipped her shawl off her head. Her red corkscrew curls shot free like bursting flames as she tilted her head and peered to the far corner of the small cemetery.

At first glance she thought the size of the Highlander was the cause of the nuns' unease. Further glance revealed the real reason for the sisters' apprehension. A grave had been violated, an unthinkable act, but worse than that, it was a grave Sara was all too familiar with.

She threw her shoulders back and her head up, and with each step she took her heart thundered more loudly in her chest. This big brute of a Highlander was somehow connected with the poor woman who had been robbed of her newborn son by order of her callous father, the Earl of Balford. The story had circulated throughout the abbey upon the woman's arrival. The earl had forbid her to wed her lover, a man beneath her station. She would deliver the babe and be done with it, never to see her son again. The injustice of the whole situation sickened Sara and made her take a decisive action she had thought someday would return to haunt her.

It looked like it had.

On closer approach, she saw that the large man, though obviously angry, had strong, handsome features and, thank the Lord, those were good teeth she spied through his snarl. His brown eyes were a shade darker than his long earthy brown hair and fumed with impatience. He looked about ready to reach out and grab her, and if he did, she had no doubt she'd get a taste of his strength. He was broad in chest and shoulders, with thick muscles in his legs and more than likely in his arms, though his long sleeves prevented confirmation. But she didn't need it. What she could see of him told her enough.

Good features and good strength equaled good husband material.

As long as he wasn't already married, she would have herself a husband, even if only for a brief time. God had been generous and answered her prayers.

Sara stopped beside the Abbess. "You wished to see me?"

"Where is my son?" The man shook the empty sack at Sara. "I have lost his mother. I will not loose my son."

Pain mixed with his angry tone and tore at her heart. This man had been deeply wounded, and she didn't wish to cause him any more pain, but she also needed him to help her. In return, she would give him what he so desperately wanted.

"You were to take care of the burial," the Abbess said accusingly.

"If there had been a dead babe to bury, I would have seen to a proper burial. The babe, however, was very much alive."

The Abbess snapped tall, as if affronted by her suggestion. "That is impossible. The babe died."

"Not true. The babe—"

"Was dead and deserved a Christian burial," the Abbess said. "Now what have you done with the child's body?"

Sara rarely held her tongue, and when she knew she was right, she never held her tongue. "You had to have heard the whispers."

"Pure nonsense—"

"The mother didn't believe, so—"

"The mother was not of her right mind—"

"Enough!" Cullen's shout brought a startled silence, and his dark eyes darted to Sara. "Explain."

"Sara knows nothing," the Abbess claimed.

Cullen's head snapped around to pin the Abbess with a cold glare. "She will answer me, and *you* will not interfere." He dismissed her presence by merely returning his attention to Sara and reiterating his query, again with a single word: "Explain."

15

"I was not present at the birth, but I lingered like most of the others, waiting, hoping, to have a peek at the babe. The whispers started as the delivery drew closer. They were not easily dismissed. Who, and especially someone in the abbey, would suggest that the babe was doomed? Why?" Sara shrugged her shoulders. "It made no sense that the child should be in danger. A tiny babe, an innocent—"

"No babe is innocent," the Abbess corrected. "He entered this world in sin and—"

"And that doomed him?" Sara snapped. "Alexander had done nothing to anyone. He simply entered this life ready to live, and his grandfather, the Earl of Balford, planned for his immediate demise."

"Hush your lies," the Abbess scolded.

Sara ignored the Abbess and focused on Cullen. "Alexander's mother—"

"Alaina," Cullen said. "Her name was Alaina."

Sara had only seen the woman briefly when she entered the abbey, but her name fit her. Her features had been stunning. Any man who glanced her way would find it hard to take his eyes off her. "I heard that Alaina pleaded for help for her child, begged that he not be harmed, and screamed when he was ripped from her arms."

Cullen turned smoldering dark eyes on the Abbess.

"She lies," the Abbess said.

"You saw my son die?"

"No, I was told of his passing—" The Abbess gasped, and with a shocked glare looked at Sara.

16

Sara grinned. "I informed the Abbess of Alexander's passing."

"Y-You lied?" the Abbess sputtered in disbelief.

"I took pity on the babe. He did nothing to deserve such a horrendous fate. So I saw that he was sent someplace safe."

"Where? Where is he?" Cullen demanded.

This was her chance, more than likely her only chance, and as much as she felt for the Highlander's loss, she couldn't let it stand in her way. Besides, it truly was a small favor in return for what he wanted. He had nothing to lose and everything to gain. It was more than a fair bargain she would strike with him, or so she forced herself to believe.

"I want to see you reunited with your son, but I need something from you first. And I feel it is best we discuss it in private."

The Abbess objected, but as Sara expected, Cullen was quick to dismiss her protests and requested they be shown privacy.

Cullen wasn't comfortable in the chapel. He stood tensely between the front pews and the altar. He had long ago lost faith, and with Alaina's senseless death, his faith had completely perished. His own actions and courage were what he relied upon, and what would return his son to him. Then and only then would he settle his debt with the Earl of Balford.

He forcibly pushed revenge out of his mind. His son required all of his attention, and he could not afford to

17

dwell on the horror of what Alaina had gone through in delivering their child and knowing his fate.

Whatever this woman wanted, he would give her. She had, after all, taken pity on his son's plight and had courageously seen to his safety. He owed her for saving his son's life. No price was too high. He would pay whatever she asked.

Wanting this ordeal over and done with, he spoke directly. "How much do you want for the information?"

"I want you to marry me."

Cullen stood stock-still, staring at her for a moment until he found his voice. "What?"

"You heard me correctly," Sara said bluntly. "I need to marry immediately, and you're the only man available."

He glanced to her stomach.

"No, I'm not with child. I've never even bed a man."

His brow went up.

"Think what you want of me. It doesn't matter. What matters is that I wed. My father demands that I marry the man he has chosen for me—" She shuddered at the thought. "Or I take my vows here at the abbey. I have been unsuccessful in securing a candidate of my own, but since I have something you want and you have something I want, I assumed we could bargain."

Cullen walked in a slow circle around her, taking stock of the woman who stood between him and finding his son. She wasn't a beauty, as Alaina had been, her features more common, unmemorable, though her bright red hair certainly couldn't be forgotten. Her curls sprung crazily around her head like flames out of control. She stood far

18

too tall for a woman, and her ill-fitted, plain brown skirt and tan blouse did little to define her body. Her blue-green eyes, however, intrigued him. He couldn't say why. The color was common enough, but there was something else there in the depths. He just couldn't quite define it.

She also was obviously outspoken, direct in her manner, and did not care if her words disturbed or shocked. To be so blatant as to tell him that she had never bed a man, or to not care if he believed her, was not good manners.

Marriage meant little to him. If he couldn't marry and spend the rest of his life with the woman he loved, then he would not wed at all. His love had died with Alaina. He'd never love as strongly as he loved her. He wouldn't even want to try to love again.

So what she required was a small price to pay for his son's safe return. He could give it to her easily, and just as easily leave the fiery redhead and join his half brother in America when his son was finally in his arms.

"Since you have yet to respond," she said, "I assume you are considering my proposal."

"A strange proposal and one I never expected," Cullen admitted.

"I've learned that life is full of unexpected events." She shrugged. "One must do the best one can with what she has in hand."

"And I just happened to be handy."

"Actually, you're a godsend."

She continued to startle him with her bluntness, but then, she was being honest with him, and he couldn't fault that.

"You mentioned your father had chosen a husband for you. Why not just marry him?"

Sara pinched her nose and waved a hand in front of her. "He stunk!"

Cullen cracked a smile, the first in a very long time. "That badly?"

She rolled her eyes. "If you put him on the battlefield, he'd wipe out the enemy in one good whiff."

Cullen laughed this time, a short burst that surprised him, but it couldn't be helped. The picture she painted was just too humorous to ignore.

"And his teeth?" She shook her head. "I thanked the good Lord when I spied yours."

He grinned, and she smiled.

"No rot and none broken. You're a gem."

"I meet with your approval?"

"It doesn't truly matter if you do or not, though I am grateful for your good appearance. More important, you're all that's available."

"So you're stuck with me," Cullen said, thinking he might just have the upper hand in this matter. Sara was quick to let him know that wasn't the case.

"And you're stuck with me, since I have what you want."

"You'll tell me—"

"After we're wed," she said.

This woman wasn't only blunt, she was shrewd, and he wondered how much he could actually trust her, and if he could be sure she was speaking the truth.

He was direct with her. "How do I know you don't tell me a bunch of lies just to get out of here?"

Sara shrugged. "You don't."

Her response startled him silent. She all but told him that he'd have to take a chance with her. He could be chasing a wild goose or he could be on the road to finding his son.

Sara sighed and shook her head.

Cullen watched her tight curls bounce around her face and spring from her head. The molten red color reminded him of the blazing sun as it settled in the sky at day's end. Then her eyes caught his and a shiver raced through him. The soft blue-green color held a compassion that stirred his own, and he knew there and then that she spoke the truth.

"I'm not lying to you," she said gently, and smiled. "I held your son in my arms. He was adorable, with a thatch of brown hair much like your own. I hushed his cries with a soft melody as I stole out into the night, sneaking him to safety. I felt so relieved when he was gone from the abbey. I knew no one would find him for they would all assume him dead and buried. I filled the sack with sand and wrapped it in the blue blanket. I dug the grave myself and fashioned the grave marker and purposely etched his name carelessly into the wood."

Cullen almost reached out and hugged the woman. She had done for his son what he'd been unable to do. She had saved his life, and with a threat to her own, for if the Earl of Balford ever discovered what she'd done, he would have had her severely punished.

While he was forever grateful to her, he was also an-

21

noyed. He wished she would just tell him where Alexander was so he could be on his way. He ached to hold his son in his arms, know he was safe, and then see that they both joined his half brother in America, where no one could hurt either of them ever again.

"I appreciate what you did for my son," he said.

"But . . . " Sara sighed. "You wished you didn't have to marry me."

Cullen answered her bluntly. "You're right. I don't want to wed you."

"You have little choice if you want to see your son again."

Her threat did not sit well with him, but he tempered his anger. He needed this woman whether he liked it or not. So, what if he wed her for a brief time? Their marriage meant nothing. He didn't love her, nor she him. It was simply a bargain struck between two people, no more, no less.

He supposed it was the thought of marriage itself that disturbed him. He had always believed that he would wed Alaina. She would be his one and only wife; he wanted no other. Then he recalled how Alaina, with her last breath, thought only of their son. She knew she was dying, and all she could think about was Alexander's safety. She had taken a chance to be with him and for them to find their son, and had paid dearly for it. She had paid with her life.

He was being asked to pay far less. He had no right to complain.

He captured Sara's eyes with a stone-hard glare. "I will wed you," he said.

Chapter 4

The ceremony was quick and simple following a lengthy protest from the Abbess. She claimed it wasn't right to wed for inappropriate reasons, and after a round of debates, she conceded out of pure exhaustion. Sara had been relentless in her reasoning and demanding in her decision. She would wed Cullen Longton and that was that.

The wedding served a purpose, or so she convinced herself while exchanging vows. Like so many young girls, she had dreamed of love, but had resigned herself to never finding it. It appeared it just wasn't meant to be for her. Since she had been young, the lads made fun of her height or ridiculed her outspoken nature, which fostered an even deeper bluntness. While they practiced with their swords, she had sharpened her tongue, until few dared even to spar with her.

Her bold nature had won her few friends and even fewer suitors. But she survived her time at Stilmere Abbey and learned a thing or two, so her stay wasn't for naught. Her time at the abbey had also provided her with the means to return home under her own terms, and for that she was grateful. However, she didn't think the Scotsman would be too pleased to learn there would be more to their agreement than she'd led him to believe. "I will get my things so that we may leave," she said moments after the ceremony ended.

"That won't be necessary," Cullen told her. "You go your way and I'll go mine. Just tell me where I can find my son."

Sara took a breath and released it with a whoosh of words. "After my father meets you and knows we are properly wed, we'll get your son."

Wisely, she took a step away from her new husband as soon as bright red splotches popped out all over his face and neck and melted into each other until his skin glowed like red amber.

Cullen lunged at her, and she halted him with a firm, splayed hand to his chest. He felt like hot metal and her palm nearly singed from his heat.

"Your son is safe," she reassured him. "Once my father knows that I am good and wed, and claims my duty as a daughter done, then I will see you to your son."

"That wasn't our bargain. We were to wed, no more."

"I didn't exactly say that."

"You tricked me."

"Would you have wed me if you thought more was expected of you?" she challenged.

He turned away from her and she heard him take a heavy breath before turning back, his face no longer aflame.

He kept his voice low. "What else do you expect of me?"

"We'll discuss it later," she said, casting a quick glance at the Abbess, who was busy at her desk, properly recording the ceremony. All the others were already gone from the room.

Cullen leaned in closer, until it looked as if he were about to kiss her, but Sara knew better and didn't flinch.

"Tell me now."

"When we're alone," she said firmly.

Rather than respond, Cullen took hold of her arm and propelled her out the door to the far corner of the arches, where no one could hear them, much less see them.

"Now!" he said, releasing her arm as if it scalded him.

"Try to understand my predicament," Sara began. "My father must know for sure that we are properly wed. Only then will he be satisfied and leave me alone. I do not insist that you must stay with me. One day you can simply vanish, be gone. Tongues will wag for a while then turn silent, and I will finally be left in peace. And you will finally have your son."

"Define 'properly wed.'"

She had thought to have more time before addressing the issue, but since he asked, she said, "I need you to bed me."

He threw his hands up in the air, paced in front of her and shook his head.

Sara was blunt. "I understand that you're still mourning your beloved Alaina. That should make it easier for you. There is no love involved, simply duty. You could do it and be done with it."

Cullen groaned, though it sounded more like a snarling growl.

"The vows must be sealed. I cannot take the chance of my father dissolving the marriage and forcing another husband on me." Sara turned silent, wanting to add more but knowing it was best to give him time to digest the information, and for her to swallow the ridiculous hurt that he didn't want to bed her.

She was offering herself to him, and he acted as if he found the thought repugnant. From what she had learned about men through observations and candid queries, they were receptive to any willing woman, so why should Cullen be any different?

He grabbed her arm once again and forced her up against the stone wall, his brute of a body near pinning her to it. She barely had room to take a breath, though there was no need to since her breath had caught in her throat, and struggled to break free.

"Explain everything it is you want of me in exchange for my son."

Breath finally rushed from her chest, near choking her. This Scotsman was not a man to cross, and for that she was grateful. He would stand well against her father, guaranteeing her freedom.

"Bed me on the way to my home, meet my father, see that he believes us wed, and you shall be reunited with your son."

"I want to be reunited with my son before I see that your father believes us solidly wed."

Sara understood he needed guarantees, but she also

needed to be sure he would honor their agreement. "I'll have your word that you will not desert me as soon as you have your son?"

"I will honor our agreement once I have my son."

"I need you to bed me before we reach—"

"I will bed you," he snapped, and stepped away, turning his back on her.

Why did she let his reluctance disturb her? It was an arrangement that would serve both their needs—no more, no less. Whether he desired her didn't matter. Perhaps she was disturbed because once, just once, she'd like a man to desire her. But then, no one truly knew her. She had made certain of that, shielding herself behind her sharp tongue so she could not be hurt.

"We leave immediately. Gather your things," Cullen ordered.

Sara nodded and rushed past him, anxious for a few moments to herself and eager to leave the abbey. She had little to take with her. Two wool skirts, two linen blouses, boots, the shawl she wore, a dark blue wool cloak, and a linen shift. With the last chill of winter still upon them, she choose to don her wool cloak, and used her shawl to bundle her clothes in, tying a secure knot that would serve well as a handle she could slip over her arm. She also added the two carved bone combs that had belonged to her mother, gone since she was twelve and still sorely missed.

She glanced around the small room, a single bed and small chest the only furnishings, and of course a lone cross, so solemn against the white wall. She wouldn't

27

miss this place or the people. It was a lonely, empty life of drudgery and duty, not at all for her. She ached to taste all of life, the good and the bad, the smiles and the tears, the happiness and the sorrow, otherwise she wouldn't feel as if she had lived.

Today, she would begin to live, would taste all she could and relish every morsel. With a brief nod of good-bye to her old life, she quietly shut the door behind her and without regret walked off to meet her destiny.

Cullen paid the Abbess handsomely to replenish his dwindling food supply and for an extra blanket for his wife.

Wife.

The word stabbed at his heart. Alaina was meant to be his one and only wife. He loved her beyond all reason, and all love died with her the day she died in his arms. He'd never love again. He had no love left in him, except of course for his son. Alexander was all that mattered to him, nothing else except finding him and getting them both to safety.

He planned to give his son a good life in America. His half brother Burke had told him of the plentiful land that was his in the Dakota Territory. He and Alexander would live well, get to know his brother, and learn more about his father, whom he'd never gotten to know.

That was why it was so important for him to find his son. Cullen didn't want what happened to him to happen to Alexander. He had been relieved to learn that his father hadn't deserted him, but rather had gone off to America after his wife had died, to build a future for him and his son. His father had left him when he was just a babe, and put him in the care of his sister-in-law. Unfortunately, his father, upon his return, learned that the sister-in-law had died and no one knew where Cullen had been sent. Burke told him that their father had never given up in his search for his son and, upon his deathbed made Burke promise to find Cullen. Burke gave his word, not just to please his father, but because he too wanted to find his half brother. They were, after all, family.

Cullen and Burke had but a short time together before Burke had to set sail, but Cullen looked forward to learning more about his brother and of his new home in America.

All he had to do was honor his agreement with Sara.

He shook his head, tying the rolled bundle after adding the extra blanket and dropping it to the ground. He hadn't bed another woman since Alaina. He hadn't wanted to think of bedding another woman. The hurt was still too new, too raw, to even consider touching another woman.

And yet . . .

His body ached for release. Part of him was grateful for a chance to bed a woman, no strings attached, and another part warned him that he would find no satisfaction in it. He would only feel emptier, more alone, missing Alaina even more.

However, he realized he had no choice, and if he were to bed a woman, at least he did so for a good reason. And at least he didn't find Sara repugnant. He actually admired her courage and bravado, especially when it had come to protecting his son. For that reason alone he knew Alaina would forgive him for bedding her.

But could he forgive himself?

"I'm ready."

Cullen turned, startled, not having heard Sara's approach. He stared at her. She was so very tall for a woman and carried her height with pride. There wasn't a slouch to her slim shoulders or her rigid stance. Her crazy hair, which refused taming, blazed bright red against the sharp afternoon sun.

And what was it about her eyes that he found so intriguing?

"Are you ready?"

She jolted him out of his musings and he nodded. "Have we far to go? Will we need horses?"

"You walked here?"

"I stabled my horse at a nearby farm."

"A horse would get us there in a week's time," she said.

"Good. I wish to be reunited with my son as soon as possible."

"You will see him. You have my word on it, just as your son has my word that I will see him kept safe."

Cullen halted just as he was about to fling the rolled bedding over his shoulder. Sara certainly was a curiosity, giving her word to a newborn babe who could understand nothing. "Tell me about my son."

Cullen began walking, Sara falling in step beside him

"Alexander was astute for a newborn," she said as

they walked through the gates of the abbey, the chapel spire shrouded by a hovering cloud while the sun shined down on their departure.

"How so?"

"He squirmed and fussed when certain people held him. It was as if he knew who he could trust and who he couldn't."

"He didn't fuss when you held him?"

Sara smiled. "Not at all. He settled in my arms as if he knew me, but then, I would always tell him he was safe with me. That he wasn't to worry. The night I crept out of the abbey with him, he slept peacefully tucked in my arms. He didn't make a sound, but I had warned him that he needed to remain silent."

Cullen grinned. "And he had heard and listened."

"Of course," Sara said, as if he were daft to believe anything else. "I told you, he's very astute."

The couple soon settled into an easy chatter and steady pace, leaving the abbey in the distance and the eyes that watched them disappear out of sight.

The Abbess finished the note posthaste and delivered it to the young lad who had been summoned from a nearby village. She gave him specific instructions.

"You are to take this to the Earl of Balford. It is to go from your hands into his, no one else but him. Do you understand?"

The young lad sniffled and nodded. "Aye, the Earl of Balford," he confirmed, snatched the note from her hand and wiped his nose on the sleeve of his dirty jacket.

"It is imperative that you do precisely as I've instructed. Let nothing stop you from getting the note into the Earl of Balford's hands."

He nodded again.

"Good, then be off with you." The Abbess dismissed him with a wave and collapsed to the hard wooden chair in her quarters. The Earl of Balford was the abbey's largest contributor. Without his generous donations, the abbey would not survive. The earl had made arrangements for his daughter to birth her child at the abbey and for the child to . . .

The Abbess shut her eyes and shook her head. What was she to have done? Deny the earl his request? No, it hadn't been a request. It had been an edict. The babe was to have been deceased by the time he reached Sara. No one was to know of the plan, but she was unable to stop tongues from running loose, and had been relieved to learn the babe had been buried and the whole ordeal was finally done.

She opened her eyes and sighed. It wasn't done. It had just begun. There was no telling what the Earl of Balford would do once he discovered the babe lived and that his father had come to claim him. She only knew it was her duty to protect the abbey at all costs, and if that placed others in danger, so be it.

Cullen Longton and his new wife Sara were on their own—and God help them.

Chapter 5

It felt good to ride a horse again. Sara loved to ride, to walk the woods and hills, to fish the streams and hunt the forest, and she could cook whatever she caught, not to mention being quite skillful with a needle and thread. She was quite proficient in many things. Growing up with limited friends, she had spent much time on her own. With curiosity that harbored on the obsessive, she was soon learning all she could about anything she could.

But though she knew a whole lot about a whole lot, it hadn't helped her find a husband. What man wanted a woman more skillful than himself at riding and hunting? Not to mention that her intelligence far surpassed most men in her clan and allowed her no patience for moronic viewpoints.

Her sister Teresa, three years older and, thank the Lord, her champion, insisted she would meet her match one day, someone who would recognize her qualities and respect her for her own worth. Sara didn't believe it possible. It would take a man of pure courage or pure foolishness to fall in love with her.

Sara glanced at Cullen's back from where she rode in a steady gait a few feet behind him. He was far from a foolish man and far more courageous than most. He had dared the wrath of a powerful earl to find his son. She admired his bravery and selflessness. He had proved that he would do anything to find his son—after all, he'd wed her.

She hadn't liked the thought of forcing him to marry her, especially so soon after losing the woman he loved, but in a way, it proved advantageous for them both. Neither actually wanted to wed or remain wed. A purpose would be served, a deed done, and a marriage ended. It was simple, a perfect union with a perfect solution.

She had admired the way he dealt fairly with the farmer who stabled his horse, offering more than a fair price for the mare he'd purchased for her. While kind in his dealings, there was strength in his actions, confidence in his stance, purpose in his silence, and he loved tenaciously.

He was an impressive man and he intrigued her.

She winced. Not good, she warned herself. Not good to let this man intrigue her. They had a business arrangement and then he would be gone. Besides, she wasn't exactly in his good graces.

How then would it go when he bed her?

The thought sent a shiver through her. She would have to remind herself it was just part of their bargain, an important part for her. It would be over and done before she knew it. He or she had no desire to make it any more than that.

The day wore on with few words exchanged between them. Sara let him have his silence. She surmised that the day hadn't gone quite as he expected; after all, he now had a wife. Dusk finally had them stopping for the night and making camp before dark claimed the land. While Cullen saw to the horses, she built a fire.

They worked in companionable silence, each settling on separate blankets on opposite sides of the campfire. Cullen divided chunks of cheese and bread and they shared a pouch of wine.

By then Sara had enough silence. She'd lived in almost relative silence for two years, and yearned to talk with someone. Who better than her new husband?

"You gave that farmer a generous price for the mare," she said, breaking off a smaller piece of cheese.

Cullen shrugged. "He needed it. I had it to give."

"You have coins to spare?" She had noticed the freshness of his garments, and his fine stallion must have been costly.

"I have my fair share."

Wealth, but no title. Is that what had kept him from claiming Alaina as his? No power, no importance. The Earl of Balford was known for his powerful connections. What better way to accrue more than having his daughter marry power?

Her curiosity, not to mention her blunt nature, had her asking, "Family wealth?"

He stopped chewing, stared at her a moment, then returned to chewing and answered with a simple nod.

So, he intended to keep his business to himself. She'd

see about that. She had a way of finding out about people without them even realizing it. She turned to a topic she was certain Cullen would discuss—his son.

"Alexander is not far from where we go."

Cullen's head snapped up and his dark eyes near bored into her.

She got him with that, and intended to keep his interest while doing a little digging. "He's safe, as I've repeatedly told you, and he'll be in your arms as soon as our bargain is sealed." She didn't give him a chance to respond. "How did you track your son to Stilmere Abbey? I would have thought the earl would have closely guarded what he thought of as his daughter's indiscretion."

"Coins quickly open sealed mouths, especially when they're hungry."

Coins again, she thought. He seemed to have an unlimited supply.

Suddenly, it seemed he was eager to explain. "Though it took a while," he said, "no one was forthcoming at first. Once I began throwing coins around, people began to talk, in whispers, of course. All feared the wrath of the Earl of Balford, and since I knew his evil ways all too well, I didn't dare place anyone in such danger. One person connected me with another then another, which finally brought me to Stilmere. I was amazed at how intricately the earl had worked his maze so that none would know my son's birthplace."

"Not even Alaina," Sara said in gentle reverence.

Cullen tossed the last small chunk of bread in the flames. "After her—"

He took a breath and sank briefly into what Sara could only imagine was a heart-wrenching memory.

When he spoke again, it was with renewed strength. "I wondered why Alaina had never told me where she had given birth to our son. Then I discovered she herself hadn't known where she was taken."

"I heard she pleaded with all who tended her to tell her where she was," Sara confirmed.

His jaw muscles flinched and hardened and his dark eyes smoldered with anger. "No one helped her. Why didn't they help her?"

"You can't blame others," Sara said defensively. "The nuns have no free will. They follow whatever orders are given them without question."

"You didn't."

"I'm not part of the abbey and I have a mind of my own. I think and speak my own opinion. When I heard the whispers about the babe's possible demise, I knew I'd have to investigate further."

"Why didn't you try and help Alaina?"

She had been expecting the accusing question. If she could help his son, why hadn't she been able to help the mother?

She brushed the crumbs off her hands and glared at him. "Don't blame me for something that you blame yourself for."

He looked ready to spring to his feet, but instead grew rigid where he sat. "I wasn't there, you were."

"I did what I could," Sara said caustically, while regret tore at her heart. She had tried so hard to find a way to help Alaina, but the earl had placed guards outside her quarters and throughout the abbey. Cullen would never truly know just how dangerous it had been for her to protect his son. However, she would never have been able to allow any harm to come to the babe. He was an innocent, and his escape was the best way for her to help Alaina. Perhaps one day, she had thought, the mother would come and reclaim her son. It was the only way possible for her to help the pleading Alaina.

But she didn't feel compelled to share any of this with Cullen. She'd done what she thought was right. It was her way, and she didn't need approval from anyone for her choices.

"And now you use this generous act of yours to claim your freedom," he said. "Did you actually save my son's life in hopes of saving your own?"

He released his venomous accusation like an arrow aimed at her heart, but she didn't flinch. She let the blow bounce off her tough facade.

"You'll think what you want no matter what I say. It saves you from your own guilt."

He fisted his hands. "I loved Alaina and would have done anything for her."

"You didn't love her enough."

"How dare you say that? You know nothing about Alaina and me. You don't even know a thing about love. No man wants you. You had to force me to wed you."

That blow she felt, though she didn't react. Besides, it was true, so how did you argue against the truth?

"Our marriage arrangement is a fair one," she said,

"and not different from many arranged marriages today."

"Our *bargain* is nothing like an arranged marriage," he spat out. "I do what I must to get my son, nothing more."

Sara quickly defended herself. "I don't recall asking you to care about me, to protect me, to love me."

"I love only one woman and will always love only one woman."

Part of her ached to feel a mere pinch of a love so strong that it transcended death. It was a foolish ache, and an ache she knew she would probably carry to her grave.

His chin went up. "*While* you're my wife I will protect you—it's my duty. I will see you're kept safe."

That rattled her dander, and she let him have it. "Don't bother. It's not part of our bargain, and besides, I don't need you to look after me. I can take care of myself."

"Not too good, since you wound up at the abbey against your wishes," he reminded her with a smug grin.

She retaliated swiftly with her own grin. "I'm not at the abbey anymore."

"It took you long enough."

"Patience pays off. I got a man that doesn't smell."

Cullen abruptly laughed, which broke the contentious mood, then shook his head. "You're a marksman with your tongue."

"I'm the same with a bow and arrow."

"What aren't you skillful at?"

"Mating."

"Do you wish to be skillful at it?"

His candid question stunned her, though it didn't stun her silent. "Are you offering to teach me?"

"Not part of the bargain," he said, and stretched out on the blanket, his head cushioned on his folded arms. "We'll have at it and be done with it."

"That's fine with me, but not tonight. I'll let you know when," she said, and stretched out on her own blanket, wrapping her cloak tightly around her.

"Fine by me. I'm too tired tonight anyway," he said on a yawn.

Sara's temper bubbled like a pot left over the flames too long. Maybe it was only part of their bargain, but he didn't have to treat it so flippantly, as if it was unimportant, meaningless.

But it was. Their coupling would merely serve to seal their vows. She couldn't expect anything more then *We'll have at it and be done with it.*

She glanced over at him. His eyes were closed, though she didn't think he was asleep. His anger had apparently returned, his jaw rigid, his lips locked tight. He obviously was annoyed and mulling it over. She didn't have experience when it came to seducing men but had watched enough women work their wiles on them. It hadn't appeared difficult; the men seemed to fall under their spells fast enough.

She didn't like the *We'll have at it and be done with it* or *I'm too tired tonight.* Her womanly pride had been stung, but then, she set herself up for the sting, so had no one to blame but herself. Of course, that didn't mean she couldn't ease the sting and practice her womanly wiles. Who knew when such knowledge would come in handy?

She had never shied away from learning anything, even when it seemed too much of a task or burden. Actually, the more challenging the lesson, the more she embraced it.

Could she seduce Cullen? Was it fair of her? Or was it unfair of her not to try? She'd never marry again; she couldn't. Her husband would disappear one day, but as far as the clan was concerned, she'd still be wed. This could very well be her only chance to enjoy a man, and at her convenience, without any ties that could possibly make things messy.

Besides, she'd feel more in charge, and he wouldn't have to worry that she'd want more from him. She wasn't looking for love, though she had hoped . . .

Sara shook her head, a sadness swelling in her chest. She had resigned herself to the fact that love just wasn't in her future. She would make the most of what she had and enjoy it. At least she was free of the confines of the abbey, and soon would be free of her father's demands. Her life would then be hers, and that filled her with joy.

"What did you mean I didn't love Alaina enough?"

She knew he hadn't been sleeping, so he didn't startle her, though his question did. "It's not important," she said.

He turned on his side to glare at her. "It is to me."

For a moment the fire's light made his brown eyes appear as if he'd recently shed tears. Had he shed tears for Alaina? It was hard to imagine this big, brute of a Scotsman crying. He appeared a warrior who could withstand the harshest battle, but battles of the heart could be the hardest of all battles to conquer.

"I loved Alaina like . . . " He shook his head. "I can't describe it. It was an ache in my heart, a twist in my gut, endless thoughts in my head, and Alaina . . . " He smiled. " . . . she was the cause and the solution. With her, everything felt good, right, perfect. She was my love, my heart, my life."

"I've wondered if love is worth finding," Sara said. "I've seen and heard how one suffers when love is lost and I ask myself if the pain is worth it."

"Well worth it," Cullen confirmed with a strong nod. "I would not give up the short time I had with Alaina for all the coins in the world." His nod turned to a shake. "That is why I can't understand why you remarked that I did not love her enough. That's just not possible, so I wonder why you thought that."

Sara looked directly at him. "If you loved her as much as you claim," she said, "then you would have walked away from her, for your love put her in harm's way."

Chapter 6

Cullen set a grueling pace the next day. He wanted this over and done with. He wanted his son safe in his arms. He wanted to be standing on his brother's ship bidding farewell to Scotland and bitter memories forever.

And Sara?

He didn't turn and look back to where she rode behind him. He didn't want to acknowledge her presence. She had made herself known early this morning, talking as soon as her eyes opened and not stopping until they mounted their respective horses and took to the road.

The woman could find anything to talk about, and it annoyed him that he found her topics of discussion interesting. Not that he joined in willingly, but damned if she didn't have a way of forcing a response from him.

Still, he was very perturbed with her unkind statement last night, especially since he'd thought the same himself. If he had loved Alaina as much as he claimed, why hadn't he walked away from her?

It was a question whose answer was not quite definable. He had tried on several occasions, but never got far. Besides, somewhere deep inside he believed, truly believed, that perhaps he and Alaina could be different. That they could manage to sneak away and share a life together, even against all odds. He had believed—Lord, how he had wanted to, needed to, ached to believe—that they would succeed. That their love would demand it, have it no other way. They would make it. They *would* be different.

He was angry with Sara for being perceptive and voicing her opinion. And what she'd said was valid, whether he wished to acknowledge it or not. If he'd had the courage to walk away from Alaina, she would be alive now. And yet, Alaina would have been the first to remind him that such a life would not be worth living.

He had fought both sides until finally realizing that Alaina had been right. Life would not have been worth living without each other. Life would be empty, meaningless, a grueling repetition of nothingness without each other.

So they took a chance and seized life with a firm grasp, and now, looking back, he would not have given up a moment of the brief time he'd shared with her. He had known true happiness, and would cherish the memories of their time together and their love, which had produced their son.

Alexander was all that mattered now, nothing else. His life would be for his son, and he would see that Alexander grew into a fine young man Alaina would have been proud of.

"It feels like a snowstorm might be brewing," Sara called out.

Cullen gave a glance to the gray sky, noticed the decidedly sharper nip to the air and had to agree. Winter might just dump one last snowstorm on them before spring buds bloomed.

"Any shelter along the way, if need be?" he asked without turning around.

"If the weather holds until early afternoon, we'll reach an abandoned farmhouse. Might be worth settling there for the day."

He agreed with a nod. It wasn't wise to be caught in a snowstorm, especially an early spring one. They hit fast and furious, dumping enough snow to trap travelers and freeze them to death and leaving just as fast. He had a good reason to keep himself alive—his son.

Not that only a few months ago he would not have preferred death. When he saw Alaina lying on the ground, blood gushing from her stomach, he wanted to scream. It hadn't been fair. They were so close to freedom, and when he held her in his arms and realized how near to death she was, he wanted nothing more than to perish with her.

Alaina had changed all that when she struggled to tell him of their son.

We have a son—Alexander.

He would never forget her words. Fighting through pain and her last breaths, she had spoken the words clearly. She fought to let him know that he had to live. She knew him well. She knew he would want to die along with her, and also knew he couldn't. He had to find their son. The child conceived from their love.

"Snow!"

Sara's shout startled him, though the heavy snow startled him even more. He'd been so engrossed in his thoughts that he hadn't even noticed it had started snowing and was now accumulating on the ground. It was falling hard and fast, and they had hours yet to go before they reached the farmhouse.

"We should pick up the pace!" Sara shouted to him.

He turned around to see that she had fashioned her shawl around her head, face, and neck to protect her from the storm. She was quick to respond to a problem, asking no help, yet offering sound advice.

He nodded and didn't bother to ask if she was all right. She obviously was, having kept up the arduous pace and now suggesting that they set an even more exhausting one.

The storm intensified, and the two riders and their horses were worn out by the time they reached the farmhouse. What remained of a partial stable was enough to house the horses against the storm.

Before Cullen could order Sara to take shelter in the farmhouse while he saw to the animals, she was already seeing to the care of her mare. Once both horses were secure from the elements, Cullen took hold of Sara's arm and, huddling together, they made their way to the farmhouse.

The wind whipped the heavy snow around them, stinging their faces and near blinding their path. With a gentle hand, Cullen eased Sara's face into the crook of his neck to protect her.

Once at the farmhouse, he gave the door a hard shove with his shoulder, and with an arm around Sara's waist, rushed her inside and fought the driving wind to latch the door shut.

They both immediately took stock of the room. Small but sturdy, it looked to have withstood its abandonment with little decay. A broken table missing a leg lay on its side, while a lone wooden chair remained unscathed. A narrow, lumpy bed, but its stuffing still intact, hugged the wall to the right of the cold fireplace, which was cluttered with debris.

"Break up the table for firewood," Sara directed, rubbing her hands. "We need to get warm." She reached for a barely usable broom tucked in a corner and began clearing the rubbish out of the hearth.

Cullen shook his head as he shed his fur cloak and hung it on a peg near the door. That she was one to take charge and capable of looking after herself was obvious, and yet when he'd offered her shelter in the crook of his neck against the wind, she hadn't objected, but had huddled against him without protest. Her warm breaths had kept the cold off his neck, and for a brief second he thought he felt her moist lips skim his flesh. Just the thought of that now, to his surprise, sent a shot of searing heat through his body.

With a gruff growl of annoyance, he attacked the table, breaking off one of the three legs with a vicious yank. He'd been too long without a woman, that was

47

the problem, and Sara was his wife—he winced at the traitorous realization.

"Did you hurt yourself?" She rushed to his side and grabbed hold of his free hand.

Before he could stop her, she was stroking his palm. He watched her long, lean finger trace a path over every inch of his palm and he shut his eyes, lost in the exotic sensation. Lord, it felt good, so damn good.

Too damn good!

His eyes sprung open, and with a yank of his hand, he moved away from her.

She caught up with him. "You may have a splinter. Let me see."

"You saw."

"Not enough. Now give me your hand," she said, holding out hers.

He shook his head. "No time. I need to get the fire started." He walked around her, avoiding getting too close, broke off the remaining table legs and then attacked the chair, breaking it into several pieces. He got busy starting the fire, not that he needed any more heat. His body already generated a sweat, and it wasn't from exertion.

How could an innocent touch spark such heat?

Too long. Too long. He had been too long without a woman. He needed to lose himself in a night of reckless passion and be done with it. He tossed a spindle from the chair into the flames.

Not so.

At one time, maybe that would have sufficed, but Alaina had changed all that.

48

"Let me see your hand now."

Cullen glanced up from where he hunched in front of the hearth. Sara stood towering over him, hands planted on her curving hips, her bright red hair a mass of flaming curls that matched the fire's glow.

He couldn't keep himself from grinning. Her unruly hair certainly matched her nature, and damned if she didn't intrigue him. Again with the intrigue. Why did this woman interest him? The question needed an answer, and if he were wise, he'd find the answer quickly.

"Afraid you may have to have a splinter removed?"

An intentional challenge, and of course one he couldn't ignore. "I can handle it myself."

"Don't trust me?"

"I don't know you."

She smiled and spread her arms wide. "I'm your wife."

He tossed the last of the broken wood in the flames, brushed his hands off and stood tall. She was near eye level with him and didn't flinch a muscle or bat an eyelash when he moved closer to her.

"Not an obedient one."

She laughed. "You know your wife well."

He tweaked her nose gently. "Not yet, but I will."

He thought the innuendo would unnerve her, but she laughed softly, as if she found him amusing.

"Yes, you will." She poked his chest. "When I let you."

She turned her back on him, and for a moment he almost reached out, grabbed her, and spun her around to kiss that smug grin off her face. He was damned sure she hadn't been kissed, or if she had, it was probably an innocent peck that did little if nothing for either party.

Wait until she tasted a real kiss. She was in for a surprise.

"I'm hungry."

His head jerked around.

Her blue-green eyes rounded, along with her widening smile. "Have you any of that cheese and bread left?"

He silently cursed his sinfully straying thoughts and nodded. "That and more."

"Good." She rubbed her hands together. "We'll picnic on the bed."

He glanced over at the single bed as he reached for the sack of food attached to the rolled bedding. They would share a bed tonight, a narrow one. Would she wish to share more?

Cullen tossed her one of the blankets, and as if she sensed his instructions, she went to the bed and spread it out. She shed her cloak and sandals and hopped on the bed, crossing her legs beneath her skirt.

He dropped the sack of food in front of her and caught the edge of the bed to sit, choosing to keep his feet planted firmly on the earthen floor. Sara paid him no heed. She was too busy untying the sack of food and spreading it out between them, while nibbling on pieces that just happened to fall in her lap.

"You did a fine job on the fire." She handed him a chunk of dark bread and a hunk of cheese.

"I have some skills." He took the food, realizing he was famished. He hadn't eaten since last night, having wanted to get an early start, and then with the snow surprising them, there had been no time for food.

"Tell me of them."

He shrugged. "My skills are no more, no less, than other men."

"There's a good quality you have."

"What's that?"

"You don't boast," Sara said. "Most men boast." She deepened her voice to that of a man's. "I can do this and I can do that and I have this and I have that."

Cullen laughed. "Is that how you see men, as boastful?"

"Pride too. Lord, there isn't a man alive who doesn't possess an overabundance of pride."

"A man should have pride," Cullen said in defense of all men.

"As long as he can handle it. Too much could be a detriment to his character."

Cullen nodded. "I agree with that."

"Good, so we've now established that you can build a fine fire, you don't boast, and you don't overindulge in pride. Tell me more."

"Enough about me. What of your qualities?"

She laughed with such glee that it caused him to chuckle. "My father would say I have not a one, and I would say I could always use more."

Cullen suddenly felt odd, sitting there on the bed with her, talking like newly acquired friends when in essence she was not a friend at all, but the woman who forced him to wed her in exchange for his son's whereabouts.

"You frown. Something troubles you," she said.

"This scene," he admitted, waving his hand out in front of him. "It is odd sitting here conversing with a stranger who is my wife."

"We are merely a means to an end for each other. There isn't any reason not to be civil about it. We both will do what we must to get what we want. You want your son. I want my freedom. We both will benefit, with no loss suffered by either of us. I'd say our bargain was a worthy one."

"Put like that, it sounds justifiable."

"It is justifiable. We've made no unreasonable demands on each other."

His brow shot up.

Sara folded her arms across her chest. "Speak your peace."

"You have dictated the terms from the beginning. I have no recourse but to follow them."

"If you viewed it as merely an equitable bargain, you'd see it as favorable and have no problem."

"It doesn't change the fact that you dictate the terms."

"True enough."

He laughed. "I don't like being dictated to."

"In this case I don't think you have a choice."

He leaned forward. "There's always a choice."

"Not this time."

Her smug, singsong tone punched him right in the

gut, and he'd be damned if he didn't retaliate. "I think otherwise."

"Really?" she asked calmly. "And what do you intend to do about it?"

He pressed his nose to hers. "I intend to bed you when and where *I choose*."

Chapter 7

Sara leaned back with a confident shake of her head. "The choice remains mine."

He laughed gruffly. "You think so?"

"Do you intend to force me?"

"I won't have to."

She wanted so badly to slap the sinfully confident sneer off his face. But such an action would only foster his self-assurance, giving him the upper hand. Of course, she could just let him have his way and be done with it.

Why didn't the notion sit well with her?

Too many people dictating to her? Too little control of her life? Too frightened of how she might feel or respond?

"Just surrender and leave it to me. It will be easier that way."

Surrender?

She didn't have the luxury of surrender. She had to look out for herself, which meant she'd need to seduce him to have it her way, on her terms.

"I agree surrender is the easier way. I'm sure you'll enjoy surrendering to me."

He laughed hysterically. She didn't think he'd stop, and of course, it was amusing to see how he so foolishly misjudged her, so she chuckled herself.

Cullen held his stomach and in between final chuckles said. "I haven't laughed until it hurt in a long time."

"So glad I could amuse you."

"Oh, you did, you truly did."

"This encounter at least served a useful purpose," she said.

"And what is that?"

"We both learned that neither of us like to be dictated to."

"It could prove a problem."

Sara smiled. "Not really."

"I'm amazed."

"Not awed?"

He shook his head. "You truly believe it will go your way?"

"Of course, but then so do you—" She stopped his protest with a raised hand. "—believe it will go *your* way."

"I need to remember that you're quick-witted."

"You need to know many things about me if you're to have your way with me, but then—" She winced as if her remark would be painful, though not to her. "I believe you referred to me as a stranger? Whereas I've already learned some things about you."

"You'd make an excellent warrior."

Sara slipped off the bed and stretched her back. "I've been one all my life."

Cullen grinned. "I've just learned something about you."

"Please, I felt sorry for you and threw you a bone." She wasn't about to admit she had slipped up and allowed him a peek at her. She had to keep her confidence high in order to rattle his confidence.

"I'll take the scrap and any more you wish to throw me."

She admired his response. He hadn't let her rattle him a bit, or at least he hadn't shown it. He remained calm, which indicated confidence on his part. He felt he'd have his way.

A strong wind suddenly whistled around the cottage, catching both their attentions.

"This storm will delay us," Sara said, feeling a bit disappointed. She was looking forward to returning home, seeing her sister, showing her father that she was capable of finding her own husband and finally living life as she chose. She also looked forward to uniting father and son. She believed the risk she had taken was well worth it and would prove even more laudable once Alexander was in his father's arms.

Cullen stretched himself off the bed. "We're going to need more firewood if this storm continues to rage."

He was a fit one, muscles tightening and stretching his shirt, reminding her that when she chose, she'd know his taut flesh intimately. She wrestled with the exciting and frightening thought, though outwardly did not show it. "You're right, the table won't provide sufficient firewood."

56

Cullen reached for his fur cloak on the peg. "I'll go see what I can find."

"Be careful," she said, joining him at the door.

"Don't worry, I'll be back."

"I have no doubt you will," she said softly, leaning forward and brushing her lips ever so faintly over his.

She noticed a stirring in his dark eyes and was pleased with herself, so much so that she dared to brush another kiss across his warm, moist lips. And to her surprise found it sent a tickle through her. Seduction wasn't difficult at all.

Suddenly, she was swooped up in his arm, her startled gasp caught in a feverish kiss that had his tongue mating with hers and her blood rushing like wildfire through her until she thought she'd spark and burst like a flame.

It was so sudden and so unexpected and yet so unbelievably wonderful. She actually didn't want him to stop. She wanted more, much more.

He tore his lips away from hers and pressed them near her ear. They pulsated against her flesh while her own throbbing lips ached from his abandonment. And when he spoke, his warm breath whispered across her face and sent tingles and gooseflesh rushing over her.

"Now tell me who will decide when we mate."

He left her staring at the closed door, the heat from her body melting the flurry of snowflakes the wind had driven in to fall around her.

She was in trouble. Big trouble. She splayed her hand against the door to gain balance and perspective. If one kiss could turn her so utterly mindless, he'd have his way with her in no time.

But that was what she wanted, so why make a problem out of it? Get it done with as he had said.

Sara pushed away from the door, her legs surprisingly weak and her body still trembling. She sat on the edge of the bed, determined to make sense of her situation, see it for what it was and make no more of it.

Be honest, Sara, you must be honest with yourself, she warned silently.

She didn't want to just *be done with it*. She wanted a memorable night, and it was because of Cullen. He was a fine-looking man with good teeth and a good mind, a man who, under different circumstances, she would have considered for a husband. If he had been similar to Harken McWilliams—she cringed at the thought—she would have bed him fast. A necessary approach since she would have had to hold her breath.

But from what she had determined thus far, Cullen seemed a good man, and good men were hard to find. So could she blame herself for wanting to enjoy him under her terms, and not feel their shared intimacy meant anything more than sealing their bargain?

Besides, she wanted to experience kisses and touches and not just the act itself. She wanted to feel it all, enjoy it all, savor it all. After Cullen, there would be no one, and at least she'd have the precious memories to keep her warm on cold lonely nights and as fodder for good dreams.

She understood his misgivings, his desire to have some

say in the forced arrangement. She had experienced the same herself when her father informed her of the marriage he'd arranged for her.

But hers had been no bargain. Cullen would benefit from their arrangement, as would she. She would get what she wanted . . .

A spark of a smile tickled Sara's mouth and grew. She didn't have a problem. He would approach her. There'd be no need to seduce Cullen. She'd experience all the kisses and touches she wanted as long as . . .

Her smile faded.

As long as she didn't surrender to him until *she* was ready.

She touched her lips, the throbbing long since dissipated, though they remained sensitive and plumped. If one kiss could almost do her in, how would she be able to keep from surrendering to an onslaught of kisses?

She stood quickly and paced in front of the bed. She would need a shield of sorts. Something she could erect when surrender became imminent. *Think, Sara, think,* she cautioned as she continued to pace.

She stopped abruptly, and smiled once again. Her mind had often drifted off when she was intent on learning a new skill, and then she'd pay no heed to anything or anyone around her. Her sister had devised a fast way of yanking her out of her musings. Teresa would pinch her hard, and Lord did she feel the sting, but it worked and that was what mattered.

A good hard pinch would do it.

She set the thought in her mind, giving it credence so

she could call on it when necessary. With her plan giving her added confidence, she set to work foraging the small cottage for anything that might prove useful.

She found a couple of candle stubs, the wicks barely sufficient to sustain a flame. A small caldron was upended in a dark corner, and she placed it by the fireplace, thinking it might be of use for cooking if they were stuck there longer than they hoped to be. That and a broken wooden bowl were her limited finds.

The last occupants of the cottage had thoroughly cleaned it out, leaving nothing but broken scraps behind, except for a single chair and the bed. She gave the bed a glance. It was narrow, barely large enough for two people.

She was far from a tiny woman, and Cullen was certainly a brute of a Scotsman in size and manner. If the two of them could manage to fit on the narrow bed, it would certainly be a tight squeeze.

Sara continued to stare, imagining them together in bed, clothed, of course, pressed tight against each other. She would be able to feel all of him, and he would feel all of her. She shivered, imagining the feel of his warm breath against her bare neck.

"Want me to satisfy your curiosity right now?"

She jumped, flaying her arms as she swung around, smacking Cullen square in the jaw and sending him and his armful of firewood stumbling back to crash against the closed door.

Surprisingly, he managed to hang onto the wood as he caught his balance and kept himself upright. She was shocked at sending him reeling, and even more shocked that she'd been so absorbed in her thoughts as not to hear him enter, or to feel the rush of cold from the open door.

Cullen rubbed his jaw. "You've got a mean elbow there."

"I'm sorry," she said, hurrying over to him. "You frightened me. I didn't know you stood behind me."

She reached out and took the firewood from him.

She was stacking the wood near the fire to dry when he shed his cloak on a peg and went to help her. "It wasn't intentional," he said.

She glanced at him. The snow that nearly covered his hair melted rapidly from the heat of the fire and left the dark brown hair to glisten; like the dark rich earth after a refreshing rain, she thought. His cheeks were stained red from the cold, and his lips bore a blue color that warned he needed warmth.

A kiss would warm them.

"I didn't frighten you on purpose."

Sara shook her head, realizing she had not responded and so he'd clarified his remark. "I didn't think you did."

They stared at each other for several silent minutes, as if wondering what to make of their situation.

She finally broke the silence. "How goes the storm?"

"It continues to rage. My hope is that it will end sometime tonight and the morning sun will rise bright and warm and melt whatever snow has fallen, causing us only a short delay."

"Snowstorms in early spring usually don't last long on the ground."

Cullen shrugged. "We have no choice but to make the most of it, and at least we have shelter. We could be huddled under a tree somewhere. Here we have a warm fire and a bed to huddle in."

She caught the deliberate, sinful little sneer of his lips. It was a quick flash and then it was gone. Almost as if he wanted her to see it and then perhaps doubt that she had. She decided her best response to his goading was to ignore him.

"Then we will sleep well tonight," she said, standing and brushing her hands off. She didn't have to look at him to know his sneer had surfaced once again and he was about ready to provoke her.

She turned with a flourish, grabbed the small caldron she had found, as well as her cloak, and hurried to the door. "Be right back."

He jumped up. "Don't go out—"

She smiled and wiggled her fingers in a wave before closing the door on him.

The immediate sting of the snow felt refreshing against the heat of her cheeks. She breathed deep of the cold air, taking in great gulps. She'd needed to place distance between the Scotsman and her. He was a calculating warrior and a foe not to be underestimated. He had found what he assumed was her weakness, and would prey on it in hopes of gaining command of the situation.

As much as she wished to experience a few moments of passion, she couldn't chance losing control of their bargain. It was imperative that she reached her home and settled this matter with her father, which came before anything else.

A chill raced through her, and she looked at the caldron hanging from her hand and was surprised to see that it was half full. The snow was falling heavier than when they first arrived at the cottage. She hoped Cullen was right. She hoped it would end and that the morning sun would chase the remnants of the snowstorm away.

Before she could turn to enter the cottage, the door was flung open and she was yanked inside.

"What is the matter with you, going out in a blinding snowstorm?"

She held up the caldron. "Melted snow will provide us with water." It was a good excuse and one he couldn't argue with.

His grip tightened on her arm and his eyes narrowed. "Until my son is returned safely to me you will refrain from placing yourself in danger. Do I make myself clear?"

"I will see your son safe no matter what it takes."

His hand dropped off her and he stared at her strangely. "Why? He is nothing to you, yet you fiercely protect him."

She shook her head in disbelief and made a flourish of ridding herself of her cloak and arranging the caldron by the hearth to heat before she even considered supplying him with an answer.

Cullen grew impatient and grabbed hold of her again,

propelling her to the bed and forcing her to sit alongside him. "There is something you haven't told me."

He certainly was perceptive.

"What is it? Tell me."

She had told no one of it. It was a secret best kept a secret. "There is nothing to tell," she said firmly.

He took hold of her chin and forced her eyes on his. "No, there is something there."

She pulled her chin free. "You want something to be there. I did what was right and nothing more, and I continue to do what is right."

"By forcing me to wed and bed you?"

"For a brief time only."

"Right," Cullen said with a nod. "A brief time only." He stood and stripped his shirt off. "Let's get the brief bedding done with."

Chapter 8

"**Y**ou can kiss me if you'd like, but there will be no consummating our vows tonight," Sara assured him with a smug smile.

"Are you sure?" Cullen asked. "You can't seem to take your eyes off my chest."

Sara stood and splayed her hand over his chest. "You have a fine chest, strong and thick with muscles." She stroked her fingers along his flesh, up and down and all around, covering every inch. "I can feel your strength, your power."

Cullen almost reached out and snatched her hand away, but had he done that, she would have known that her touch affected him, and he wouldn't give her the satisfaction. Besides, he didn't want to believe that he could respond to her. But then, he was a man who had been months without a woman. What had he expected?

Certainly not the heat that scorched his body to life. He felt a traitor to Alaina's memory. Their love had developed slowly, shyly. Their first kiss was hesitant and unsure, and it had been an ongoing process before they came completely together and finally made love. It had been a beautiful joining, one he would never forget. She was a virgin, and he was gentle and slow with her.

Presently, he wasn't thinking slow and gentle. He was thinking of hiking up Sara's skirt, plunging into her, and satisfying his lust, nothing more. It would settle their bargain and settle his need.

She walked around him, running her fingers along his shoulders, down his back, across his waist, and back up again in a playful rhythmic touch.

"You are a fine man," she said softly. "Few scars mar your skin and I so admire the strength of you."

Cullen had had enough of her teasing. He grabbed her wrist, shoved her to the bed, and fell down on top of her. She was pinned helplessly beneath him, and he waited for a spark of panic to light in her eyes.

She smiled and aimed for his heart with a single question. "Were you this rough with Alaina?"

He was off her in a flash, spewing a flurry of oaths as he snatched his shirt and slipped it on. "You are nothing like her."

Sara sat up, bracing her hands on either side of her. "No, I'm not, and it would do you well to remember that."

"*Her* tongue was gentle!" Cullen snapped.

"What you want to say is that my tongue is sharp and unpredictable," Sara accused. "And you don't find me appealing."

"We don't have to appeal to each other to solidify this bargain."

"True enough, but you will need to let go of your grief long enough to seal our bargain."

Cullen stood silent, staring at her, knowing she was right yet wondering if he would ever be able to step out of his grief, out of the memories, out of the pain of losing Alaina.

Sara sat on the bed. "Tell me what happened to Alaina. I often wondered of her fate."

Cullen obliged her, though he didn't know why. Maybe it was his need to speak of his pain and finally release it. He sat alongside her, again silently questioning why. He only knew if he didn't share some of his pain, his heart would certainly burst from his suffering.

"Alaina helped to rescue me from Weighton."

Sara's eyes rolled in shock. "I heard Weighton was an impregnable prison that no one escaped."

"Thanks to my brother Burke and the infamous outlaw Storm—"

Sara grew excited. "Storm! I've heard tales of her bravery and how she rescues the innocent."

"Storm is a pint-sized bundle of courage and skill, and my brother fell helplessly in love with her, as she did him. He is taking her to his home in America where she will be safe. Alaina worked with them, providing them with important information that helped lead to my escape."

A sadness marred Sara's nod. "Alaina was a brave woman."

"Braver than I ever imagined, though her courage cost us dearly." Cullen paused, recalling Alaina's smiling face, her violet eyes, her gentle ways and her last breath. "We were all on the last portion of our journey to freedom when we were attacked by soldiers, the Earl of Balford's men. I lost sight of Alaina during the clash, and when it was over, the stench of blood and death heavy in the air, I spotted her."

He drew a much-needed breath before continuing, but it did little good. The stench of that battle still stung his nostrils, and he knew it always would. "She had been run through with a sword. I rushed to her side—" He choked on his words and fought the tears that tore at his eyes. "I knew—" He shook his head roughly. "I knew at first glance she was dying. I held her in my arms and she fought with every painful breath to tell me of her love for me and of our son. I promised her that I would find him."

Cullen hadn't realized that she had laid her hand over his or that he'd taken hold of it and gripped it tightly. He did know he needed an anchor right now. Something to keep him sane and steady, and Sara, with her stout courage, could do that.

Sara gave his hand a squeeze. "She left a part of her here with you in her son."

Cullen took their clasped hands to rest at his heart. "She left part of herself here as well. I can never forget her."

"There's no reason you should. In time you will heal and the pain will ease."

He let their locked hands rest in his lap. "You sound as if you speak from experience."

Sara shook her head. "I have not been lucky enough to find love, but I have observed others around me who have loved and lost. It is not easy, but then life is not easy. We do what we must whether we like it or not."

"Like us marrying?"

"It serves a purpose for each of us, a good purpose. So why complain?"

"You have a practical nature," Cullen said.

"What else am I to do? I have learned through trial and error that there is a time to fight and a time to surrender."

Cullen smiled. "Then you will know when to surrender."

Sara laughed softly and slipped her hand out of his. "Hear what I said, not what you want to hear."

A gust of wind shook the cottage reminding them both of the storm. Cullen left the bed to go to the door, open it and check on the weather.

He returned after latching the door. "The wind remains but it looks as if the snow is letting up. It may just stop before morning, which means we can be on our way."

"That is good news. I look forward to seeing my family again. It's been too long."

"You aren't angry with your father anymore?"

"I have no reason to be." She poked his chest. "I have a husband, so I have fulfilled my duty. He will bother me no more."

"What happens when I leave you?"

Sara shrugged. "I'm not concerned with that since in

69

the eyes of the church I am still wed. My father might bluster in anger, but eventually he'll calm down and leave it be, leave me be."

"Do you have sisters or brothers?"

"A sister, Teresa." Sara grinned. "We were inseparable growing up. After she took a husband, Shamus, a man she had long been sweet on, and whom I think is wonderful for her, we didn't spend as much time together. But we manage to see each other often enough. She lives on a farm not far from the keep."

"You haven't mentioned your mother."

"She passed many years ago, when I was twelve. Many say I resemble her, though they're quick to point out that I was endowed with my father's audacious nature."

"Then by the time we reach your home I will know what to expect from your father," Cullen said.

Sara chuckled and shook her head. "I am not all like my father. He can be sly and secretive."

"Not so you?"

She gasped dramatically. "I am stunned that you should even ask that of me."

Cullen had to laugh. "Forgive the implication and thanks for the insight."

"How can you be so sure it is insight, if you believe me sly and secretive?"

"I believe I should add manipulative to the list."

"What of your list?" she asked.

She was a quick one, and Cullen told himself he needed to remember that. "We'll work on mine another time. Right now, I think it would be a good idea for us to get some sleep. If the snow abates before morning we'll be able to get an early start."

Cullen retrieved the other blanket and with some maneuvering, they settled into bed together. It was a tight squeeze. They could only manage to occupy the bed if they rested side by side. Cullen took the side closest to the wall with Sara's back planted firmly to his front. He kept his arm wrapped around her to make certain she didn't slip off the bed.

His cheek rested against her hair and he favored the sweet scent of her silky curls. It reminded him of freshly bloomed spring flowers. He didn't mind the feel of her either. It actually felt good to be wrapped around a woman and though he would have preferred her to be Alaina, that wasn't possible.

"Comfortable?" he asked.

"Surprisingly yes."

"You enjoy sleeping next to me."

"Actually flat up against you," she amended with a wiggle.

Her tight bottom was pushed flat up against him all right and fit him with snug perfection. He took a breath and steeled himself not to respond. If he did, she'd feel it.

She moved again, innocently enough, but any movement was too intimate.

He tightened his arm around her waist, flung his leg over hers and whispered in her ear, "Lie still or I'll bed you fast enough."

Sara stiffened against him, which didn't help him

any since it forced her bottom to press harder against him.

He groaned.

Sara moaned.

The next thing he felt was Sara's hand wandering down near his leg or was it her leg her fingers reached for when—

"Ow!"

"I'm sorry. I'm sorry. I didn't mean to pinch you," Sara said frantically.

"Then whom did you mean to pinch, *yourself*?" he hissed in her ear.

"Yes," she said on a sorrowful moan.

Chapter 9

"**I**'m not going to ask why," Cullen said.

"That's good, since I don't intend to explain," Sara said, annoyed. She had gotten so hot and bothered feeling the length of him against her, smelling the earthy scent of him and feeling content in his arms, that if she hadn't accidentally pinched him, she'd have attacked him. And that wouldn't do since he'd already assumed she wanted him. Besides, with so much talk of Alaina, she was feeling guilty about having forced him to bed her, let alone forced him to wed her.

"You are a strange one," he whispered in her ear.

"That I am," she agreed, though if she was not mistaken, it sounded as if he admired her for it. "We should sleep."

His yawn agreed, and while she felt his body go limp and a slight snore drift from his lips, she remained wide awake, her mind lost in a clutter of thoughts. Two days she had known this man she called husband, yet surprisingly, she felt as if she'd known him many years. Hour by hour he had become more familiar to her, and she admired and respected what she'd learned about him.

Guilt continued to weigh heavily upon her. Here was a man who searched for his son after losing the most precious love of his life, and she forced him to marry her.

But hadn't God sent him to her? She'd prayed so very hard, and hadn't He answered her prayers? Who was she to question the wisdom of the Heavens? Cullen had probably prayed as hard to find his son as she to find a husband. And while she would have accepted whatever man was sent, he would have accepted whatever was necessary to find his son.

They would make it through this bargain, she thought, for it was the answer to both their prayers. Guilt would serve no purpose, nor would regret. What was done was done, and what would be done would be done. She had to accept that this bargain was right for them, and she believed that Alaina would have felt the same. This bargain would reunite father and son, which is what Alaina had wanted.

A bevy of thoughts continued to haunt Sara until, finally exhausted, she fell into a heavy slumber.

She woke with a wide stretch and jolted up in bed when she realized she was alone. The cottage was empty, the fire cold, and the blanket tucked around her. She fingered the coarse heavy wool and thought how Cullen must have taken the time to tuck the blanket around her after getting out of bed.

A thoughtful gesture that touched her heart.

She finished her stretch with a yawn and bounced out of bed to slip on her boots and busy herself rolling up the blankets. She felt refreshed, though suspected she'd gotten only a few hours sleep. She was eager to continue their journey, eager to return home, and that alone was enough to renew her spirit.

Sara freshened her face with several splashes of the now cooled water in the caldron and ran her fingers through her curly hair. She couldn't wait to get home and wear other garments, rather than only the plain skirt and blouse that had been her wardrobe for the last two years. She and her sister had spent winters huddled before a fire talking, laughing, and stitching some fine garments. It would be nice to have a selection to choose from once again.

The door burst open and Cullen entered without any snow flurries.

"The sun shines bright and the snow melts fast," he announced. "By noon I wouldn't be surprised if there was not a trace of it left on the ground." He grabbed for their few parcels. "I say we leave right now and make the most of the daylight."

"Agreed," Sara said. "I'll grab some bread to nibble on along the way."

"Grab some for me too while I gather the horses."

Sara had bread enough for both of them, and handed Cullen his share after they mounted their horses.

"We'll keep a steady pace, stop to rest the horses, then be on the road again. I'd prefer not to stop until near nightfall."

"That is fine with me, but we need to take the bend in the road up ahead—"

"I know," Cullen said with a nod. "I recalled this morning my father taking me on a trip to deliver bows he had made for a Laird McFurst—"

"The Clan McFurst borders our land to the north."

"I recalled my father mentioning the Clan McHern, and I remember a market we passed through where he treated me to a sweet cake. A memorable, mouthwatering treat."

"Two days journey from here."

"Good," he said with a smile. "I will buy you a sweet cake."

Sara nibbled on the dry bread, her mind on the sweet cake. It wasn't the cake she actually gave thought to, but that he would buy her one. No man had ever bought her anything, had ever even given her anything. She felt a tug at her heart and warned herself not to think anything more about Cullen's simple act of kindness.

After the bend in the road, the path opened wider and Sara directed her horse beside Cullen's stallion.

"Your father, the man who raised you, was a bow maker?"

Cullen grinned. "He made the finest bows and arrows you'd ever know, and was as skillful in using them as he was in making them. I recall him telling me that patience was the key to a fine bow maker and a skillful archer."

"And are you patient?"

"What do you think?"

76

Sara erupted in a spurt of laughter. "I think you have patience with a bow and arrow and nothing more."

Surprisingly, Cullen laughed along with her. "I believe my father would agree with you."

"You cared for the man who raised you," she said softly.

"He was the only father I knew. The only person who treated me kindly and cared for me."

"What happened to him?"

"He took ill. I cared for him, though he told me to go and make my way now that he had taught me all the skills I needed to survive."

"But you didn't leave him."

Cullen shook his head. "I couldn't. I didn't want to. He had taken me in when I was ten. He taught me that there are caring people in this world. It was my turn to care for him, and I did. Once he passed and I saw to a proper burial, I left and made my way as he wanted me to."

"Then he was a true father to you."

Cullen nodded. "Yes. Yes, he was."

Sara thought about him being ten, alone and frightened, taken in by a man who probably gave all his time to his bow making. He no doubt took Cullen in to help him, and somehow along the way, the older man began to care for the lonely lad and offered him what he could in the way of caring. He taught him how to survive.

In a way, the strange pair had helped each other much like she and Cullen did now. They would give each other what was needed and then part ways.

"Tell me more about your childhood," she asked curiously.

"Nothing much to tell."

"I'll tell you about mine," she offered, and in minutes she had Cullen laughing with tales of a rambunctious girl who forever was off doing what she pleased.

Near noon, they found a secluded spot by a stream where the horses could rest and quench their thirsts and they could feast on dried meat and cheese.

"You chatter endlessly," Cullen said, brushing crumbs off his hands. "I don't think you've been silent once since we left the cottage."

"What do you expect? I've been in an abbey for two years."

Cullen grinned and shook his head. "Somehow I don't see that stopping you from chatting."

Sara shook her head. "How do you get to know anything if you don't talk with people? It makes no sense to sit idly by and not partake of life. You didn't, and either did Alaina. I respect her for going against her father and loving whom she chose to love. If she hadn't, she would have never tasted love at its finest."

"Yet you admonished me for not loving her enough to leave her so that she would be safe."

Sara shrugged. "I believe true love can never separate couples. They will always find a way back to each other against all odds. Therefore, even had you left Alaina, she would have found her way back to you. Love would not have permitted your separation, and of course, it didn't. Even with you in prison and Alaina imprisoned by her father, love found a way to reunite you both. I merely wanted to know if you had given the question thought. I never believed it was a viable solution."

Cullen rubbed mindlessly at his chin.

"You did give it thought, didn't you?"

His hand fisted tightly as it fell to his side. "How could I not? I was responsible for her protection, and yet I was putting her in harm's way. What kind of man was I?"

"A man in love. In love enough to let her go, and she in love enough to refuse to let you go."

Cullen shook his head. "You truly are perceptive."

"It's more logic than anything."

"On the contrary, nothing is logical."

"Love displaces logic, or so it seems from what I've observed," she said, dropping her head back and allowing the sun's warmth to toast her face.

"I need to be logical now," he said quite firmly.

Sara turned to look at him. His handsome face had taken on a worried appearance. "But you are being logical. You wed me so you could find your son."

"Some would believe that stupid."

Sara frowned. "Someone who cared naught for their child. Only an unselfish parent would sacrifice so much for their child. I admire your courage." A sudden smile quickly swallowed her frown. "Of course, I also admire your surrender for the greater good."

Cullen burst into laughter. "You so amuse me."

"Good, surrender will be that much easier for you." She chuckled like a young lass teasing a young lad.

"That, you can count on," he said, and grabbed quick hold of her shoulders to tumble her back on the blanket while his mouth came down on hers.

Sara gasped, leaving her mouth open, vulnerable, and he took full advantage, hitting his target dead on. His tongue mated with hers in frenzied madness before slowing to an erotic pace that had her panting and writhing beneath him.

Damn, if the man wasn't a great marksman. One shot and he had her.

His hand explored along her waist, up to her breast, without ever growing too intimate. He simply teased her into thinking he'd touch her intimately, damn him!

Trouble. She was definitely in trouble.

Pinch! Pinch! She screamed silently to herself, reached out to pinch her arm and caught his neck.

"Ow!" he yelled, pulling away from her while rubbing his neck. "Don't tell me you meant to pinch yourself again?"

She had, but actually it worked a whole lot better pinching him. "We should be going."

"You didn't have to pinch me to tell me that." He grinned smugly after standing and offering his hand to her. "Enjoyed that little plunge into intimacy, did you?"

Sara ignored his hand and stood on her own, gathering up the blanket that had thankfully rested on a dry spot of grass. "It had its moment."

Cullen's grin vanished in a flash. "What do you mean by that?"

She made a fuss of folding the blanket, a necessary

diversion since her heart was beating madly and her trembling legs were sure to give way at any moment. "It was adequate."

Cullen snatched the blanket from her hands. "How would you know adequate when you've never been kissed?"

She opened her mouth to spew out a defense and stopped abruptly, her mouth remaining open.

"Aha! I'm right," Cullen said, grinning widely. "You have never been kissed."

"You're right," Sara admitted with no reluctance. How could she deny the truth, and why would she want to? "I haven't ever been kissed."

"Then how would you know if a kiss was adequate or not?" he challenged.

"Easy," she said, yanking the blanket out of his hands to finish folding it. "It's how a kiss makes you feel that determines its potency." Since her legs had finally stopped trembling, she should be admitting that his kiss near did her in, but that would be surmountable to surrender, which was not an option.

Cullen walked up to her and took firm hold of her chin. "Are you going to stand there and tell me that you felt nothing when I kissed you?"

Sara smiled sweetly, her hazel eyes dancing with merriment. "I felt enough to pinch you."

Her remark, though actually meant as a compliment, was taken as she had expected. Cullen released her chin as if she'd just pinched him again, while his own chin tightened in an effort to fight his annoyance.

He raised his finger as if to scold her, stopped, turned, then turned back again. "I can certainly understand your father wanting to find you a husband. The poor unlucky soul."

Her smile grew even sweeter. "It's unkind to speak of yourself that way."

He cringed, reached out his hand toward her, stopped midway, grumbled something incoherent, then snapped, "It's time to go."

"I couldn't agree more," she said, handing the rolled blanket to him. Then, with a lift of her skirt, she hurried past him to her horse.

Afterward, deciding that silence might prove beneficial, she remained quiet for a time, giving him a chance to settle his annoyance. Just when she thought she would go crazy remaining silent any longer, they both jolted to a stop when the ground quaked beneath them from the sound of approaching horses.

Cullen signaled her to take cover in the woods. They had no sooner disappeared amidst the trees than a wagon heavily loaded with barrels came rumbling down the worn road, a skinny friar driving the team.

Something wasn't right about the scene. The friar was sweating profusely, his thin face splotched red and a nervous glint in his eyes, and he drove as if the devil was chasing him.

Cullen signaled her to stay where she was, and she couldn't agree more. As the friar disappeared from sight, a troop of soldiers came barreling down the road, their horses' hard, steady gait like thunder.

Shouts, demands, and pleas split the air, followed by a round of laughter before silence finally ensued.

"It's not wise to trail the soldiers," Cullen whispered. "Do you know of another way to reach your home?"

"There's a less traveled path. Certain areas we will need to walk the horses, but it will bring us to the market, though add several hours to our journey."

"I would rather be safe."

"Soldiers hunt you?"

"I can't be sure," he said. "I hoped the Earl of Balford believed that I sailed to America with my brother, but he must have gotten word by now that someone has been asking questions regarding the birth of his grandson."

"Do you think the Abbess will alert the earl to the situation?"

"I'd count on it. The only thing in our favor is that she doesn't know our destination, doesn't know my son's whereabouts. That will give us time, though how much, I can't be sure, which means we can't take any chances. We trust no one."

She nodded, feeling the same. She wanted Cullen to reunite with his son and escape to the safety of America with him. She had kept Alexander from the Earl of Balford once; she'd do it again. Only this time she would also protect the father along with the son.

He signaled her to follow him but remain silent.

As much as she would have loved to chatter with him, she kept a tight rein on her lips. They took it slow, and just as the path divided, they caught a glimpse of where the wagon had been stopped. A couple of barrels lay broken on the ground, wine staining the patches of remaining snow. There was no sign of the skinny friar, and Sara didn't want to imagine what might have happened to him.

The road they now traveled had been far less traveled, and it impeded their progress to forge a path where there appeared to be none.

They weren't far along when out of the woods popped the friar, waving his hands, only now he wasn't wearing friar robes, his garments threadbare and haphazardly patched.

"Take pity on a poor man and help me?" he begged.

Chapter 10

As soon as he caught sight of the man emerging from the woods, Cullen instinctively reached for his sword, drawing it from the sheath attached to his saddle. Then he boldly pranced his horse in front of the man, purposely keeping him away from Sara.

"I mean you no harm," the man urged, his thin frame trembling.

"Do the soldiers hunt you?" Cullen asked, ready to put substantial distance between the stranger and them.

The man quickly shook his head. "No. No, they let me go, thinking me a friar unwilling to share his brew. If they knew I was a farmer who had stolen the brew to sell to help feed his hungry family, they would have done me in without a thought."

"Where is your farm?" Cullen asked, being cautious until he could be sure that the man spoke the truth.

"A good distance up the road."

"What do you want of us?"

"Nothing more than to travel with you," he pleaded. "It is safer in numbers than alone. I only wish to get to my wife and daughter, and you are welcome to take shelter in my home for the night, though—" He hung his head. "I have no food to offer you."

Cullen glanced at Sara and saw that she appeared as cautious as he of the man. In the event that his story should prove true, Cullen intended on helping him. He'd see no family go hungry when he had coins enough to spare. If, however, the man meant to steal from them, he would feel the end of the sword.

Cullen leaned down and offered the man his hand. "You are welcome to join us. I am Cullen and—" He glanced at Sara. "—this is my wife Sara."

"I am Jeremy," he said, accepting the offer with a shake. "And I am grateful for your help."

The terrain proved a challenge, forcing the animals to a slow stride, and so Jeremy was able to keep pace with the horses.

Cullen kept a steady conversation with the man, and was surprised and pleased that Sara merely listened, but then, she was no fool. She understood Cullen's intention, for she probably thought the same herself. Find out what you could about the stranger.

Wasn't that what they had been doing since they met? she thought. Finding out about each other? Getting to know and understand each other, yet not trusting—not just yet, or perhaps never. Only time would tell.

"How did you come by the wine?" Cullen asked, almost feeling Sara nod approvingly behind him.

"I had taken to the road in an attempt to find a safe place to hunt for food," Jeremy said. "The manor lords are getting worse in protecting their lands against those who they deem poachers. Tenants cannot survive on the harvest alone, especially when the harvest proves bleak and the manor lords take more than their fair share."

Cullen had seen all too often how the poor suffered while the wealthy feasted.

"I had no luck until I happened upon a friar taking his brew to market. He offered me a ride and I accepted. The friar never woke the next morning, and I buried him after taking his robe. I thought it a sign from the Heavens. If I could sell the brew at market, I could possibly get enough money to feed my family and maybe even buy us passage out of Scotland."

"Do you hunt with a bow and arrow?" Cullen asked, and felt another nod of approval from Sara.

"Yes, I do."

"Where is your weapon?"

"Lost along with the wine. I tucked the bow between the barrels. It would have been foolish of me to pull the weapon on the soldiers, and even more foolish to let them know the weapon existed. They would have never believed me a friar if I carried a weapon."

Cullen knew he was right about that. Friars were men of God and needed no such protection. They would have suspected he was a fake immediately; if the man was now telling him the truth, of course.

The path suddenly opened wide and Cullen signaled Sara up beside him. He wanted her opinion of Jeremy's story. When her mare came alongside his, Jeremy picked up his pace to walk a few feet in front of them.

"He looks familiar to me, though I can't recall ever meeting him," Sara said. "And he looks like he has gone hungry."

"I thought the same myself. His clothes hang on him as if he's lost weight."

"Or he has stolen them. He could be nothing more than a thief."

"Or a hungry man trying to feed his family."

Sara shook her head. "I wish I knew why he appears so familiar."

"Give it time. It may come to you. For now it's better we remain cautious."

They were alert to every suspicious sound and kept their guard high. Cullen wanted to take no chances. For all he knew, the Earl of Balford could have discovered that he'd never left on the ship to America, and the earl could already have offered a generous bounty for his return or death.

They stopped hours later for a rest and to eat. Jeremy took the proffered food, breaking the bread apart to shove more than half in his pocket.

"My family needs to eat," he explained.

"We have extra to spare," Cullen offered.

Jeremy's dark eyes glistened and he near choked on the piece of bread he swallowed. "You would share with us?"

"Of course we would," Cullen said, thinking the stranger might well be telling them the truth. He was a simple farmer trying to feed his hungry family.

Sara asked the question that was about to slip from

Cullen's lips. "Don't you have a clan to look after you?"

Jeremy shook his head. "My cousin isn't much of a leader. He boasts and promises and does nothing to improve the lot of our small clan. Ginny and I hope someday to go to America. I hear that people like us have a chance at a better life there, a chance to own land of their own. We want to provide a better life for our daughter Gwen."

Jeremy brushed his hands free of crumbs. "I don't mean to rush you but if we keep a good pace we can reach my farm by dusk, and I am eager to see my family."

Cullen stood and extended his hand to Sara. "Then let's be on our way."

He had half expected her to refuse his help, but then, she had been quieter than usual and subdued in her manner. She was either up to something or acting the good wife in front of the stranger.

That he was aware of the noticeable change in Sara reminded him of just how familiar he'd become with his new wife in such a short time. She wasn't a woman easily ignored, though beauty wasn't her draw. Her features were classic, defined like the sculpted statues that graced the churches. She appeared a pillar of strength and confidence, a woman a man could rely on.

When he glanced over at her where she rode alongside him, she seemed lost in thought. No doubt that was the reason for her silence, since she talked endlessly, and surprisingly, her discussions were always of interest to him. She was a well-informed woman with strong opinions and the brightest, most unmanageable red hair he had ever seen. Actually, her hair was much like her; it did as it pleased, whether it curled tightly, sprang out oddly, or fell softly around her face and shoulders. Its unpredictability matched her perfectly.

"He's slovenly," Sara said, her eyes fixed on Jeremy, who kept several paces ahead.

"That sounds like an observation not an accusation," Cullen said for clarification.

"It is more like a clue."

"To help you recall what's familiar about him?" Cullen scratched his head. "Slovenly is familiar?"

"That's it," Sara said, thrilled, and reached out to squeeze Cullen's arm. "You're a genius, I love you."

His heart broke a little bit at hearing *I love you*. The last time he'd heard those words, they trembled off Alaina's dying lips. He knew Sara meant it in a grateful sense, not a loving sense, but it had drudged up memories, reminding him how much he missed hearing it.

"Jeremy," she called out, excited.

The man stopped and instinctively spun around and crouched as if bracing for attack.

"It's all right," she assured him. "I was merely curious about your clan and wondered if I knew your leader, since I've been through these parts before."

"Harken McWilliams. I doubt a lady like you would know the likes of him. He's a slovenly one." He brushed at his soiled garments. "Not that I'm much better, but it's been a hard trip in my search for food, and Ginny is going to have a fit when she sees the filth of me. My Ginny is a good wife and keeps what meager family garments we have in good repair, and clean as well. I'm a lucky man."

"You're right. I don't know him," Sara said, with a raised brow to Cullen.

He understood her silent message and her unwillingness to share the fact that she was the woman that Harken McWilliams, his cousin. had planned on wedding to improve his clan's lot. Not that he expected Jeremy to be upset with her. More than likely he would be upset with his cousin for even thinking a woman like Sara would consider a careless man like Harken.

Sara leaned closer to Cullen to whisper, "I feel I owe Jeremy and his family."

It certainly hadn't been her fault that Harken was a poor leader and an idiot, Cullen thought, though he knew Sara would see it differently. She would feel responsible, simply because she had a caring heart and the courage and confidence to follow her convictions.

Thank the Lord she did or his son would have been dead.

"I'm sure we can help them somehow," Cullen said in agreement.

Sara smiled, pleased. "You are a good man. I am proud to call you husband for the short time we have together."

Her sincere words touched his heart, and then he grew annoyed at himself. Why should he care what she thought of him? She had forced him into marriage and . . .

He let his glance drift to Jeremy. Taking in his appearance as if for the first time, he could see how his journey had taken a toll on his already worn garments, not to mention his sweat-clad body. Grime and sweat mixed to produce a pungent odor, and hearing Jeremy comment on his own disheveled appearance had made Cullen wonder if that was why the man kept a considerate distance from them.

Cullen looked as if to rub his chin, but instead he pinched his mouth to keep from laughing, not at Jeremy, but at the thought of Sara's reaction when her father had presented her with his choice of a slovenly husband. He would liked to have seen her reaction, but then it must have been a powerful one since her father's reaction was to send her to an abbey.

Grudgingly he had to admit that maybe Sara did have good reason for forcing him to wed her. After all, she hadn't asked for a lifetime commitment, he was simply a way out for her, and she was courageous enough to have taken it.

Cullen turned upon hearing her yawn. "Tired?"

Sara let another yawn escape before answering. "I didn't sleep well last night."

"Thinking about me?" he asked with a teasing laugh.

"Yes, I was."

Not a grin, not a laugh, just a candid answer; damned if she wasn't too confident to rile. Damned, though, if he wouldn't try.

"Losing sleep over me tells me surrender is near."

"Only if my thoughts centered on sex, which they didn't," she said frankly.

She had slept planted tightly against him and had no sexual thoughts? He certainly didn't want to hear that. Not only was it a blow to his manly pride, but to his confidence in attempting to seduce her.

"Then if not sexual, what were your thoughts of me?" he demanded.

"I thought how relieved you will be once reunited with Alexander, and how pleased Alaina will be that her son is safe with his father."

His heart lurched, his stomach rolled, and he almost would have cursed himself if he hadn't bitten down on his tongue. He felt as if she'd cut his legs out from under him with her sincere response. There wasn't an ounce of malice or smugness to her tone, nothing but pure honesty.

"I guess Jeremy reminding me of Harken made me realize how lucky I am that you came along when you did. And how grateful I am that I can give you something in return for your help."

"You forced me," he reminded her—as well as himself, else he'd be thanking her for marrying him.

She dismissed his response with a careless wave of her hand. "Stop being childish. It is a good bargain and what is done is done."

He shook his finger at her. "You know, just when I think—"

"I'm the best thing that ever happened to you, I surprise you with even more reasons to think good of me," she finished with a smile.

A smug smile at that, and one he would love to wipe off her face with a kiss. He wasn't wrong about how he affected her sexually, whether she'd admit it or not. She was inexperienced and eager to sample sex, and pragmatic, wanting the vows sealed firm so her father couldn't have them annulled.

She figured she'd have it her way, but she was in for a surprise, and he knew just what he was going to do to have it *his* way. Sara was right that what was done was done, and it would be done in his good time. And all he had to do was nothing.

He'd sit back and wait and have it his way.

He smiled.

"Methinks you're up to something," she said with a laugh.

His grin spread as they turned off the path and adjusted their pace to keep up with Jeremy, who was now running and waving frantically at the slim woman and small lass who themselves rushed to greet him home.

Chapter 11

Sara was amazed at how neat and clean Jeremy's wife, Ginny, kept the two room cottage, and that both parents limited their food intake to provide sufficient sustenance for their daughter Gwen, a vibrant little three-year-old with curious, bright green eyes and soft honey brown hair that her mother kept neatly braided.

Like Jeremy, Ginny's garments hung on her dwindling frame, only her voluntary loss of weight left her looking ill. However, it didn't stop Ginny from being hospitable and offering the only thing available—a hot brew of herbs.

The short, thin woman almost wept when Cullen dropped the remainder of their food on the table.

"You are overgenerous," Ginny said, grabbing her daughter's arm as she reached for a hunk of bread near the edge of the table.

Sara snatched the bread and tucked it in the little girl's hand. "Nonsense. It is our way of thanking you for allowing us to remain the night."

Gwen grinned from ear to ear, her full cheeks turning rosy as she munched on the bread.

Ginny didn't argue. She repeatedly thanked them as she dressed the table with dishes and bowls, making a grand affair of the meal.

The two couples ate and drank and laughed and talked, Gwen taking turns sitting on everyone's lap and nibbling off their plates. No mention was made of Jeremy's confrontation with the soldiers. It would have only worried Ginny, and Sara could see that the woman was already fatigued with worry. It showed in her less than sparkling eyes and her forced smile.

Ginny eyed the dwindling food regrettably, and Sara knew that she was thinking if only some were left, it would sustain them for a while at least. It was a short-term fix to their problem, and for a brief moment Sara felt a twinge of guilt for not marrying Harken. At least their joining would have served a purpose, feeding his starving clan, though she wondered if Harken cared that his clan suffered.

"I wish to pay for the shelter you offer us tonight," Cullen said, drawing coins from the purse tucked at his waist.

Jeremy's eyes rounded at the mound Cullen stacked on the table and seemed to struggle with his response. "Sharing of your food is payment enough."

"Nonsense," Cullen said, pushing the coins in front of the man. "You provide us with a roof over our heads and a bed. You deserve compensation, and don't bother to argue. I'll have it no other way."

The color drained from Jeremy's face as he scooped up the coins and his wife hugged tightly to his arm, tears shining in her dark eyes.

"Put that way, how can I refuse?" Jeremy said.

Ginny bounced off her chair. "I will dress the bed with fresh bedding for you."

Before Sara could protest, the woman hurried out of the room with Gwen close on her heels. If it made her feel better to supply them with clean bedding in exchange for the coins, then so be it. Besides, she was feeling mighty tired from their arduous journey thus far and a clean bed would be most welcome.

With Cullen and Jeremy deep in conversation, Sara rested her head back against the rung of the high-back chair, closed her eyes and allowed the warmth of the hearth directly behind her to loll her senses.

She was proud of her new husband. His offer to them was more than generous and was made in such a way that it didn't appear a handout. Besides, she couldn't believe how patient and tender he was with Gwen. No matter how many times the little girl got on and off his lap, he never once grew annoyed with her. He'd smile and scoop her up, and when she wiggled off his lap, he'd assist her to stand, only to have her hold her thin little arms out to him again.

He'd scoop her up, give her a hug, and off she would go again, and through it all, Cullen maintained his calm and his conversation at the table. Why hadn't she been able to find a man with his fine qualities when searching for a husband?

She could understand why Alaina had fallen in love with the man. He had a caring heart while retaining his strength and courage. She hadn't failed to notice how he had positioned his horse between her and Jeremy when the man appeared out of nowhere on the road. And he had tucked the blanket around her when leaving her to sleep, not to mention how he respected her intelligence by not treating her like a woman incapable of taking care of herself.

Then there was his generosity with the less fortunate. She truly admired his unselfishness, of which she was hearing once again, as he spoke with Jeremy.

"You had mentioned your wish to go to America," Cullen said.

"A mere dream," Jeremy said sadly.

"I know of a ship that could get you to America."

Jeremy shook his head. "I haven't the coins."

"That can be worked out."

Sara smiled softly. Her husband was a wise man. He was allowing Jeremy to keep his pride while offering him a way out of his suffering.

Jeremy leaned forward, his arms resting on the table. "I would work for passage for me and my family." He shook his head vehemently. "I will not leave them behind and send for them later. I know of too many families who never reunite because of such a poor choice."

Cullen nodded slowly, and Sara knew he was thinking of his own father and the years they had lost.

"I agree, and I don't think there'll be a problem. I'll write a note to the captain and explain where you and your family are to go. The ship should be reaching port soon, so I will give you enough money for lodgings until then."

Jeremy was shaking his head before Cullen finished. "I can't take any more. I will be forever indebted to you."

"I have a farm over in America in the Dakota Territory. I could use help with it. Of course, it comes with a cottage I'm sure will be sufficient for your family, and with wages for the work."

Jeremy scratched his head. "How can you pay me wages when I owe you for passage on the ship for my family and me?"

Cullen smiled, though it faded as he spoke. "A very special person once told me that no good deed goes undone. I hope when my times comes that someone does a good deed for me."

Jeremy held out his hand. "I have no doubt it will."

They shook, and Sara tucked Cullen's words away for safekeeping. If the time came when she could do Cullen a good deed, she would, and with gratitude for what he'd done for her.

A yawn hurried out of Sara before she could get her hand to her mouth.

"My wife is fatigued," Cullen said, standing. "I think it is time for us to retire."

Jeremy stood. "I don't know what to say. Your generosity astounds me and I am forever grateful."

"Are you a hard worker?" Cullen asked with a smile.

Ginny stepped next to her husband, their daughter in her arms. "We both are."

"Then we will all work hard together so that we all may have a better life," Cullen said.

After Cullen closed the door to the small room that housed a bed with a chest at the foot and a small hearth that kept a chill from the room, Sara said, "That was more than generous of you."

"I could not leave them to starve," he answered, slipping his shirt off. "Not when I have it in my power to help them."

He yawned and stretched his arms up and then out to his sides, every muscle and fiber growing taut while his flesh glistened from the flames' flickering light.

Sara's mind turned to instant mush. She couldn't think straight, couldn't remember what they had been discussing, and didn't care. Her only thought was how deliciously appealing he looked.

Her own nipples grew taut and a rush of heat permeated her body, settling smack dab between her legs until she thought the moisture would run right out of her. She plopped her bottom on the bed and took a breath.

He hurried over to her, taking her hand. "Are you all right? You look flushed."

Sara snatched her hand out of his. "Just fine."

He brushed a stubborn red ringlet off her forehead and battled its refusal to stay put.

She didn't give a hoot about the stray hair, but the havoc his gentle touch caused was another matter.

And one she knew she'd better address soon or else surrender—and wouldn't he like that?

She gasped when his fingers rushed across her lips only to return in a whisper when his lips stole the faintest of kisses, almost as if she wasn't sure he had kissed her and yet at the same time could not doubt that he had.

Then just as suddenly he was gone.

She opened her squinted eyes and didn't see him anywhere.

"Get in bed."

His abrupt order startled her right off the bed, and she swerved around to find him stretched out beneath the covers, his kilt sprawled across the end of the bed. He was naked beneath the blanket.

She stood there a moment, not certain of her next move, then quickly shed her boots and made ready to climb into bed.

"Take off your clothes."

She thought to speak but couldn't. Her voice froze, along with her movements. Maybe it was the bold, I'm-in-command look in his dark brown eyes that had turned her throat dry. Or her thudding heart, which beat so loudly she couldn't hear herself think. Or maybe it was the way her body was responding so eagerly to his demands.

She managed to gather her strength, then said, "I'm not in the mood to consummate our vows tonight."

"Who said we would?" he asked, yanking the blanket back just far enough for her to spy part of the thatch of dark hair that nestled his manhood. "You'll be too warm beneath the covers fully clothed."

Sara shrugged. "Then I'll sleep atop the blanket."

He laughed. "Coward."

"Pragmatist," she argued.

"Then shed your garments and join me beneath the blanket."

She shook her finger at him. "There'll be no joining tonight."

"I agree. Not tonight."

Why didn't she believe him?

She decided she couldn't be a coward, and besides, she didn't want him thinking he was in command, so she shed her skirt and blouse, glad she had donned a shift before leaving the abbey.

It was plain white linen and hung like a sack on her.

Cullen shook his head. "That is an ugly shift, take it off."

"I will not."

"Afraid to stand naked in front of your husband?"

Again a challenge, but one she wasn't certain she could match.

He threw the blankets off him. "I have no trouble baring all in front of you."

She almost choked on the lump that rushed to her throat. The man was built large and firm, oh so firm, and she couldn't take her eyes off it—him—his body.

Damned if he hadn't confused her. Who was she kidding? He got her hot and bothered with one naked look.

If she were truly courageous, she would have met his

challenge and thrown her shift off, but unfortunately she wasn't that brave, or secure that she wouldn't surrender to him.

He obviously planned this seductive scene figuring she couldn't resist a challenge and she'd surrender to him in no time. Well, he was in for a big surprise.

"The shift stays on," she said, and climbed into bed.

"Have it your way," he said and smiled, pulling the covers over them.

"I intend to."

He chuckled as he snuggled around her, pulling her to him so they rested against each other as they had done the night before.

"What are you doing?" she barked accusingly as she struggled against him.

He threw his leg over hers, stilling her struggles. "Snuggling with my wife."

She spun around to face him, her finger poking his naked chest. "Don't think I don't know what you're doing. We'll mate when I say we'll mate."

"You think so?"

"I know so!" she said in a harsh whisper.

"The way you're caressing my chest tells me you're ready."

Sara yanked her hand away, not having realized her poking had turned to stroking.

"Those flushed cheeks also caution me that you're ready to do the deed."

Sara groaned and turned to lie flat on her back. "I don't want to do the *deed*."

He leaned on his side and poked at her hard nipples. "There's another sure sign of a woman's readiness."

"Ready or not, we're not doing the deed," she said with a firm whisper, though she'd rather have screamed it at him, and would have if not for the family in the other room.

"So then you are ready, you just refuse to give in to your needs?"

"I have no needs."

He grinned and tweaked her hard nipple.

She swatted his hand away. "Stop that."

"The evidence speaks for itself. You're ready."

She crossed her arms over her breasts, concealing her erect nipples. "Though not willing."

"What you mean is you're not willing to surrender. If you had started this, you would be willing."

"When I'm ready—"

"You are ready."

"Not that way," she said.

"Then what way?" he asked.

Sara gave it thought. What did stop her? What foolish game did she play? All she needed to do was be done with it, as he had reminded her more than once. What did she truly want from him? Expect from him? Or from herself?

She turned and stared at him. "I'm not sure in what way."

"Then don't question, simply surrender," he whispered softly.

She shook her head. "I prefer to have my wits about me."

He gave her ear a playful nibble before whispering, "You'll lose your wits in the throes of lovemaking."

Sara swatted at his face, just missing his retreating mouth. "I doubt that very much, since we won't be 'making love.' We'll merely be sealing our vows and making our marriage official."

Chapter 12

They left early the next morning, and Cullen was glad to see that Ginny was already eagerly packing their meager belongings, ready to embark on a new life. Gwen had given him a big hug and a sloppy kiss on the cheek, and he couldn't help but think that she and his son, two years younger, would grow up together in America free from starvation and hopelessness.

Jeremy reminded him to be careful when arriving at market. It was a place heavily frequented by thieves and soldiers alike, a place to be cautious. He had been cautious since leaving his brother's ship, taking no chances and guarding his identity. He'd been watchful of whom he approached and questioned, and left no trail that could be followed.

That precaution had come to a screeching halt when he wed Sara, since he had no choice but to sign his name to the marriage papers. He thought to give a glance back at his wife to see how she fared, but instead kept his eyes on the road ahead of him. It was an uneven terrain with unexpected obstacles in their path, a fallen branch, rocks, and overgrown foliage. He felt as if he was being warned to travel a different road, this one too littered with obstacles.

A wife being one of them.

Sara was not the type of woman he would have chosen as a wife, and yet he found she had many fine qualities, honesty one of them. He knew where he stood with her. She didn't play him for a fool. She was outright in her intentions and challenges, and confident with herself.

She had reminded him last night there would be no lovemaking between them. They would simply seal their vows and make their marriage official, no more, no less. That suited him fine, though strangely, it also annoyed him, when he should have felt relieved.

It had been almost five months since Alaina's death, her passing still fresh in his mind and heart. He hadn't given thought to finding love, which was why it had been so easy to wed Sara. Love had nothing to do with their union. It had been a practical decision.

So why be annoyed over the fact that it was simply sex they would share? He just needed to be done with it, and what did it matter how, when, where, or who decided what?

A crack of thunder startled his horse, and Cullen's troubled thoughts were diverted to dealing with the skittish stallion. After he resumed control, he realized how dark the sky had grown and knew it would be only minutes before the sky opened up and drenched them.

"We should find shelter," Sara called out to him.

He nodded. "Jeremy mentioned that there were many abandoned cottages not far off the path."

"Which way?" Sara asked.

Cullen felt the first drop of rain splat on his head. "You choose."

Sara smiled and turned her mare toward a path that could barely be spied through the overgrown debris.

Cullen followed and, surprisingly, they emerged into a clearing where a tiny cottage sat snuggled by two large trees. They quickly secured the horses under the canopy of thick branches and made a dash for shelter.

The place was cold and empty, not a stick of furniture in the one room, and the hearth so small it could barely hold one log.

"I'll gather what firewood I can," Cullen said after dumping his rolled pack on the earthen floor. "Leave the window shutter open until I get back or it will be pitch-black in here."

Sara agreed with a nod and shut the door behind him.

Cullen snatched up broken branches and sticks with a sense of annoyance. The trip thus far had seen too many delays. He was eager to get to his son. He had purposely avoided dwelling on his child, knowing it would do him little good to think about it, and besides, Sara had said Alexander was safe, and he trusted that she told him the truth. He had to; he had no other choice.

His concern now was to settle this bargain with Sara, for then he could give his full attention to his son, whom he ached to hold in his arms and never, ever let go. He had sworn to a dying Alaina that he would always keep their son safe, and he would keep his promise.

Cullen returned to the small cottage, dumped the broken branches and twigs in the small hearth, and set the wood to burning with a grumble and a groan.

"Something troubles you?" Sara asked, sitting cross-legged on the blanket she had spread on the ground.

"Delays," he barked. "There have been too many delays."

Sara shrugged, toying with a stick in her hand. "Unavoidable, and besides, we reach the market by tomorrow, and three days from there we arrive at my home."

Cullen reached for the stick in her hands. His fingertips touched hers and for a moment neither one of them moved.

Then ever so slowly Sara stroked her finger along his. "You are a strong man."

Cullen snatched his hand away, the jolt from the innocent touch sending a shot of heat through him that landed tight in his loins. He turned, ignoring her remark and seeing to the fire, though he certainly didn't need any more heat.

Damn, but he truly did need a woman if a simple touch fired his loins so quickly.

He almost jumped when Sara hunched down beside him in front of the fire, her side squashed to his.

"The heat feels good," she said, holding her hands out to the flames.

He nodded, tossing in the last of the sticks, and drew in a breath, which he immediately regretted. The scent of her invaded his senses like an unexpected punch to the gut. She smelled of rich earth, pungent pine, and a hint of fresh rain, a potent combination, and damn if he could ignore it.

But why should he? She obviously was working her wiles on him, so why not take control of the situation and have it his way?

He turned, slipped his arm around her and dropped back on the blanket with her, his lips going for hers.

He was shocked when his lips met her hand.

"What are you doing?" she asked.

"Giving you what you obviously want," he snapped.

"You thought I wanted you to kiss me?"

"You touched my finger, hunched beside me—"

She shoved him aside and sat up. "I thought you needed comforting. You looked upset."

"So you tell me I'm a strong man?"

"I only wished to remind you of your strength and how it would help you, nothing more."

"You need to get close to me to do that?"

"I offered you comfort, or is it that . . . " She grinned teasingly. "Is it that you simply can't resist me?"

His annoyance erupted in anger. "Resist you? You're a bold, demanding, irritating woman who I was forced to wed and now I'm forced to bed. I have no problem resisting you."

Cullen regretted his cruel words as soon as they left his mouth, and more so when he watched all color drain from Sara's face. Her remark had been made in jest, while his had meant to sting.

Sara scrambled to her feet. "You need not bed me. Your wedding me was enough. I will take the chance of my father not finding out that our vows were never consummated." She walked over to the window and pushed open the partially closed shutter to stare out at the rain.

Cullen felt like kicking himself. He hadn't meant to be cruel. He'd been upset and taken his misgivings out on Sara. He had been infuriated with her from the start, when she forced him to wed her, and gotten even angrier when she had told him he would have to bed her. But he had fast come to realize that Sara had done what was necessary for her freedom. Just as he'd done what was necessary to find his son.

In judging her, he'd judge himself, for he would have done whatever it took to free himself from that prison and find his way back to Alaina.

He needn't be cruel to her when they'd both been faced with difficult decisions and made the necessary choices, like them or not.

He walked over to her, his steps mindful, an apology on his lips.

"Save your breath," she said before he reached her. "I've heard enough apologies in my life to know they mean little and are meant to soothe the fool who spoke cruelly."

"I was—"

"Angry with yourself," she finished. "I've heard that time and again from my father while reminding me that if I were a dutiful daughter I would obey him and not upset him. And while I had little choice but to listen to my father's lame excuses, I do have the choice of listening to yours. You're my husband in name only, and that is the way it will remain. Take me to my home, spend a few weeks, and my father will have no problem accepting that you abandoned a demanding woman like me."

"That wasn't our bargain."

Sara turned cold eyes on him. "It is now."

"I will fulfill the bargain we agreed upon," he insisted.

"No. You won't!" She shoved open the shutter all the way. "The rain has stopped. We can leave and waste no more time."

Cullen reached out to her as she walked past him, but she shoved his hand away from her.

"The fire needs dousing. I think I saw a bucket outside." She went to the door.

"I'll get it—"

She ignored him and walked out the door.

"Damn!" he mumbled, raking his fingers through his hair. How the hell was he going to repair the damage he'd done? Should he even try? Was it better to keep her at a distance and be done with it? Or did he fulfill the original bargain that guaranteed his son's return? He'd made an agreement, given his word, and in return he would have his son. How could he not give her what she needed when he would get what he so desperately wanted?

Sara entered struggling with the overflowing bucket. He hurried to take it from her, and when she protested, he covered her hand with his.

"Let me help you," he said sincerely.

"I don't need your help."

Cullen pressed his nose to hers. "You'll get it anyway."

"I don't think so," she argued.

He smiled and gave her lips a quick kiss. "I know so."

She grinned slowly, much too slowly, so much so that it had Cullen easing his face away from hers, but too late. Her tongue darted out, stroking his lips before she claimed his mouth in a bone-crushing kiss.

Damned if he didn't respond.

The bucket hit the ground and the two were in each other's arms in an instant. Cullen cupped the back of her head, wanting, needing, to keep her close, keep the kiss lingering, keep their feverish tongues mating.

When she pressed her body against his, he answered by rubbing up against her, and her soft moan echoed in his mouth, hardening his loins.

Then suddenly she tore away from him and stood, her chest heaving, staring at him with such a painful look in her eyes that it felt like a knife to his heart.

"You had asked me last night why not now? I told you I couldn't say. I wondered why myself. Why not be done with it, as you had said. I foolishly believed that perhaps—" She hesitated. "—I might find pleasure with you, if only for a short time. To taste seduction and what followed." She laughed sadly. "I even enjoyed our combative challenge of surrender." She shook her head as though she thought better of saying any more. "I will not force you to bed me."

She walked out of the cottage, and Cullen almost went after her. Instead, he took the bucket and doused the flames. It was better this way, he thought. He would have merely used her to satisfy his manly needs. But then she would have at least gotten to taste intimacy. Wouldn't that have satisfied both their needs?

He tossed the bucket across the room. She hadn't been the only one who had enjoyed their little bouts of combat. She had managed to spark life back into him with a strange challenge, and he'd enjoyed outmaneuvering her attempts to have it her way.

She hadn't only managed to be a thorn in his side, but a constant in his mind, usurping thoughts of Alaina. The realization shocked him, and he stumbled out of the cottage determined to keep his mind focused on . . .

Damned if Sara didn't pop into his head before Alaina.

Sara, however, who sat her horse, waiting, was presently giving him the most grief. Or was it the most challenge?

"Finally ready?" she daringly accused.

"Oh, I'm ready," Cullen said, mounting his horse with powerful dexterity.

"Good, then let's be done with this." Sara directed her horse in a steady gait away from the cottage and to the road.

Cullen followed. He couldn't have agreed more. This needed finishing for them both, but certainly not to her way of thinking. He had entered into a bargain with her and would not see that bargain absolved due to foolishness.

If she gave him what he needed, then he would make certain that she got what she needed. It was only fair.

Besides, he was feeling an idiot for having hurt her the way he had. He'd struck out at her when angry with himself—not that her candid nature had helped, but then she had only been honest with him.

Cullen rubbed at his chin. Damn, if she didn't confuse him.

It had all been simple to start with. How had it grown so complicated? Wed, bed, get his son. Why hadn't he simply stuck to that? Why had he allowed her to challenge him? Why had he allowed her circumstances to affect him?

Why had he opened his heart to her?

Then realization struck him.

He had been numb since Alaina died and certain he would never feel again. And this brash, wild redhead had managed to stir his feelings.

"You needn't bother to buy me that sweet cake," she said from her stiff perch on her mare.

Cullen couldn't resist a grin. She was a prideful woman, and a determined one, no withering flower on the vine, and he couldn't help but admire that.

"I want to," he said firmly.

"Why?"

Her sharp, curt query startled him, but his reply was simple. "Because *I want to*!"

"And if I refuse?" she said, not turning to look at him.

He laughed. "You won't be able to. The sweet cakes are too irresistible, just like me."

Chapter 13

They broke camp early the next morning after an uneventful and quiet night. Sara saw no point in speaking with Cullen. There wasn't anything left to be said. He'd made himself clear.

And it had stung!

She hadn't wanted to admit it stung, but it had. She should have expected it, she told herself. What did she think, that this was some fairy tale union where love would conquer all?

She sneered at the foolish thought.

She had mistakenly thought to enjoy the intimacy the sealing of their vows would bring, and why? Idiotically, she had found him appealing. Even his undying love for Alaina had touched her heart. She'd thought that for a moment she would be able to sample love-making, but that was never a possibility, only a silly dream.

She was much better off sticking to the practical, making plans for a future alone and filling it with worthy achievements.

"We'll need to be cautious at market," Cullen said from behind her.

Sara didn't turn around. She kept a steady gait along the well-worn path. "I know."

"We'll need to appear the loving couple."

"I can be sly when needed."

"Aha! You are like your father."

Sara heard the teasing in his tone and chose to ignore it. "Like my father, I use my skills against an enemy."

He made no reply, for which Sara was relieved. She was in no mood to banter with the Scotsman. She simply wanted to return home and finally resume her life. Cullen could go wherever he chose once he made a good show of short-lived marital bliss. She expected nor wanted any more from him.

"We'll replenish our food supply and be on our way," he said.

She nodded her agreement, thinking it best they didn't linger and be remembered, just in case someone searched for them.

When the path opened wide, Cullen brought his horse to trod alongside her mare.

"I didn't mean to hurt you."

Sara understood he meant it as an apology, but it didn't ease her pain. "You spoke the truth. I prefer it to a lie." Even though in the end both could cause suffering. Where, then, was the line drawn?

"It was unkind of me."

"True, but the truth is often unkind." And she didn't

want to feel its sting anymore. It had been with her long enough, his words replaying in her mind until she had felt moved to tears. She had been rejected enough. Why had she let one more rejection bother her?

"It's no excuse," he said gently.

True as that might be, it had already consumed far too much of her thoughts, leaving her vulnerable, which she didn't like. It was time to redirect her strength. "There is a farm just outside the market where we can leave the horses under safe keeping, for a price, of course."

Cullen nodded. "Good idea, and be sure to stay close to me. I don't want us separating."

"At least not yet," she purposely reminded him.

She knew her intentional barb had hit its mark when he winced.

They traveled on in silence, and for once she was comfortable with it. Enough had been said. Now was the time to move on toward the end of their bargain and the reuniting of father and son.

A tear formed in the old farmer's eye when Sara watched him stare at the generous amount of coins Cullen deposited in his gnarled hand as payment for keeping their horses safe.

"We'll be no more than a couple of hours," Cullen told him.

"Take what time you need," the old man said on a choked cough. "Your horses are safe with me. I give you my word."

That was all most Scotsmen had left, their word, their honor, and it was something that would never be taken from them. Sara understood since it meant the same to her. She had given her word once, and she intended to keep it, no matter what it cost her.

They walked hand and hand into the market, Sara wearing a bright smile and a wool shawl, since the day had grown sunny, a hint of warmth in the air. Winter and spring were at odds, one refusing to let go, the other pushing to take over.

Either way, it didn't matter. She felt a jolt of joy at the sights and sounds of the busy market. It had been too long since she was here, the last time with her father, though she'd spent a good portion of the time on her own and had loved it.

"Stay close," Cullen whispered in her ear as he gave her cheek a peck.

She would have liked to believe he meant to keep her safe, and of course he did, but not because he was a concerned husband. He couldn't chance anything happening to her, for then he'd never be able to find his son.

She took firm hold of his arm. "I'm not going anywhere."

"That you're not," he said, and dragged her over to a table loaded with smoked fish.

They nibbled, ate, and talked their way through the market, all the while keeping watchful eyes on their surroundings. A few soldiers meandered throughout but paid no heed to a loving couple. They were more interested in the lone females, especially the ones willing to sell their wares.

Their purchases mounted, mostly foodstuff, though Cullen stopped and convinced an old man whittling a horse to let him purchase it. The man thought him daft, but the coin convinced him he was serious, and Cullen grinned with pride when he held it out to Sara.

"For my son."

Sara smiled and strolled on.

She lingered at a table heavy with silks and linens, wishing she could bring a gift to her sister Teresa, especially a deep blue silk. The color would look perfect on her, Teresa being much fairer, with sun-colored hair and half her size.

"You like that?" Cullen asked, slipping his arm around her waist.

"It's perfect for my sister. I would love to bring a gift to her."

"I'll buy it for you."

"I'll repay you," she said quickly.

"No need," he said, and bartered with the merchant for a fair price.

She was about to thank him when he took hold of her hand and dragged her across the narrow aisle to a market stall protected with a makeshift canopy and concealed by a crowd of people.

He grinned. "Sweet cakes."

They waited, and when finally reaching the front of the line, Cullen purchased four of the round sticky cakes, devouring one in seconds after handing one to Sara.

She nibbled at hers, though it was a fast nibble since the cake was simply scrumptious and hard to resist. They both ate the remaining two in no time, standing off to the side in between two stalls where they wouldn't be disturbed or disturb others. The one stall had fresh baked breads from dark to light to crusty and soft.

While Sara licked her fingers and watched the throes of people passing by, Cullen purchased a few loaves. He took her arm as they maneuvered into the crowd and stopped just as quickly, to hurry her over to a table where he insisted on buying her several brightly colored ribbons for her hair and a beautifully carved ivory comb, much too expensive.

They stepped aside as Cullen planted the comb firmly amidst her curls as she objected. He silenced her lips with a firm finger.

"I'm sorry. Forgive me," he whispered, moving his finger to kiss her gently. "You truly are a beautiful woman."

Sara stood speechless, her heart swelling with a flutter. He sounded as if he meant every word. His apology was from his heart, and not just meant to placate her and mend their rift.

"Sometimes men are simply fools, though not an excuse, but the truth, and I realize that you recognize the truth when you see it or hear it. Please, forgive my stupidity."

She remained speechless, though her hand drifted to the comb tucked snugly in her curls. She touched it, felt the beautiful carvings on the rim, and knew he had offered it as a truce.

Unable to speak, she simply nodded.

He smiled and kissed her cheek. "You do the comb justice."

How many compliments could the man deliver and continue to sound sincere? Did she question his sincerity, or accept it and savor it?

He took her hand and brushed his lips near her ear. "We only need make a few more purchases and then I think it would be wise to be on our way."

"Agreed," she said, though wishing they could linger and enjoy their time together. It had been such a pleasure being at market with him, her husband, instead of alone.

They meandered throughout the stalls, Cullen making certain he refurbished their staples, while a young lad, no more than eight, caught Sara's interest. She watched wide-eyed as a merchant swung him by the back of his shirt, his ties catching at his throat and choking him.

With Cullen engrossed with the purchase of wine, Sara drifted toward the scene, where she heard the lad being accused of stealing.

"I took nothing," the lad pleaded.

A frantic woman approached, cutting her way through the crowd, screaming for her son. "Patrick's a good lad. He would not steal."

"He stole a fish from me," the merchant spat at her while shaking her son.

"No. No." She shook her head. "I tell you he would not steal."

"Then pay for the fish and be done with it," the merchant demanded.

The woman's ragged appearance confirmed her reply. "I have no coin."

"Then what do you at market?" the merchant accused.

"I came to barter," she said.

"Then give me what you bartered for and we'll be done with it," the merchant sneered.

"No, Ma, no!" the lad cried.

The woman hugged the small bundle she carried to her chest and tears pooled in her tired eyes.

Sara had enough. The bundle probably contained barely enough food to feed the woman's family. She marched forward and with a sharp tongue said, "Let the lad go, you stupid fool!"

There was a collective gasp that Sara ignored as she walked right up to the brute of a man. She near gagged and took a quick step back. Good lord, didn't men ever bathe?

"Watch your tongue, woman," the man snapped, and purposely shook the lad again.

Sara planted fisted hands on her hips. He didn't intimidate her at all. He barely reached her chin and had more fat than muscle. She was confident he'd pose her no problem.

"I won't tell you again." Her menacing warning sent mumbles rushing through the crowd.

"You need to be taught your place, woman," the man threatened while he held the lad steady.

"It would take a *man* to do that."

Her challenge hit its mark. The man grew red in the face and spittle flew from his mouth as he tried to retaliate, but words seemed to fail him.

Sara marched up to him and with a firm yank dislodged the lad from his grip. The lad ran to his mother, who hugged him tightly.

It took a moment for the stunned man to react. "You'll pay," he screamed, and raised his meaty hand.

Sara sidestepped him with a laugh. "Your lard-filled ass will never catch me."

The crowd's roaring laughter only served to infuriate the man, and he took another swing, which Sara easily avoided.

She knew insulting him any further wouldn't be wise, but she couldn't help it. "Told you it would take a *man*."

He charged at her, and though she moved swiftly, his fist grazed her chin and she stumbled, though quickly righted herself.

His cheeks puffed red, his eyes bulged, and his feet pawed the ground.

She grinned and urged him forward with the wave of her hands, knowing her boastful tactics would only serve to anger him more and render him a careless fighter. "Come on, make yourself look more a fool."

The man charged at her, and she waited until he was

close enough to sidestep him safely while tripping him with her foot.

He went down hard and the crowd cheered.

Sara smiled and bowed her head graciously, accepting the many accolades.

The man turned over slowly, screaming oaths at her, and the crowd gasped when they saw that he was about to fling a knife at her.

Before he could discharge the knife, however, a heavy sandal-covered foot came down on his shoulder, pinning him hard to the ground.

"Drop it!" Cullen ordered. "That's *my wife* you attack."

The man released the weapon and crawled to his feet in order to stand. His manner was far different with Cullen, though he made no bones about telling him how her interference had cost him, pointing to the young lad whom he claimed had stolen from him.

Sara had joined her husband, standing beside him and listening to the man's tirade. She wasn't certain what Cullen would do, possibly pay the man off just to quiet him or to protect the boy. But wouldn't that make her look the fool?

When the man finally finished, Cullen turned to Sara and said, "What will you have me do with him? The choice is yours."

The man paled, and Sara stood stunned that he should leave the choice to her. She couldn't help but smile. Her husband made certain she retained her pride, and she wanted to kiss him for his thoughtfulness.

"I don't want the lad to suffer, and while I don't believe he stole from this idiot, I say we pay him and be done with it."

Cullen's smiling eyes and curt nod told her he admired and agreed with her decision, and while the matter was settled and the crowd dispersed, Sara spoke with Patrick and his mother.

The woman thanked her profusely, and Patrick kept repeating that he hadn't stolen anything and that he never would. Cullen soon joined them and gave the mother a few coins, though she protested, saying they had done far too much for her and her son already.

Cullen wouldn't have it any other way, and he was quick to take Sara's arm and tug her away. She realized he was urging that they leave quickly, and saw why when she turned where his eyes looked in the distance behind her. A troop of soldiers were heading into the market.

They both moved quickly off, ducking into the woods at first chance.

"We need to put a good distance between us and the market," Cullen said as they hurried through the woods.

Sara kept pace with him, taking the burden of a few of the parcels he carried.

"I appreciate what you did back there," she said.

He shook his head with a laugh. "At first I thought to interfere, but you seemed to have matters well in hand."

"You watched?" she asked with surprise.

"How could I not? You had gathered a large crowd, and I could understand why. You were making a fool of the idiot, and everyone was enjoying the show, including me."

She smiled as her sure footing matched his along the uneven terrain. "You let me deal with him?"

"You were doing a good job and I was prepared to help you when the time came."

Sara was even more surprised. "You were confident I could handle the situation?"

Cullen stifled a laugh. "Confident? Good Lord, anyone with eyes could see that you were intimidating that fool."

"So you waited?'

"I wanted to see how you would finish him off." His smile soured. "When he pulled the knife, that was the end. There was no way I'd take a chance of you being harmed."

Her heart soared, though her practical side reminded her that he needed her. If anything happened to her, he'd never find his son. Still, for whatever reason, he had protected her and her pride.

He had in essence been her hero when no one had ever defended her.

She reached out and touched his arm briefly, their hurried pace not allowing for more contact. "Thank you."

His reply came quick as he ducked a low branch in his path. "You're my wife."

It was simple to him. Whether the vows were spoken

in earnest or in need, he took them seriously. He would allow no one to harm *his wife*.

He obviously was a man of his word, and that she could count on him wasn't a question. He was a good man and would make a good husband.

The thought saddened her, for she knew he would not long remain her husband.

Chapter 14

They camped at dusk, a good distance from the market and the soldiers, exhausted from their arduous pace. Cullen settled the horses and wasn't surprised to see that Sara had seen to building a campfire. She wasn't the type of woman to sit around and wait for a man to do for her. She took charge and got things done even if it meant placing her life in danger.

He had been shocked to see her confronting the man in the market. He had first thought to intervene, then was amused at how easily she had handled the fool. So he had watched and waited and enjoyed the show.

She was a remarkable woman, who stood her ground with courage and confidence, and he admired her more each day.

With a fatigued sigh, he collapsed to the blanket beside the fire. She sat on the opposite side munching on bread and dried fish. He saw that she'd arranged a portion of the food for him and left it on his blanket.

She looked exhausted, her blue-green eyes lacking their usual luster and curiosity, but then, it had been a long day.

"You're tired," he said.

She licked fish crumbs from her fingertips. "We both are. We need a good night's sleep. In three days' time we'll arrive at my home, and soon after you will be reunited with your son."

"Alexander is close by?"

She nodded. "He is near and you will be with him soon."

Cullen felt a twinge of guilt. She would keep her part of the bargain; not so he, and he didn't like the thought. He had given his word, and today had protected her. How could he walk away from her and leave her unprotected, vulnerable to her father discovering the truth, once again placing her in danger?

Perhaps seeing her courageously defend the young lad had made him realize she depended on no one but herself. And why? Had it been a necessary learned trait? Had she always had to depend on herself? Alone? No one to help her?

And had it been that learned strength that enabled her not to think twice about rescuing his son?

"I can't wait to be with him," he said, eager yet grateful.

"It is good he is so young, just about eleven months, he will know only you and not remember the people who cared for him the first year of his life."

"Good people, right?"

"The best," she said with an affirmative nod.

Her confidence gave him confidence as well, and while he would have liked more information, he knew she'd give him only what she deemed necessary. He'd been patient, having no other choice, and besides, he trusted her. She had proven herself truthful and trustworthy, and he was grateful his son had landed in her arms.

A sudden thought hit him. "The couple won't mind me taking him?"

She shook her head. "Not at all. They expected me to come for the child."

He eyed her strangely. "You intended to raise my son?"

Her head snapped up. "Of course. I didn't plan on deserting him after having rescued him. Besides, I had hope that his mother would return for him."

"And his father?"

"I knew nothing about him. Had he truly loved the woman giving birth to his son or had he merely used her? I planned to be cautious where he was concerned. If the time ever came."

"It has, and you've certainly been cautious."

"I didn't protect him to see him hurt in the end." She yawned and stretched.

"You should sleep."

Sara stretched out on the blanket. "So should you."

"I will," he said, and thought to say more, to thank her for her bravery and unselfishness, but he didn't feel he could, not unless he gave as unselfishly as she had. How he'd be able to do that, he wasn't sure. He only knew he had to try. He owed her so much more than she realized.

He watched her drift off to sleep, her eyes closing slowly, her breathing growing steady. She rested on her side facing the fire, facing him. The fire's heat tinged her cheeks pink and gave softness to her sharp features.

Something in him swelled and twisted his gut. He didn't know what to make of it, or if he should make anything of it. He'd been so busy tracking down his son that he had paid little heed to anything else, especially his feelings.

He stretched out on his back on the blanket and gazed up at the night sky sprinkled with stars. Alaina had been his world. and when he lost her, he'd lost himself. If it hadn't been for his son, he wouldn't have wanted to live.

As the months passed, his pain subsided, thanks to his determined search for his son. That was all he thought about, all he wanted to think about—finding Alexander, leaving Scotland, and most of all, avenging Alaina's death.

He had not intended to marry. He turned and looked at his wife.

It still unsettled him to think of Sara that way—as his wife—and yet today at market his first instincts had been to protect *his wife*. She had good qualities and was a woman a husband could depend on.

If he chose to wed for the mere sake of having a wife, a companion, Sara would be a good choice. She had even cared enough for his son to protect him, a motherly instinct. She was a good woman.

Her anxious moan caught his attention and he turned on his side. She scrunched her face as if in pain and her sorrowful whimpers attested to her suffering. Did nightmarish memories haunt her? Or did dreams of the future cause her unrest?

A heart-wrenching cry had him up and over to her in no time. He stretched out beside her, his arm going around her and easing her back against him.

"Shhh," he whispered in her ear. "You're all right. I'm here. You're safe."

She pressed her fisted hands against her chest. "Nothing will stop me. I promise. I prom . . . "

Her words faded, along with her dream apparently, and she settled comfortably in his arms, a fitful sigh escaping now and again. She felt good wrapped snugly against him and it felt good for her to be there. He liked being wrapped around her, the feel of her springy red curls tickling his face.

He had looked forward to sharing intimate moments like this with Alaina. They'd merely had stolen moments, each one all too brief. He had dreamed of so much more, but his dreams were replaced with nightmares after her death.

In the first few weeks following Alaina's passing he had rarely slept. He didn't want to close his eyes for fear of reliving her death or to have dreams in which he held her in his arms.

He tightened his hold around Sara, drawing her as close to him as he could. He had hated waking from the dreams where he felt Alaina so alive, so real in his arms, only to open his eyes and find himself alone, with her gone forever.

He couldn't replace Alaina; he didn't want to, would never want to, but couldn't help relishing the feel of Sara in his arms, knowing they could sleep side by side, wrapped around each other all through the night, to wake together in the morning.

He might not love Sara, or she him, but at least they weren't alone. She helped fill a void, an emptiness inside him that was tearing him to pieces, and for a while he wanted to savor having a woman in his arms, a good woman at that.

And what of Sara?

Hadn't she wanted to experience intimacy with her husband while sealing their vows and guarding her future?

He squeezed his eyes tight. The simple bargain they struck had suddenly become complicated. He shook his head. He couldn't allow that to happen. His first and foremost thought, action, and deed had to be his son. Nothing else could stand in his way.

He breathed deep and caught a whiff of pine, not a heavy scent, but a light, barely discernible one, and yet appealing. He wiggled his nose to dislodge the red, pine-scented curl that tormented his nostrils. It remained stubborn, refusing to budge.

He finally had no choice but to swat at it with his fingers, but that only managed to release two other curls joining the stubborn one. He grabbed hold of all three and stilled, rubbing the strands between his fingers.

They were silky soft, and he rubbed them against his cheek, then over his lips while drinking deep of their intoxicating scent.

"Damn, damn, damn," he whispered, and buried his face in her hair.

He got lost in the scent of her, and claimed by intoxication, fell sound asleep.

"No! No!"

Cullen was jolted awake by Sara struggling in his arms. She was dreaming again, and he sought to soothe her.

"Shhh, be still, it's all right."

She didn't listen or didn't hear, and struggled harder.

He had to stop her thrashing or one of them would get hurt, and so threw his leg over her legs and, with a firm arm around her, held her tight, all the while trying to reassure her.

Her eyes sprung open and she glared at him until recognition finally struck and her fear gradually subsided.

"A bad dream?" he asked after giving her time to calm.

She confirmed with a nod and a relieved sigh.

"They've haunted you since you've fallen asleep."

"They plague me now and again."

"Want to talk about them?' he asked.

"No, I want to forget them."

Cullen wasn't surprised when she turned in his arms and cuddled against him. She buried her face in the crook of his neck while grabbing handfuls of his shirt and pressing tightly clenched fists against his chest.

He rested his cheek atop her head. "You're safe."

He couldn't make out her muffled reply, but the way her body grew taut in his arms, he sensed that she didn't agree.

"I won't let anything happen to you," he said, wanting to ease her fears, whatever they were. He had woken too many times from nightmares wishing he wasn't alone, aching for a pair of comforting arms. At least, he thought, he could give that comfort to her.

Cullen woke with the break of dawn, that first light easing away the darkness and promising a new day, a new start. And it was certainly that, for he woke with Sara's head rested on his shoulder, her arm snug around his waist and her ankle crossing his.

It took him a moment to remember how he had come to be beside her, and he was glad that they had remained together throughout the night. Their bodies were warm from the shared heat, and his sleep undisturbed by nightmares.

He felt good, as if he'd slept soundly for the first time since Alaina's passing. He felt strangely renewed and comfortable. So much so that he just wished to remain as he was, relishing the peaceful moment.

A groan and the beginning of a stretch interrupted his brief peace, and he smiled when Sara suddenly realized where she was, her body springing taut like a bow.

She lifted her head to stare at him, startled out of sleepiness.

"Good morning," he said, hoping to ease her concern.

His innocent ploy didn't work; she popped up but remained sitting beside him, looking bewildered.

"You were having nightmares, and I attempted to comfort you." He shrugged. "I fell asleep alongside you in the process."

She appeared speechless, which he found hard to believe. The woman was never at a loss for words, and he could only assume that sleep still partially claimed her.

She reminded him of a cornered animal frozen in fear. He reached out, laying his hand on hers. "You settled peacefully in my arms and I settled peacefully into slumber."

Her face turned soft then, her eyes gentle, and her whole body seemed to breathe a sigh of relief.

"Thank you," she said, to his surprise.

He thought she might rant at him and tell him to keep to himself, that she didn't need his concern, his comforting. He had never expected a thank-you.

"I remember now you asking me if I wished to talk about my disturbing dreams."

"I did, and the offer still holds."

"I appreciate it," she said with a tentative smile. "Perhaps some other time."

"I'm all ears."

"That you're not," she said with a grin. "You are a good-looking man."

"And you are a beautiful woman."

Suddenly, once again, she appeared a cornered animal. "I am not."

He playfully squeezed her hand. "Do you call me a liar?"

His teasing accusation startled her silent, and as he took in her eyes, wide in disbelief, and her rigid posture, he realized that it was likely she had never been told she was beautiful. He felt a twinge of sorrow for her and for all those who had failed to see the beauty in her.

Still holding his hand, she finally found her voice. "You can't mean it?"

"I simply speak the truth. You are a beautiful woman."

"Have you rubbed the sleep from your eyes?" she asked with a laugh.

"Whether in the dawn of first light or the gray of dusk, your beauty remains the same."

"That is so very lovely."

"Finally," he grinned shaking their locked hands, "you accept my sincere compliment."

A tinge of pink painted her cheeks, and the idea that he could make her blush delighted him and widened his already foolish grin.

She gave a quick nod and turned her head for a moment, he assumed to hide her cheeks' staining a deeper pink. The blushing response reminded him that she was a woman in all ways possible. She merely masked her various aspects as a safeguard, and probably more so for no doubt having been hurt more than once.

"I was thinking," he said. "We struck a bargain and I gave my word, and I believe it also prudent that we consummate our vows so that your freedom is guaranteed."

Sara eased her hand out of his. "I appreciate it, but it's not necessary."

"I gave you my word." He heard and felt his irritation. Why would she argue with him? It was for the best and she knew that, which was why she had made it part of the bargain. Why, suddenly, didn't it matter anymore?

"I release you from that part of the bargain."

"A bargain is a bargain," he found himself arguing.

"My bargain, my decision," she said, and scrambled to her feet.

He followed by jumping to his feet and grabbing hold of her arm. "Our bargain, our decision."

With a huffed laugh and a shake of her head, she said, "Spit it out, Scotsman, what you're really saying is you want to have sex with me."

Damned if she wasn't right, but then what had she expected when they flirted with challenging each other to surrender? How could she not have expected sparks to fly and some to ignite? Especially since, for his own part, he had been so long without a woman, just as she had never been with a man. It had always been a situation bent on an explosive ending.

He yanked her up against him. "And *you* want to have sex with me," he declared.

Chapter 15

Sara almost exploded, but instead tempered her anger when she begrudgingly admitted to herself that he spoke the truth. She had forced the issue of him bedding her as a practical one. They had then taken on a challenge of their own, both of them wanting to take charge of the situation until finally it became obvious that by sealing their vows it would settle all issues, the most important one being that it would protect her. Her father would not be able to annul her marriage and force another husband on her.

What she hadn't counted on was that the more she learned about Cullen, the more she liked him and wished she could have found a man like him to wed permanently.

"No answer?" he asked, his lips brushing dangerously close to hers.

"I'm thinking."

He laughed, caught her around the waist, swung her around, then planted her on the ground as he put a forceful kiss on her lips.

She grabbed hold of his broad shoulders, her fingers grasping solid muscle while her body drifted against his, with help from his guiding hands.

She didn't struggle; she didn't want to. She liked the taste of him, the feel of him against her, the way his heat melted over her and tingled her flesh to life, and the way his tongue danced with hers.

When he finished, he rested his forehead to hers. "We have a bargain, you and I, one that will benefit both of us in more ways than one."

He was right, and she could either be a foolish female who denied the obvious and have him chase after her, which of course they had no time for, or she could be practical and enjoy what time she could with him.

"Agreed," she said before she changed her mind.

"Three days, if there are no delays," he said. "Three days for us simply to enjoy each other, sealing the deal and allowing both of us to have what we want, me my son and you your freedom."

"Three days," she repeated. Three days to live her life and gather memories before she would once again be on her own.

They were on the road in a couple of hours when the path turned dense with overgrown foliage and they had to dismount and guide their horses, hoping it cleared not too far ahead.

"You handle a horse with experience," Cullen said as they maneuvered their way around the dense foliage.

Sara held tight to the reins, guiding her mare slowly and carefully, the animal trusting and obeying her every directive. "My father thought me foolish for wanting to ride as well as a man."

"Is that what you told him?"

"You seem as surprised as he did. What good does a horse do me if I can't handle it on my own? My father insisted I would need no such skills." She laughed. "I guess he was wrong."

"Did your father always let you have your way?"

"My way?" she asked curiously. "Why is it that I must forever seek permission from my father or a husband? Why can't I make my own choices? I'm not an idiot like some men, and yet the fools are still free to make their choices."

"Alaina felt the same," he said.

"And what of you?" she asked as he followed in her footsteps, the terrain more even where she stepped.

"Surprisingly, I found myself discussing things with her, both of us working together to find solutions to our problems, neither fighting to be right, just fighting to be together."

"You respected her," Sara said, and he agreed with a nod. "You both were lucky to have found each other."

"Or unlucky?" he said sadly.

"Do you think Alaina would have traded her life for the brief time she spent with you?"

"Never!"

"You didn't even hesitate in answering. You knew her well, and I suspect that you wouldn't ever trade having known her for your suffering in prison."

"Never!"

"I envy the love you had for each other. It is so very priceless."

"That it is, and I will never know it again," he said regrettably.

"That's selfish," she snapped.

Cullen looked affronted. "How dare—"

"You do an injustice to Alaina's memory," she barked. "She loved unselfishly, not caring for the consequences, simply loving with all her heart, and she taught you the same. How dare you not strive to keep what she taught you alive and pass it on so others may share in its beauty."

Cullen stopped. "You know not what you say."

Sara halted her horse and her steps. "You are right, I don't, but I would love to know." She turned and walked on, her horse following without hesitation.

They stopped when the sun was high in the sky to water their horses at a cool stream and fuel their own bodies with cheese and bread and quench their thirst with the tasty wine purchased at market.

They sat on a blanket Sara spread out near to the stream, the food separating them, the overhead sun toasting them nicely. It seemed as if spring had suddenly sprung.

"Will you miss Scotland?" Sara asked, receiving a startled look from Cullen, as if he'd just realized he would be leaving his homeland. "You did say you would be going to America. I just wondered how you felt about leaving."

It didn't take him long to dismiss any concerns. "I

have more unhappy memories here than I do good, and my first thought is for my son's safety. If I remained in Scotland, I would always worry that the Earl of Balford would discover Alexander's identity and kill him. In America, we can build anew, and with my inheritance, I can give my son a good life."

"You sacrifice for your son. You are a good father."

He pointed at her with a hunk of dark bread. "You would do the same."

"Sacrifice for my child?" she asked, and nodded. "Of course, without hesitation. I would protect my child with my life."

"You took your life in your hands to protect Alexander."

"I suppose, though the soldiers saw me as no threat— the idiots. I was simply a woman stuck there by a family who didn't want her. What threat could I be to them?"

Cullen laughed. "If only they knew."

"One felt my wrath when he attempted to corner me and have some fun."

Cullen bolted upright from his lounging position on the blanket. "A soldier attacked you? Did you report him to the Abbess?"

"She would have blamed *me* for initiating it since she knew I searched for a husband." She shook her head. "No, it was much better that I handled it myself, and quite easily at that."

"Dare I ask what you did?"

"Showed him the error of his ways with the strategic placement of a dagger to his loins."

Cullen shook his head with a laugh. "Embarrassment probably kept him silent."

"He never said a word and never dared look my way again, nor did the other soldiers, which worked to my advantage when I abducted your son."

"How did you get your hands on him?"

She had relived that night many times in her thoughts and dreams, the outcome not always the same, and she was grateful they were merely dreams.

"I pestered the sisters so much about seeing the babe that they reported me to the Abbess. She then informed me that the babe was ill and wasn't expected to last long, though I had learned otherwise. I went into action, made the necessary arrangements with a local couple who were desperate for money and promised them even more if they made certain the babe reached the destination safe and sound."

"How did you know the person you sent my son to would take him in?"

"She's a good woman, and I knew she wouldn't refuse my request. I set up a plan so that I would be chosen to see to the babe's burial arrangements—" Her raised hand prevented his query. "I said as much in order to protect the babe from harm. It helped that only two sisters were permitted to tend Alaina and your son, and I found them crying often enough to know that they weren't happy with the situation."

"So not all the nuns were involved in the deceit?"

"Oh my, no. The Abbess couldn't risk that many tongues keeping the secret."

"Who was to kill my son?" he asked with a harsh anger.

"One of the two who tended him, though I could tell neither wanted the chore, and besides, one of the guards had to confirm the babe's death."

"How did you get a live babe past the guards?" he asked incredulously.

"That part presented a serious problem, for I feared what the guards would do to make certain the babe was dead." She grinned and puffed her chest in pride. "Alexander was so very patient with me while I used crushed red berries to mark his skin to make it appear that he had the pox."

"How did you keep him silent and still?"

Sara laughed. "That was easy. I screamed and waved his little red-pocked arm outside his blanket. 'He's dead, he's dead,' I kept screaming, while holding him tight to me and waving his little arm at the guard who stumbled backward." Sara laughed some more. "It was hilarious. Alexander even wore a smile, though no one saw his cute face. The guard ordered me to be rid of him—bury him quick is what he told me. Even the sisters who had tended him kept their distance, worried for their own health."

"And you simply walked off with my son?"

"Past the lot of the terrified idiots," she boasted, "and had Alexander whisked away to safety in no time, and made certain that no one would dare dig up his grave until you came along."

"Why didn't the Abbess tell me of this, to prevent me from unearthing a contagious grave?" Cullen asked.

"She didn't know. The one guard insisted that we tell no one for fear of being left behind, quarantined and secluded at the abbey, and the sisters agreed readily enough. They feared the same treatment."

"So you all agreed to a lie?"

"It worked to my advantage."

He shook his head and smiled. "You went to great lengths and took a dangerous chance to save my son. I truly appreciate it."

Sara shrugged, grateful for his appreciation but uncomfortable with it. "Your son deserved to live. I simply did what was necessary."

He stared at her a moment before saying, "You seem to always do what is necessary, and it's not always simple."

"Necessary decisions are simple, it's the action that is difficult," she argued. "But then I believe you have learned that lesson yourself." She stood, stretching her arms up and out. "We should be going."

Cullen stood more slowly and eased his solid arms into a stretch. "We should find a cottage to shelter us tonight."

Sara protected her eyes from the bright sun with her hand. "There's no threat of rain. Bedding beneath the stars should be no problem."

"If you want to be bedded beneath the stars, that's fine with me. I just thought you might want more of a secluded spot."

Her head whipped around and her eyes turned wide. "We might as well—"

Sara yanked the blanket off the ground. "Don't dare say be done with it." She shook the blanket in his face, bits of dirt and grass flying out from it. "Why not just stretch me out here, hike my skirts and have at it?"

"Is that how you want it?" he asked, his brows arching.

Sara groaned angrily, threw her hands up, discarding the blanket, and mumbled as she stomped off to pace a few feet away.

Cullen approached cautiously. She could tell since his steps were hesitant and measured, as if he feared being caught in a snare.

He whipped his hands up in surrender when she turned a hard glare on him.

"I give up. Whatever I did, I'm sorry. I didn't mean it."

Sara smirked. "If you don't know what you did, how can you be sorry?"

"Simple," he explained. "I never meant to offend you from the start, so since it wasn't intentional, I'm safe apologizing."

Her hands smacked her hips. "You think so?"

"I'm not safe?" he asked with uncertainty, and took a step closer.

She threw back her shoulders, her breasts stretching tight against her blouse. "You should know."

He nodded slowly and eased closer, reaching out to take her hand. "You're right. Explain and I'll fix it."

His fingers locked with hers while his thumb stroked her palm, and magically she felt her body ease and her temper abate.

"You want me to fix it, don't you, Sara?"

He kissed her lips gently before she could respond.

"And I want to fix it. I want it to be right for you."

He eased their locked hands behind her back and drew her in against him, all the while kissing her tenderly, until suddenly the kisses turned hungry.

He fed off her like a starving man, not only tasting her lips, but nibbling along her neck, around her ears, and returning to feed once again at her mouth. She found her appetite just as ravenous as his and enjoyed every morsel he had to offer her.

His free hand cupped her backside and pushed her hard against him, their bodies eager. Her hands raked through his long hair, digging into his scalp, drawing their mouths closer, to feed like frenzied lovers.

One of the horses snorted loudly, snapping the both of them apart. Cullen's hand went to the dirk sheathed at his waist as he quickly scanned the area. Sara did the same, until they both returned to where they started, staring at each other.

Sara's breathing had yet to calm, while Cullen's chest heaved a rapid tempo.

She couldn't help but touch her lips, which pulsed wildly, tingling her fingertips.

Cullen remained where he stood, staring at her.

Neither of them said a word, and then he began to gather the food on the remaining blanket and pack it away, after which he rolled up the blanket and secured it to his horse.

Meanwhile, Sara didn't move. She wasn't certain she

could. Her legs trembled and her stomach rolled and she wasn't at all sure if she could take a step without toppling.

She continued to stare at Cullen's back, broad, muscled, and . . .

He turned around in a flash and headed for her, his feet pounding the ground, stirring the dry earth. The determined look in his narrowed dark eyes almost made Sara run in the opposite direction.

But she stayed where she was, and when he walked up to her, he took hold of her arm and walked her back to the horses. She almost stumbled a few times but he kept her firm on her feet, thank goodness, since her legs trembled more now than they had before. Once in front of her mare, his large hands settled around her waist snugly and, with one swift lift, he placed her on her horse and handed her the reins.

When she thought he was about to step away, his hand came down to rest on her knee, hard and firm.

"We'll get this right, you and me," he said, as if giving his word, then reaffirmed it. "We'll get this right."

Chapter 16

Cullen had much on his mind. There was his son's safety to consider, his plans of revenge, and yet for the moment he thought about Sara and how much he owed her for saving his son's life. At least he attempted to convince himself that was the reason she plagued his thoughts.

The horses meandered along the unobstructed path, the sun bright, the air fresh with spring, and his mind on making love to her. He shook his head, hoping to clear it, yet worried it wouldn't work.

They hadn't shared a week together and yet he felt as if they had shared years. How could that be? When she had spoken of rescuing his son, he felt as if he'd been a part of it. He had held his breath with the telling of the tale and sensed the danger that surrounded her, and still she had taken a chance, placed her life in jeopardy, to save his son.

She'd done it again when she protected the lad at market. She was either very brave or very foolish, and somehow he didn't see Sara as foolish.

She was a remarkable woman whom he greatly admired and respected, and he felt her loneliness, perhaps because he shared it with her. How he had gotten to understand this complex woman, he couldn't say. He only knew that little by little she had revealed herself to him without even realizing it. And the more he uncovered, the more he cherished knowing her.

Perhaps that was why he found himself attracted to her, something he hadn't expected. But she had grown on him like a persistent root that took firm hold and didn't reveal its beauty until it blossomed. And Cullen knew that Sara had yet to blossom.

Three days until they reached McHern land, and he wanted to make certain their wedding vows were sealed by then. He wouldn't take a chance with Sara's safety. When he met her father, he would be sure that no one could dispute that she was in all ways his wife. He would see her safe before taking leave with his son. He owed her that much.

The road opened to a wider path, leaving the forested area behind them and mostly meadows ahead. He was glad they could avoid the gloomy barren moors and travel in the richness of the Highlands. He wanted to scorch the brilliance of the Highlands in his mind so he could describe his son's birthplace to him someday.

He waved Sara to ride beside him, and she obliged, bringing her mare alongside his.

She sat firm and steady in the saddle. Her exceptional skill with a horse amazed him. She rode her mare with confidence, in full control, not the least bit intimidated by the animal. She saw to it that the horse did as she directed, and brooked no objection, just as she had handled the man at market. Her fearlessness filled him with pride for her—his wife.

He turned the conversation far from his thoughts, not yet ready to openly admit his admiration to her and certainly not wanting her to misconstrue it.

"I never imagined leaving my home," he said, his honesty mixing with his sorrow.

"I have learned it is best to expect the unexpected," she said, "for then change is not so difficult."

"Being practical doesn't work when it comes to love," he informed her, and noticed how the gentleness in her blue-green eyes belied her brash nature. Hers was an empathetic soul combined with a passionate spirit.

She shrugged. "I wouldn't know."

"You resign yourself to an empty life," he said with a twinge of guilt, though he wondered why. It had been by her choice that this arrangement was made.

"Is that what you think?" she asked incredulously. "You believe my life will be empty because I will never truly love?"

"Love is a driving force that few escape and that most ache to find."

"True enough," she agreed with a sharp nod. "But I would prefer to find a rare love, one that is everlasting, than to be left with the bad taste of a brief offer that means nothing."

He smiled and nodded. "Now I understand why it

was so difficult for you to find a husband. You actually searched for a man to love."

"Of course," she admitted without hesitation. "If I was committing to spending the rest of my life with this man, then I intended to love him, or at least respect him at the onset so that love had a chance to develop. How else would I have been able to commit to him?"

"And not a one struck your fancy?"

She rolled her eyes and head to the Heavens. "Sweet Lord, not a one."

"None with the slightest potential?" he asked seriously.

"Nothing," she stressed with a firm shake of her head.

He couldn't help but tease her. "Then you found me."

"Hah! You wish," she said.

He felt the bite of her rejection, and damn if it didn't annoy him. "Am I not better than any you have come across thus far?"

Sara looked him up and down, pursing her lips, narrowing her eyes as if she took serious stock of him.

He near choked on his own laughter. "You have to think about it?"

"What I know of you thus far would put you near the top of the list."

"Not the top?" he asked, wounded.

"The top is reserved for the man I love," she said seriously. "I may never find him, but he will remain forever there, first in my heart and mind."

"How lucky for him," Cullen said caustically, wondering why it irritated him so much.

"Lucky for us both," she corrected.

"Then it's equality you search for in a husband?"

"Equal respect and patience." She chuckled. "From watching my share of marriages falter, I realize that if a husband and wife don't have patience with each other, their marriage is doomed."

"You do a lot of observing?"

"I found it not only a wise skill but a beneficial one. Know your foe and friend alike and you are less likely to be hurt or disappointed."

He realized why she intrigued him. She was far more intelligent than the average woman, which produced her confident nature, which certainly would threaten most men, at least men of little character and even less intelligence. No wonder she had had such difficulty finding a husband. He doubted few men existed who could call themselves her equal.

"I also found that by observing others, I learned much about myself," she said with a gentle smile.

"What did you learn?" he asked curiously, amazed at how much he enjoyed talking with her.

"You may not believe it," her eyes sparkled with glee, "but I can be stubborn at times."

Cullen dramatically smacked his hand to his chest. "No, not you."

Sara laughed playfully. "At least I admit it."

"Are you suggesting that I'm stubborn?" he asked, finding her merriment contagious and smiling even though he was certain she had just accused him of being stubborn.

"I think we're equally stubborn."

"*That*, I can admit to!"

He often found strength in his own stubbornness. It had gotten him through more difficult times in his life than he cared to remember. His stubbornness had proved a quality he couldn't afford to live without and therefore helped him to understand the quality of her stubbornness.

"Do you also know you have a generous heart?"

She glared at him, her burgeoning eyes displaying her disbelief. "No—" Her bewilderment impaired her response, and she faltered before finally admitting, "I've never been told I have a generous heart. 'Cold and self-ish' are the words I've heard more often than not in describing my heart."

"Then obviously the person doesn't know you, or perhaps it is himself he describes."

Her eyes saddened, and it saddened his heart.

"It is nice to have someone who defends me."

"You are my wife," he said firmly. "And the truth is always easy to defend."

"You may find yourself constantly defending your wife once we reach my home."

Her serious remark made him realize he wasn't as prepared for the encounter with her father as he should be. He knew little about the man or her home. If they planned to convince her father of their wedded bliss, then he needed to know more and they had to appear a loving couple.

"If that's the case, then make me aware of what I need to know before we arrive, and we need to start acting the newly wed, loving couple."

Sara sighed. "I've been thinking the same myself."

"Consummating our vows would be a good step—"

"How so?" she was quick to ask, though it sounded more an accusation.

"Intimacy brings a certain amount of comfort between couples. It establishes a natural bond, which your father will not be able to deny."

Sara let lose another sigh. "You're right."

Cullen knew that Sara possessed the rare ability to recognize the truth, or perhaps they simply saw things the same way. Regardless, she never argued the truth of a situation. She bluntly stated facts and solutions and that was that. Even if her logic could irritate at times, it was simply because she was right. As she had been about sealing their vows.

"Actually, you've been right all along." He paused, figuring she'd want to speak a few victory words here, and when none came, just a curious smile, he admired her resigned confidence even more.

"We need to protect our vows. It is the wise thing to do, as was my choice in wedding you to gain custody of my son. We have a bargain, and I intend to fulfill my end, as I know you will fulfill yours."

"It's simple that way." Her eyes saddened again, and again it hurt his heart. "It's a bargain we've struck, no more, no less, and we'll be done with it soon enough."

Cullen nodded, his heart growing heavier with sadness. He had tasted love with Alaina and it was like nothing he ever experienced before. He wondered if he could truly find pleasure with a woman he didn't love, though he cared for Sara. She was a good woman with a good heart. How would he feel making love to her?

No, not love, as Sara had reminded him. They'd simply be done with it, and that thought didn't sit well with him at all.

They found a stream to stop by for the night and set up camp, each familiar and comfortable with their chores by now and completing them without question or complaint.

They had established a comfortable bond, and while it wasn't actually an intimate one, it was a close one. He had come to rely on her in sharing the burdens of their journey, and she on him to keep her safe. At least he wanted to believe she felt that way, since he took his wife's safety seriously.

The night air brought with it a chill, and the fire's warmth was most welcome, along with the food they shared.

Cullen noticed that Sara had arranged their blankets on opposite sides of the campfire, and he wondered if it was her way of informing him that they wouldn't be done with it tonight. He didn't believe she feared their joining, so perhaps she was merely shy.

The thought almost sent him into a fit of laughter. Shy was not a word he would use to describe Sara. She was a curious woman who didn't shy away from learning or experiencing anything.

Just from the few kisses they had shared, he sensed she would be a willing and curious lover. She was a woman who had passion for everything she did, and he had no doubt she'd approach sex with the same enthusiasm.

He wasn't surprised that halfway through the meal she was blunt with him about the placement of the blankets.

"I don't know if I'm ready for intimacy with you."

"I can understand that."

"You can?" she asked, astonished.

"Of course, we barely know each other—"

"No," she interrupted, shaking her head. "Many couples wed barely knowing the other. I think the problem is that *I do know you* now."

"Don't find me appealing?" he teased, hoping to lighten her concern.

"You are appealing, again another problem."

It was his turn to shake his head. "Explain."

Sara brushed her hands free of crumbs and sighed. "It was easier when I didn't know anything about you. You were a man in search of his son."

"I still am."

"Yes, but you're also a man still deeply in love with the woman he loved, and a man willing to go to any lengths to rescue his son, a man of strength and character. A man to be respected."

"Then what is the problem?"

"You're a man I could easily fall in love with."

Cullen was shocked silent.

"And I don't want to do that, for then it would be

hard to say good-bye to you, and know I would never see you again."

"We've only met. You can't possibly know that—"

"How long did it take you to know that you could love Alaina?"

He was hesitant to answer, but he did, and with honesty. "I knew I could love her when I first laid eyes on her."

She smiled.

How did he argue with her? And why did he feel angry with her?

"This is nonsense," he snapped, and tried to talk sense into her. "I was there when you needed a husband, and you are simply grateful for the rescue. You are feeling gratitude, nothing more."

"Then why do I enjoy your kisses?" she asked with a soft distress.

Damn, if that knowledge didn't stir his blood, and he was fast to dismiss it before it threatened him. "Because you've never been kissed before. It's only natural you'd enjoy it."

"I feel comfortable in your arms."

He enjoyed the feel of her there. He near cursed himself for the intruding thought, and continued to try and convince her otherwise. "No man has ever offered you comfort, so of course you would favor the feel of my embrace. I am your first in many ways. It is common to feel as you do. It will pass."

"Will it?" she asked with urgent hope.

"Yes," he assured her. "Besides—"

"You could never love me."

He shut his eyes a moment, and when he opened them, her blue-green eyes rested sadly on his face. She knew his answer.

"I loved Alaina."

She nodded. "I know."

"It isn't love. It's gratitude. Trust me," he urged, while sadness squeezed at his heart. He didn't want to hurt her, but he had to be truthful. She respected the truth. She would understand in time.

"I'm glad you clarified it for me," she said with a weak smile. "And I'm glad you didn't make jest of it."

"I would never do that."

"I didn't think you would, which is what gave me the confidence to speak to you about it. You are an honorable man, another quality I so longed for in a husband."

"I am your husband," he said, and stood. "And it is time to seal our vows."

Chapter 17

Sara didn't budge or prevent Cullen from joining her on the blanket. She had discovered pleasure in the few intimate moments they had shared together and could only imagine how wonderful the depths of intimacy would be with him. Now, however, she didn't know if she wanted those memories. They would most likely haunt her for the rest of her life and leave her feeling empty and lonely, and she was lonely enough already.

"There's nothing to fear," he reassured her softly, linking her fingers with his.

She regrettably broke the link, easing her hand away from him. "I don't fear being intimate with you. I fear what would follow, and having lost the woman you love, you know what I refer to."

"I am glad to have loved briefly than never to have tasted love at all."

"Then you are stronger than me," she admitted freely.

His grin turned to a tender laugh. "I'd say more foolish than strong."

Sara chuckled along with him. "But isn't it fools who truly love, for they don't allow fear to stop them?"

Cullen nodded and reached once again to take hold of her hand. "Neither of us are fools, and love doesn't have anything to do with our agreement. You are grateful to me and I to you, and we do what we must for the benefit of us both." He slowly traced circles in the palm of her hand. "Enjoy the moment and think of nothing more."

How could she think straight? His simple touch created havoc within her, causing tingles and shivers to race over her flesh and throughout her body. He leaned toward her and she knew he meant to kiss her, and as much as she wanted to taste his kiss, she knew it would be a mistake, and a costly one.

Regretfully, she eased away from him, her hand sliding out of his grasp. "I can't do this."

"But isn't it best that you do?" he asked.

"It would seem so, but it matters less to me than it once did."

Cullen looked perplexed, his brow scrunching. "Why so?"

Sara was direct and determined, fighting the impulse to surrender and deal with the consequences later. "I gave it more importance than was necessary, or perhaps it was simply that I wished to know intimacy before condemning myself to an empty life." She shook her head. "I never realized that it was love I wished to taste, and I owe that revelation to you and Alaina. Hearing you speak of your love for her made me understand how I longed to find such a love and not simply experience sex."

She smiled at him with saddened eyes. "I want to love. I don't simply want to couple."

"You don't have much choice at the moment," he said. "Not if you hope to protect yourself from future repercussions."

"My choice; my consequences."

"Not anymore."

His curt response startled her. "What do you mean?"

He shrugged. "It's really quite simple. You're my wife and I take my husbandly duties seriously."

"Since when?" she snapped, not believing him, or perhaps wanting to believe him.

"Since I've come to admire you."

He admired her? When had that happened? He had wed her under duress and for a specific purpose. There was no reason for him to feel one way or another about her. When had he looked at her differently? What had caused it? She was who she had always been, but then, hadn't she thought the same of him?

He had simply been a means to an end, and now suddenly he seemed more than that, and not because she found him appealing. He was a handsome man but that mattered little to her. His character interested her. Had he come to feel the same about her?

He eased her back on the blanket and she quickly splayed her hand against his hard chest. She felt his strength; it seeped into her invading her flesh and her senses. It tingled her fingers and sent gooseflesh rushing up her arms and over her body.

She reached up to stroke a small dent in his chin. She hadn't noticed it before, but in this position with him near on top of her and the firelight casting a wicked glow on his face, she could see all of him, dents, nicks, and crannies.

"We are much alike."

"It would seem so," she said, agreeing with the obvious and feeling more than comfortable with it. It was as if they were old friends, knowing the good and the bad of each other, and none of it making a difference. In the end they would, without a doubt, be there for one another.

He kissed the finger that teased his dent. "I would never hurt you. You have my word on that."

"I think I've known that all along. I believed you a good man from first we met."

"Then you trust me?" he asked softly.

"Aye, I do," she said without hesitation.

He brushed warm lips across hers. "Then let us seal our vows and protect you."

Her smile was slow to surface and she ran a finger along his moist lips. Her words did not come easy, but they did come firmly. "I can't."

He took her hand and rested it over his heart. "You wound me."

She sighed with pleasure and disappointment. "And you tempt me beyond belief."

He took her hand and kissed her palm. "Then why not surrender?"

Her eyes danced with merriment. "I would prefer to know victory."

"What makes you think you wouldn't be victorious?"

"Easy," she said with a twinge of regret. "Love can be the only victor in this skirmish."

His eyes turned sad. "Love died with Alaina."

"Only if you let it."

He rolled off her and sat up. "It wasn't by choice."

Sara rested her hand on his arm, and as usual, the strength of him permeated her flesh and sent shivers racing through her. "It is if you let it be."

He got to his feet. "You don't understand. You've never loved."

Sara sat up. "Perhaps, but I've known emptiness."

Cullen hunched down beside her, his hand gliding up her neck to cup her cheek. "Then let me fill you."

How easy it would be to agree. She'd then know the joys of intimacy without the complications. But recently she had given it second thought and believed if she tasted intimacy with Cullen, it would produce more complications than she was able or willing to handle.

He was a good man, and she had so wanted to find a good man to share her life with. Since that didn't seem a possibility, she didn't want to open herself to more disappointment.

"That's not a good idea," she said.

"Why?" he asked with a quick kiss.

She took hold of his wrist. His wildly beating pulse quickly had hers matching his own, then he moved his hand away from her. "I've explained the best I could and we'll leave it at that."

He didn't mask his disappointment or resign himself to it. "We have two days yet."

"Uneventful days to be sure."

He stood, walked to his side of the campfire and stretched out on the blanket. "We shall see."

"You have more pressing matters to consider," she reminded him. "You must act the good husband—"

"I am trying," he said, shaking his hands to the Heavens, "but I have a stubborn wife."

"A sensible wife," she corrected with a sweet grin.

"Not this time," he argued.

"I'm always sensible. You can count on me being sensible."

He turned to rest on his side. "Sensible is getting yourself stuck in an abbey for two years for refusing to obey your father, forcing a stranger to wed you so you could escape, painting pockmarks on my son to get him past the guards? And I have no doubt there is an array of other times your sensible actions were thought otherwise."

"I can't help it if I'm more sensible than anyone else."

He laughed. "So that's the way you explain your insensible actions?"

"I have never made an insensible decision in my life. Not marrying a smelly fool was good common sense.

Marrying a stranger who would place no demands on me and I could rid myself of was great common sense and a promise—"

Sara stopped abruptly and Cullen sprung up, his handsome face contorted by the firelight, giving the impression that the devil had just risen from the fires of Hell.

"Promise? Who did you promise what?"

She hadn't meant to mention the promise, not just yet at least. Besides, no one truly needed to know about it, it would serve no purpose.

"I want an answer, Sara."

"I hadn't planned to tell you this. I saw no reason to."

"I want to know," he said sternly.

His body grew rigid as if he braced for a blow, and Sara was certain her words would hit him hard, so she delivered them fast. "I promised Alaina I would keep her son safe."

Cullen jumped to his feet. "You spoke with Alaina and never planned to tell me about it? In God's name why?"

"As I said, I saw no reason. It would serve no purpose."

"You didn't think I would want to hear what she said to you?"

"And what would those words do for you? Bring you more suffering?"

He shook a finger at her across the fire. "Regardless of what it brought me, I had the right to decide for myself. Now tell me what she said." He shook his head.

"And how in God's name did you get to speak with her? You told me there were guards at the door. And why? Why did you see her?"

"To promise her I would keep her son safe from harm if someday she ever wished to return for him."

Cullen's eyes turned wide. "That's why she had insisted Alexander was alive. She knew what you had done."

"That was all she knew, and she had agreed that she should know no more. If questioned for any reason, she'd be able to speak truthfully and never fear bringing harm to her son."

"You didn't tell her your name?"

Sara shook her head. "I simply informed her that her son was safe and would remain so until she came to claim him."

"And Alaina said to you?"

Sara hesitated.

"Tell me. Please, I must know."

Feeling his ache as if it were her own, Sara nodded and spoke Alaina's words. "She said, 'I will return for my son.'"

The impact of her words hit Cullen like an arrow to the heart and dropped him to his blanket. Sara stood and walked around the fire to join him. She sat beside him, her arm going around his slumped shoulders.

"I had but a few moments with Alaina. My concern was that she knew her son would be safe. There was no time for more since I arranged for the guard and the sister who normally tended her to go on separate fool's errands. The timing had to be perfect and I had to be gone before they returned. I couldn't take the chance of being discovered there. After all, I was the one who buried the babe, and I didn't want to cast doubt on the situation."

"Again you took a chance with your life, and this time for Alaina."

"It tore at my heart to think that the child's mother would forever think her son dead. It wasn't fair, and I couldn't allow her to suffer when I had it in my power to ease her pain and give her hope of one day reuniting with him. It was the right thing to do."

Cullen took hold of her hand and squeezed tight. "You did right by my son and Alaina. I will do right by you."

"You have," she assured him. "You wed me."

"But I haven't protected you."

"I have no problem in seeing to my own safety."

"You have me now to see to that," he said adamantly.

"For now I do, and I appreciate it."

"I promise you that I will see you safe before I leave you."

Leave you.

The two words rang loud and clear in her head. He would leave her, and once again she would be alone, and that was all right; after all, it had been their agreement. She couldn't ask for more.

Unfortunately, over the last few days she had grown accustomed to having a husband, and a good one at that. She had even allowed her mind to wander now and again, but only for a very short time, thinking on what it would be like if she went to America with Cullen and Alexander and was able to be a true wife and mother.

It was a foolish dream, no more, and she didn't linger long in the foolishness. It hurt much too much to spend time in such nonsense. Her destiny was here in Scotland, and his was in America. That was why she didn't want this ruse to go any further. It would pain her too much to say good-bye. She preferred he remained a stranger, though she had grown to know him enough that he could never be a stranger to her.

"I mean what I say," Cullen said, squeezing her hand.

She nodded, knowing he did, which was what caused her heart to hurt a little more. "I know and I thank you."

She attempted to stand, but he held her firm.

"Stay," he said softly.

"I am tired and need sleep—"

"Sleep with me."

Her eyes rounded.

He shook his head. "I just want to hold you next to me."

He didn't want to be alone, and neither did she.

"Let me get my blanket," she said.

He stayed her with a soft touch. "No, stay, I'll get it."

As soon as the blankets were settled, he took her in his arms and together they stretched out beside the fire, Sara closer to the warmth, since the air had chilled considerably, and Cullen's arms tight around her.

"Thank you for giving my Alaina peace," he whispered in her ear, and gently kissed her temple.

A response wasn't necessary, and she didn't know if she could speak if she wanted to. A lump had lodged in her throat, threatening tears if it remained as it was—a hurtful pain.

She did what she had done since she was a child, chasing the pain away with fanciful dreams. Dreams could produce magic for her. She would think of wonderful things that she could do, and more often than not she had found a way of doing them, like learning to ride better than most men or crafting a special bow for herself.

She had even dreamed of a good husband, and had gotten him, but just wasn't able to keep him.

The lump grew larger, and she quickly changed her thoughts. But Cullen somehow continued to invade her dreams, and soon she was envisioning a happy life with him and Alexander. The thoughts brought her such joy that she couldn't chase them away. Besides, they refused to be ignored, so she gave them free rein and imagined sailing off to America with them.

Every now and again Cullen would tighten his hold on her and mumble incoherently. She assumed he dreamed of Alaina and his son. It had to have torn his heart apart, being unable to save her, and unable to be there to protect his son. All he loved had been ripped away from him, and now she thought of him fighting

173

to get back the most precious of gifts lovers can share—
their child.

No matter what it took, she would help him and his
son to safety. It was the right thing to do.

And she?

She would have her dreams.

Chapter 18

Cullen's sullen mood mirrored the gray skies, and try as he might, he couldn't escape his brooding. He had barely spoken to Sara since rising a couple of hours ago, and once they took to the trail, he hadn't said a word to her. She had tried to engage him in conversation, but he sat silent on his horse and she eventually gave up.

He blamed his surly mood on his dream. He often dreamed of Alaina, and actually looked forward to those dreams where she seemed so alive, so real to the touch. He had expected to dream of her last night after what Sara told him, but instead he had dreamed of Sara.

A rumble of thunder portrayed a measure of his grumbling anger. It seethed beneath the surface, ready to erupt, and yet he wasn't certain who he was angry with.

No, he told himself. That was a lie. He was angry with himself for betraying Alaina by dreaming of making love to Sara.

He cringed at the betrayal and near swore beneath his breath at the fact that he had actually enjoyed loving

Sara. She'd been so responsive, so giving, so honest in her desire for him.

Could he say the same?

That was what angered him the most—his desire for Sara. It felt stronger than he remembered it being for Alaina. How could that be? Had he simply gone too long without a woman?

He mumbled incoherently, berating himself for believing his dream held any validity. He was a man in need of a woman, plain and simple.

Cullen gave a quick glance to Sara, riding beside him. She was more of a beauty than he had first realized, but then, he hadn't known her at all. Actually, he hadn't wanted to know any woman. He was forced to get acquainted with Sara, and was grateful that he had.

He smiled slowly, her fiery red curls springing out of control from her head, never obeying a pat or a tuck but simply doing as pleased and looking completely natural on her. And fitting her pale skin perfectly, while a smatter of freckles stained the bridge of her nose.

Then there were her eyes, which had intrigued him from the start. At first he'd assumed the blue-green hue had gotten his attention, but it was so much more. Caught in the depths of her eyes was the essence of her character, so rich and vital that it refused to be disregarded or masked.

He looked away, afraid his eyes would steal down along her body and make him face what he had tried to ignore—that he found her appealing. Tall, shapely, with curves and mounds he ached to explore and plunder.

He shook his head.

He needed a woman, he told himself again. That was the problem. He needed to satisfy his lust and be done with it. It would settle everything, and then he'd want Sara no more. She was simply available and convenient.

He growled beneath his breath, the selfish thought disturbing him, and yet he was unable to rid himself of it.

"Are you all right?' she asked bluntly. "You've been mumbling and groaning since we left camp hours ago. Talk to me. Tell me what troubles you."

He near grinned, thinking of telling her how he'd like to yank her off her mare, take her to the ground, toss her skirts up and take her like a man too long deprived. A tumble between friends, no more.

But she looked for more, and he couldn't give it to her.

He rubbed his stiff shoulder. "It's nothing. I just woke in a dour mood."

"You want me to believe that?"

"Believe what you want," he snapped.

She shrugged. "Have it your way and stay miserable. It makes for such pleasant company." She gave her horse a nudge with her heel and moved a few feet in front of him.

He cursed himself for being abrupt with her, but he was in no mood to discuss his mood. Besides, it wasn't any of her business, and she had a way of getting people to reveal themselves through casual conversation. Before you knew it, you were confiding in her like a trusted friend, and he wasn't about to share last night's dream with her.

The ground shook before thunder rumbled, and just as Cullen hurried to Sara, she turned wide eyes on him.

"Riders approach," she said.

Her eyes followed his, darting around the area, searching for cover.

Their only chance was to blend into the woods that bordered the trail on both sides and hope to get far enough within the forest so as not to be seen. Unfortunately, the trees were sparse upon entering, and he wasn't sure they had enough time to reach the dense brush that would provide sufficient cover.

"We need to hurry," he said, urging her to go before him.

He was grateful she didn't argue, but that gratitude faded fast when he caught sight of the ragged looking group of men who rounded the bend in the road and, as soon as they spied them about to enter the woods, gave chase.

"They've seen us," he said, and gave her horse's rump a sharp slap. "Get yourself to safety and hide."

Cullen drew his bow and an arrow from the sheath attached to the saddle. He needed to even the odds some. They were either robbers or mercenaries, and the latter were a dangerous bunch. They hired out to whoever would pay the highest fee and do whatever bidding they wished. No one was safe around them, man, woman, or child.

He readied the bow and took careful aim as they descended on him. If he took two out then drew his sword on the other two, he'd have a fighting chance. He let loose the arrow, and it hit its mark dead on in the chest, sending the rider toppling to the ground.

Cullen was quick with the next arrow and took another rider down. But as he grabbed his sword to face the other two, one of them rode into the woods after Sara.

"I'll have my fun with her," he said aloud, wearing a huge grin.

Cullen nearly went after him, but knew he needed to take the other man down first. He had to trust that Sara could hold her own until he could get to her. They battled from their saddles, swords clashing, and Cullen meanwhile had only one thing in mind: Sara.

His thought for her safety nearly drove him mad. What if he got to her too late? What if she suffered at the man's hands? What if she died? He'd never forgive himself.

His worry fueled his strength, and he fought like a madman, finally driving his sword through the man's stomach. When the man slumped over, Cullen gave his chest a shove with his sandal to dislodge his sword.

The man toppled off his horse, dead, as Cullen quickly turned and went after Sara.

Prayers that he'd be on time fell from his lips as he flew through the woods at breakneck speed in the direction he'd seen her disappear.

It wasn't long before he had to slow to almost a

crawl, the woods having grown dense. That was when he heard a cry like that of a wounded animal and his heart clinched in his chest.

Another high-pitched scream had him slipping off his horse and running the rest of the way, scrambling over a boulder and pushing past heavy pine branches to emerge in a small clearing where he came to an abrupt halt.

"I'm dying," the man said with an angry glare at Sara, who stood not far from where he sat on the ground, her sword dripping blood.

"That you are," she confirmed bluntly. "But didn't you mean to do the same to me once you had your way with me?"

"That be different," he snapped, and held his stomach, blood pouring down over his hands.

"I don't think so," she said. "You got what you deserved, and from a woman nonetheless."

"I agree," Cullen said, stepping beside her.

"The others have been seen to?" she asked.

"All taken care of," he assured her.

"You got us all?" It was the man's last words. His eyes rolled back in his head and he fell over dead.

"I'm glad to see you're safe," Cullen said.

Sara pointed to the dead man with her sword. "His ignorance did him in."

Cullen smiled. "You mean he underestimated you."

She nodded, then shook her head. "The fool actually laughed when I drew my sword to fight him, and then—" She shook her head, recalling the scene. "Then he proceeds to tremble in fear as he approaches me, telling me he's so very frightened of me, and when I actually demonstrate my skill with a sword, he gets angry and stupidly charges at me."

"Landing right on your sword?" Cullen asked with a grin.

"Right on it. I didn't even work up a sweat. The fool did himself in."

Cullen laughed and threw his arms around her, hugging her tight. "You're precious, Sara, precious. And Lord, how relieved I am that you're safe."

Sara stepped away from him to wipe her sword clean on the man's trousers. "You must have worried that if I died you wouldn't know where to find your son."

Cullen was shocked silent, not by her remark, but because the thought hadn't entered his head. His concern had been solely for her safety. He hadn't given a moment's thought to his son.

She walked up to him. "I made a promise that I intend to keep. I had thought to keep Alexander safe until his mother returned for him, but now I will see father and son safely out of Scotland, so my promise to Alaina will be fulfilled so she may finally rest in peace."

Cullen stared after her and his heart swelled. Sara was a remarkable woman with more courage than some men. She faced life with common sense and personal pride that many lacked, and she did it with no expectations. She was who she was, and she let no one rob her of her character and honor.

She helped him drag the bodies deeper into the woods.

Deciding that the horses would make a nice gift to her father from Cullen, they disposed of their saddles.

In no time they were on their way again, traveling along the road as if nothing had happened, though the gray clouds continued to follow them.

Cullen remained silent, with even more on his mind now than before. First, he'd dreamed of Sara and not Alaina, and then he thought of Sara's safety before that of his son. The woman was beginning to affect him. But why?

Perhaps if he bedded her and had done with it, his thoughts would once again be his own. He remembered how he could think of nothing but Alaina when he first met her. She plagued his thoughts day and night and—

Cullen nearly spit out a wicked oath. What was the matter with him? He had fallen in love with Alaina. It was only natural he'd constantly think about her. He wasn't falling in love with Sara, so why did she haunt his thoughts?

He glanced over at her, saw that she looked upset and cursed himself for not having given thought to her ordeal. Even though she'd handled herself well, it didn't mean it hadn't affected her, especially if . . .

"Is he your first kill?" he asked.

Sara nodded without looking at him. "I never had a reason . . . "

"Of course you didn't. Men are the warriors, not woman."

Her head whipped around. "We're all called on to

be warriors one time or another, to defend our beliefs, what we hold dear, or to protect ourselves. For whatever reason, we become warriors out of necessity."

She was right. In the end, he realized, Alaina had become a warrior out of necessity. She hadn't shied away from the fight, but embraced it out of love for him and their son.

Strange that this woman was teaching him about love when he thought he had known all about it. He'd assumed he had learned it all with Alaina, but could see now that he had merely touched the surface. He hadn't peeled away the intricate layers and gone deeper. He and Alaina had such a brief time together, they had barely gotten to know, truly know, one another. Short interludes, stolen moments, hurried touches, hungry kisses, and little if no time to talk with each other.

Still, they fell in love in spite of it all, and he would cherish their love for eternity. Perhaps having experienced that love allowed him to examine love more closely now, he thought, and to seek more from love than he ever thought he could.

The idea startled him and he quickly pushed it out of his mind. He didn't need to be thinking about love. He had more important matters to see to, the most important being his son.

"You are an excellent warrior," he commended.

She hesitated as if uncertain. "Thank you."

"What's wrong?"

She stared at him.

He could see the ache of uncertainty in her eyes and

wanted her to know she could trust him. "You can tell me. We're friends."

After a moment, she nodded as if accepting his friendship and his shoulder to lean on. "I was frightened."

"So was I," he admitted. "Any warrior who enters a battle fearless is a fool."

"Then I am a good warrior," she said, accepting the truth.

"I'd be honored to have you by my side in battle any time."

She seemed surprised. "It is generous of you to say that."

"We've both agreed that the truth never remains silent."

She nodded slowly and spoke her own truth. "I am glad we are friends."

"So am I," he said, realizing how much it meant to him that she accepted him as a friend. It seemed more important to him than that they were husband and wife.

Though he hadn't known the man who raised him as well as he would have liked, he had taught him that a best friend could be counted on, would always be there for you without question, and would fight by your side to the end.

Sara was his best friend.

The thought made him feel good when suddenly another thought struck him hard.

He had never gotten to be best friends with Alaina.

Chapter 19

They came upon a deserted cottage, and after bedding down the horses in a broken-down lean-to for the night, entered the cottage. It had been a long, demanding journey in so many different ways. One more day and it would be over. She would return home after two years and with a husband, her long struggle for freedom at an end.

"It's been abandoned for some time," Cullen said, his glance sweeping the room.

Sara looked around the one-room cottage and agreed with a nod. The place reeked of emptiness, not a stitch of furnishings or personal belongings. Had a desperate family given up? Had they gathered their things and simply moved out? Had they abandoned home and hearth because they had no choice?

How many families were making extreme choices out of necessity? Hadn't she done the same herself? Hard times called for hard choices. She had made her hard choice, and with no regrets.

"We'll camp outside," Cullen said, handing her the rolled bedding. "I'll see to the fire."

Sara took it without thought. They had established a comfortable routine between them and one they could count on. Actually, it spoke volumes. It was an unspoken promise that they could count on each other under any circumstance, as she had counted on Cullen coming to her rescue from the mercenary who attacked her.

She harbored no doubt or fear that Cullen wouldn't come to her aid, just as she would come to his. It was strange how they had established an undeclared promise between them. She could believe it was because they were husband and wife and therefore it was his duty to protect her, but she knew better.

They were friends. They had forged a bond, though neither of them had planned on it. It had developed on its own and with a common goal—to save his son. They had both pledged to see him safe, and the innocent child brought them closer together, as had Alaina.

Alaina's strength and courage through the entire ordeal had been a shining example of love at its best. She had been unselfish in her zest to love, and in the end had given unselfishly for that love . . .

Alaina had given her life.

Sara couldn't imagine a greater love, and she envied Cullen and Alaina what they had shared.

She yawned as she spread out her blanket on the other side of the campfire from where he had placed his own, then set out dried fish and bread for them to satisfy their hunger.

"You're exhausted," Cullen said, joining her on the blanket.

"One day and it's over and I'll be home in my own bed."

"*We'll* be home in your bed," he corrected, "and for a few weeks."

Startled by his remark, which was all too true, she simply nodded. How was she going to sleep in the same bed with him for the next few weeks and not expect anything to happen? Actually, she had expected something to happen, but her decision on the matter changed and now posed a problem.

"I can see you hadn't thought about that," he said, a grin flashing across his handsome face.

"I hadn't thought it a problem until recently," she answered honestly. "But we will make the most of it."

His grin resurfaced and turned wicked. "I hope so."

Sara smiled and shook a finger at him. "Don't get your hopes up."

"Hope is all I have," he teased.

Sara laughed and nibbled at the food. "Don't think you can tease me into your bed."

"I want you safe."

Her eyes caught with his, and for a moment they locked in silent battle, until Sara took command. "I am safe."

"You know you're not," he said bluntly. "Protect yourself and seal our vows."

It would be easy, so very easy, to surrender and do as he suggested. What did she have to lose?

Her heart.

It was foolishness for sure, to think she could fall in

love with this man. She barely knew him, and yet had to admit she knew him better than anyone she called friend. They shared common interests, opinions, and courage. He was everything she searched for in a man and more. How did she commit intimately with him and simply walk away?

"I can take care of myself," she assured him.

"You don't have to. You have a husband to do that."

What a wonderful thought that was. That she wasn't alone; she had someone to look after her, and she him. But it wasn't real. It was a ruse near over, and then once again she'd be alone. Why torture herself with brief memories? It was better she had none.

"Not a real husband," she reminded.

"As real as you let him be."

She reached out a hand to him. She didn't know why, perhaps because she simply could. "It's so strange how we were brought together, and even stranger that you are no longer a stranger to me. You are a good man."

"I am a better lover."

She laughed softly. "You try to tempt me."

"Is it working?"

She shook her head and with a smile said, "Let it be, Cullen. I am fine."

He leaned into her and brushed his lips across hers. "Does it make a difference that I want you?"

Sara's eyes rounded in surprise. No man had ever wanted her, and while the thought thrilled her, she couldn't help but wonder if he meant it, or did he merely mean to entice her into his bed and see to sealing their bargain?

She whispered in his ear, "Does it make a difference that I want more?"

Cullen kissed her lips gently and pressed his cheek to hers. "I'll give you what I can."

She thought him generous for even trying, and considered that perhaps she was selfish for not accepting his generosity. But she knew she couldn't. She had had done so much out of necessity that she'd thought bedding Cullen would be easy, but she hadn't counted on the ache to love and be loved to interfere.

She wondered why it had, and why she should give it credence.

Cullen placed a tender hand to her cheek. "Let me love you."

"If only you could," she whispered.

"One night," he said.

His mouth brushed across hers, stealing a kiss and her breath.

He cupped her face in his hands. "One night, just you, me, and nothing else. Two strangers loving, touching, healing each other, and afterward . . . ?" He kissed her firm on the lips. "Parting with no regrets, only beautiful memories."

Wasn't that what she was afraid of?

"Don't think," he warned in a murmur. "Just let yourself feel."

His hand slipped around her neck to take firm hold, and she was soon lost in a kiss that devastated her senses and heated her flesh. While she thought to protest, she didn't make a move to stop him from lowering her onto the blanket and stretching out beside her.

"This is right," he whispered, unlacing her blouse ties to slip his hand inside and cup her generous breasts.

Did he need to convince himself of his actions? Did he doubt himself?

Her own misgivings dwindled with each touch. She couldn't, nor wouldn't, deny that she liked his touch. His large hand was warm and gentle, and yet so firmly cupped her breast and squeezed lightly, his thumb caressing her nipple to life.

"So right," he whispered as he lowered his lips to hers.

His lips met her palm, and his eyes spread wide open.

"You wonder if this is right?" she asked, easing away from his mouth and trying desperately to fight the sparks of passion igniting her body.

Confusion scrambled over his face. "Of course it's right."

"Why?"

He answered sharply. "We need to seal our vows. You need protection. I want you. Take your pick."

She pushed him off her with regret but resolve and sat up. "I don't want to take my pick."

He rolled to his feet. "Be reasonable."

Sara laughed. "Oh, but I am."

"Reasonable is leaving yourself vulnerable to your father?"

"Reasonable is respecting myself in the morning."

Cullen pressed his hand to his cheek. "That stung."

"It was meant to," she assured him firmly.

"We're married," he said, as if making sense of the situation.

"Precisely." She nodded sharply. "I need no more from you."

He looked about to argue, his mouth dropping open then snapping shut, then moved to the other side of the campfire. "Fine, have it your way."

"It's been my way from the start," she reminded him.

"It certainly has, which means if your plan fails, it's your fault. I still walk away with my son."

"You met your end of the bargain. I'll meet mine."

"You'll get no argument from me." He dropped to his blanket. "You do realize, though, that people will be expecting us to be a loving couple. That means hugs, kisses, and displays of affection. After all, we've just gotten married."

"We can manage that since it won't be long before our marital bliss shows signs of problems. Of course most people will be expecting it," she said with a resigned sigh.

"Why?"

"No one believes me capable of keeping a husband. Even with my father doubling my dowry, few were interested, and those who were lost interest when they realized I would be no—"

"No malleable wife," he finished with a chuckle.

"Not one of them had a backbone—"

"To stand up to you," he interrupted again.

She narrowed her eyes. "And you do? It seems to me you *had* to marry me."

His chuckle grew. "Tongues are going to wag over our rushed wedding."

"There'll be not a smidgen of a chance of me being with child," she said forcefully, making certain he didn't detect her regret.

He responded with equal force. "That's for the best since I'd never abandon my child."

"Then this obviously works for the both of us." It actually put an end to their continuing debate on sealing their vows. In her zeal to satisfy her father's demands, she had forgotten about the possibility of becoming pregnant. While she loved children and wanted a slew of them, she would never intentionally raise a fatherless child.

"Anything more I need to know about your father?" he asked.

She thought a moment. What could she say about her father? While he was a good man, she and he had been at odds most of her life. He accused her of challenging him straight from the womb, though he also defended her many times.

She answered him strangely, or perhaps she was looking for an answer herself. "I believe he loves me, though he rarely shows it and more often than not I think he prefers when I'm not around." She shook her head slowly. "I never truly understood my father. He seems a good man, many speak highly of him, but when it comes to me he seems . . . "

"You don't really know, do you?" he asked when her silence remained.

"Not really," she said regrettably. "And I believe my refusing to wed Harken McWilliams broke my father's patience."

"Then you admit you have tried your father's patience on a regular basis?"

"Without a doubt," she said with a hesitant smile that grew with the memories of her many adventures or misadventures.

"Somehow I believe my sympathy should go to your father," Cullen said with a scratch of his head.

"I suppose I gave him a wee bit of trouble," she admitted.

"Wee?"

"Maybe more," she said with a laugh, then regaled Cullen with tales of her youth, starting with the time she was five and first learned to climb trees—big trees, to everyone's dismay—though it took her a good many months to learn how to climb down.

Cullen laughed. "So you managed to scale these large trees with ease, but it took you longer to learn to climb down, leaving your father to forever rescue you?"

"Yes, that's right." She grinned, proud that she had accomplished such a feat, even if descending them took more effort and time to learn.

"Your father rescued you every time?"

"Every one of them."

"Even though he warned you each time not to do it again and you did, he still climbed the trees to get you down?" Cullen asked.

"Yes," she assured him.

Cullen yawned and stretched out on his blanket. "That takes more than patience. That takes love."

Sara sat silent, digesting his remark. She had always thought her father angry with her after rescuing her from the trees. She had never given thought to the fact that he had never refused to rescue her or sent someone else to do it. He had always come for her himself.

She yawned and laid down on her blanket to think about her father.

Hours later Sara jumped up out of sound sleep, her eyes as round as full moons, her body trembling. With a terrified glare, she quickly scanned the surrounding area.

Cullen joined her, her abrupt actions having woken him though she hadn't made a sound.

"What's wrong?" he whispered.

She pressed a hand to her heaving chest. "I believe a nightmare."

He went to her and slipped his arms around her trembling body.

She quickly grabbed hold of him, her arms going around his waist and hanging onto him for dear life. He was warm, solid and real, and she had no intention of letting go.

A sharp owl hoot caused her to jump, and she dug

her face into his hard chest and was relieved to hear the solid, steady beat of his heart. He wasn't afraid, which was good, very good, because she was terrified. She wasn't one to frighten easily, and yet the dream had left her shaken to the core.

"Want to tell me about it?" he asked.

She was relieved he didn't let go of her. She didn't want him to. She wanted him right where he was, with her arms tight around him.

She shook her head.

"All right, but remember it was only a nightmare. It wasn't real. You're safe."

She nodded and didn't dare tell him that her dream was real, all too real.

"Why don't you sleep beside me tonight."

"Yes. Yes," she repeated, bobbing her head.

Cullen continued to hold her tight as he lowered them both to his blanket, placing her closer to the fire and then wrapping himself around her. She didn't object. She welcomed every part of him, from the leg he threw over hers, to his chest pressed firm against her back, to the arms that circled her with strength.

"Sleep," he whispered in her ear. "You're safe."

She nodded, but doubted she would sleep a wink. She didn't want to. She didn't want to chance returning to the dream. It had frightened her so badly, and worse, left her with a fear she didn't think would subside anytime soon.

She tried to chase the dream out of her head but the memory of it kept returning to haunt her. In it, she'd been running in the woods with Cullen, Alexander tight in his arms. Soldiers were everywhere and she knew they would soon be caught and killed. She had to do something. She had to save them. She had promised Alaina she would keep her son safe.

A man suddenly appeared in front of the three of them, sword in hand. Cullen had no sword, no way of defending him and his son. Without thought, Sara jumped in front of father and son and screamed for them to run as the man drove the sword deep into her stomach.

The last thing she remembered was seeing Cullen and Alexander fleeing to safety. She had saved them.

Had it been just a nightmare, she wondered, or a vision of the future?

Chapter 20

They woke early and left camp with the first light of dawn. Cullen followed Sara, the extra horses behind him in single file, attached by a rope to keep them from wandering off. Sara had spent a fitful night in his arms, getting little sleep, as did he from her constant restlessness. The sleepless night didn't disturb him as much as did his concern for her. He had wondered over her dream. Why had it upset her so much? And why wouldn't she speak to him about it? She spoke to him about everything. The woman rarely lacked for conversation. Even her silence spoke volumes, because it warned him that something bothered her.

She had been silent since they left camp. Something definitely preyed on her mind. He told himself not to worry about her. Sara had made her choice, and she would keep their bargain. There was no need for concern.

All last night, however, she had remained cradled in his arms, burrowing deeper against him during fitful episodes. She sought his comfort and protection, and he had been glad to give it to her. Actually, he felt an overwhelming need to protect Sara, just as he had when the mercenary had chased her.

Then, while he'd known that she could hold her own, he had been enraged that she would need to defend herself even for the short time it took to get to her. He wanted her safe and secure. But then, he'd wanted the same for Alaina.

Not for the first time, that he compared his feelings for Alaina with those he had for Sara startled him. He told himself that it meant nothing more than wanting to make sure he was there to defend a friend.

It comforted him to think of it that way, since he did count Sara as a friend. Friends, especially good ones, weren't made easily, though Sara was the exception. Their friendship might have begun out of necessity, but it had flourished and deepened out of respect.

He knew that Sara would help him regardless of the circumstances. It relieved him to realize that, for if anything should happen to him, he knew she would see to his son's safety. She would even get Alexander to his Burke if he asked it of her.

Cullen realized then that it wasn't going to be easy saying good-bye to her. Strangely enough, he would miss her.

"If we keep this pace, there's a good chance we can reach my home by nightfall," she said with a quick turn of her head.

"Are you sure you don't want to spend the night alone, just the two of us, and return home in the first light of morning?" he asked. She would know he was asking if she'd changed her mind, and telling her that there was still time and the choice remained hers.

"I want to get home as soon as possible," she answered, and gave her horse a nudge.

He didn't catch a smile or a frown as she turned her glance back to the trail ahead. Was she ambivalent about her decision? And why did he continue to concern himself with her choice?

He kept telling himself it was because he wanted her protected before he left her behind. He had agreed to that from the beginning, and wanted to fulfill his end of the bargain. A nagging voice, however, told him that he wanted to make love to her. That he wanted not just to give her that one night of love she ached for, but that he himself ached for. And it disturbed him, that by wanting to make love to Sara he was betraying Alaina. It left him feeling guilty.

How had everything become so complicated? It had all been simple when he started his journey. Find his son and return to St. Andrew Harbor, where his half brother would have a ship waiting to take them to America.

He would have never dreamed that a woman would enter his plans and send them astray. He hadn't wanted another woman. Hadn't wanted to feel anything for another woman. His hurt was too new and raw. Yet Sara had somehow managed to enter his heart—as a friend of course, nothing more.

A friend you want to bed.

Damn that voice and damn his betraying thoughts

and feelings. Sara's decision was best for them both. He should be grateful she had more sense than he did. He would play the loving husband, annoyed husband, distant husband, whatever kind of husband Sara wanted and be done with it.

"Be done with it!" he mumbled harshly.

"Did you say something?" Sara asked with a quick glance at him.

Was that a tear at the corner of her eye? She had turned around so fast he couldn't quite be sure and it damn well disturbed him.

Sara just wasn't the type to cry.

"I didn't say anything," he answered. "Are you all right?"

"Fine," she called out much too cheerily.

She hadn't conversed with him all morning and now this false cheeriness in her voice. What was going on?

"We should stop to rest the horses and ourselves," he shouted.

She turned after brushing her hand at her eyes and he grew even more suspicious.

"Later," she insisted.

"Now!" he demanded. "Isn't there a brook nearby? I seem to remember stopping at one with my father."

"Yes," she answered reluctantly. "It meanders through much of the hillside in these parts, the water cold and clear."

"Just what we need," he said, and directed the horses off the trodden path. He knew Sara would follow, albeit grudgingly. He wanted to know what troubled her and he was determined they wouldn't take another step until she shared her concern with him.

The horses drank at the brook while he placed a blanket near the water's edge. Sara laid out some bread and cheese, though appeared uninterested in the light fare. Cullen was famished, their morning fare inadequate.

"You're not hungry?" he asked, reaching for the bread and tearing a piece off.

"Not really," she said, sitting crossed-legged on the edge of the blanket and staring at the babbling brook.

"Tell me what's troubling you," he demanded so sharply that she whipped around to face him. "And don't bother to tell me it's nothing. I know better."

"Do you now?" she asked curtly.

He nodded. "You being silent means something is troubling you, so tell me and be done with it."

She let out an agitated sigh and shook her head. "I don't have to share my upset with you."

"But you do," he insisted with a soft smile. "You see, somehow I've grown concerned for your well-being. Maybe it's because I'm your husband and I take my duties seriously. Maybe it's because I consider you a good friend and I don't want to see you hurt, or maybe I care for you and want to help. Whatever it is, I don't intend to budge from this spot until you share it with me."

"You don't have to feel any such way for me," she said with a dismissive wave of her hand at his face.

He shrugged. "Regardless, I do, and that's that."

She puffed her chest and looked ready to protest.

"Don't bother arguing with me. It only wastes time."

Sara deflated fast enough, her shoulders slumping. "It's the dream."

"Tell me," he offered gently.

Her reluctance remained obvious as she shifted uneasily from side to side and dug her fingers deep into her unruly red curls.

He dusted bread crumbs off his hands then reached out, locking his fingers with hers, and simply waited. He noticed then that her eyes bore signs of tears, so contrary to her confident nature, and it annoyed him that she had grown so very upset and chosen to suffer alone.

"Let me help ease your hurt, Sara," he urged.

"It's nothing more than a nightmare that haunts me," she insisted, dismissing his help.

"Share it with me and perhaps we can make sense of it together."

He watched the play of mixed emotions flash across her face, questioning whether that was a wise choice. Until finally she seemed to surrender, the faint lines around her narrowed eyes fading, her tight jaw relaxing and her taut chest softening with a sigh.

"The dream seemed so real," she said.

"I've had a few of those myself."

"You have?" she asked anxiously.

He nodded. "It was madness, but I dreamed I was rescued from Weighton prison by a young lad." He shrugged. "It turned out to be a young woman in disguise."

He meant his story to ease her concerns, but it appeared to disturb her, her face growing tense once again.

"Then your dream did come true."

He realized that hers hadn't been a dream, but a nightmare, and she obviously feared it coming true. He moved closer beside her and slipped his hand from hers to drape around her shoulder and draw her against him.

"It can't be that bad. Tell me."

She snuggled against him, slipping into the crook of his arm. "Soldiers surrounded you, me, and Alexander."

He didn't like it already, but remained silent.

"There was no way out and you carried no sword. A man appeared wielding a large sword. He charged at you and Alexander. I jumped in front of you both and screamed for you to run as he ran me through with his sword. I watched you reach safety before I . . . "

Cullen felt a jolt to his heart and his gut. It took a moment for him to compose himself before he chanced speaking. Otherwise, he knew he'd use endless oaths to make her understand how that would never happen. He'd never let her give her life for him.

"That would never happen," he said.

"How do you know?"

"I would never allow you to give your life for me," he said bluntly.

"It was my choice."

"It was a rash decision in a moment of panic," he corrected.

Her mouth dropped open and her eyes rounded. "It was a decision made out of necessity. How else would you and your son have survived?"

"I would have found a way," he assured her firmly.

"I couldn't be sure of that," she argued. "My first thought was for yours and Alexander's safety."

"And what of your own?"

"It was expendable."

He pulled away from her, shaking his head. "It most certainly isn't."

"At the time I thought it was."

"You were wrong," he near shouted.

"My nightmare, my choice!"

"A foolish choice," he said, shoving his face in hers.

"I save you and your son's life and you tell me I'm foolish?"

"You will not give your life for me," he ordered sharply.

"I will if I want to," she said, her nose pressed to his.

"You will not. I *will not* allow it. I *will* keep you safe."

"What if you can't?" she asked softly, and pressed her cheek to his before kissing his lips gently.

Instantly, the memory of Alaina dying in his arms flashed in his mind and overpowered him with raging grief, leaving him momentarily speechless. He had to find his breath, his wits, and his courage to speak.

He squeezed her chin between his thumb and fore-finger. "I will. Never ever doubt that I will not keep you safe."

"And what if I say the same to you?"

He released her chin and ran his hand down to caress

her smooth neck. "Enough nonsense. You had a nightmare, no more. You have nothing to worry about. I will see to our safety. Trust me."

"It isn't you I don't trust." She shivered. "The man in my nightmare was pure evil, and I knew he would stop at nothing in his hunt for you."

"It means nothing," he said with a reassuring massage to her shoulder.

"What if Alaina's father hunts you? It would be only a matter of time before he arrives at my home. Then what?"

She had a point, and one that had silently plagued him since they left the abbey. He was almost certain the Abbess would alert Alaina's father of the babe's miraculous resurrection and the subsequent details. It was only a matter of time, as Sara had said.

The earl would find them and he would want them dead.

"You and Alexander are not safe here for long," she said. "I figure you have a month or two at the most, since it will take time for a letter from the Abbess to reach the earl and then he needs to discover our whereabouts, which won't be too hard. Two months, and that's taking a chance. We need our marriage to end fast."

He squeezed her shoulder lightly. "Then let me make sure our vows are secure before I must leave you."

Sadness rushed across her eyes, though she smiled. "For a man who first objected to our bargain, you are now quick to seal it."

He took her lips in a hot, hungry kiss, savoring it

before ending it all too soon. "That's before I got to know you."

She licked her sensually swollen lips, her narrow tongue driving him wild as it slowly circled her mouth. "And got to like kissing me."

"I very much like kissing you," he admitted, then stole a few more, ranging from hot and hungry to soft and slow.

"I like kissing you," she admitted when he stopped.

He leaned in to steal another kiss. "Then let's kiss some more."

Sara wiggled out of his reach and away from him. "I'd like to reach my home before nightfall."

"Last chance, Sara," he warned, holding out his hand.

She stood then, and stared at him, and he knew she debated with herself. He remained with his hand stretched, inviting her to rejoin him on the blanket, and he watched as her face softened, her eyes lost their fight and her body its stiffness.

She was about to surrender.

Suddenly, a strong wind whipped across the land, the branches of the trees bending and swaying, at first as if in dance and then reaching out as though shooing them away, wanting them gone.

Sara jumped, startled as a branch swept near her face.

"We should leave," she said and hurried to the horses.

Cullen mumbled beneath his breath, cursing the

damn wind as he got to his feet and rushed to gather up everything. She had near capitulated. One moment more and she would have been in his arms, and then they both would have been lost in a haze of passion.

Now they would reach her home by this evening and his chance would be . . .

He grinned. His chance would just be beginning, he realized. He'd be sleeping every night in a bed with her. It wouldn't take long for things to turn intimate.

But first he'd learn the whereabouts of his son.

Chapter 21

Dusk claimed the land when Sara and Cullen entered Clan McHern village. After her two-year absence, Sara was quick to see that the place hadn't changed all that much. A new storage house, which her father had spoken of building before she left, and fresh roof thatching on several of the cottages, but all in all the village looked much as it had when she'd left, prosperous and healthy.

Only a few villagers were out at this hour, and those who were stared at her in disbelief before scurrying off to spread the news of her return.

Cullen wasted no time in letting everyone know they were husband and wife. He had reached out, taken firm hold of her hand and smiled at her like a newly-wed man eager for his wedding night.

Which, of course, had Sara wondering what he was up to, but she had little time to dwell on it. They arrived at the keep soon enough, situated at the end of the village and tucked between two hills. Word had obviously already reached her father, his big-framed body running down the steps followed by a few of his anxious servants and a slew of his warriors.

"This best be your husband that's bringing you home, lass, or it's back to the abbey for you," he announced sternly after stopping in front of their horses and crossing his massive arms over his barrel chest.

Cullen dismounted and immediately went to Sara. He reached up, gripped her around the waist and swung her off her mare, planting a firm kiss on her lips before he hugged her close.

"Sara is my wife right and proper, and proud I am that she is," he boasted, and held out his hand to her father. "Cullen Longton."

Even though Sara knew he simply played his part and his remark was meaningless, her heart still swelled with the sheer joy of seeing her father's surprised yet pleased expression.

"Donald McHern, chieftain of the Clan McHern," her father said, giving his hand a firm shake. "And how do I know that you're wed good and proper to my daughter?"

Cullen left Sara's side to retrieve their marriage paper from the satchel and present it to her father. "Sealed and signed by the Abbess herself," he said, handing the rolled-up document to the clan chieftain.

Donald McHern made a fuss of unrolling it and scanning the page, his eyes growing wide along with his smile as he silently read the words.

Watching her father, Sara noticed that he had aged during her absence. More wrinkles claimed the corners of his eyes, numerous lines had deepened and spread across his face, and his hair, which matched hers in color, was now sprinkled with gray. His eyes, however, so like hers, had not changed a bit. One could still detect a hint of kindness in their depths.

"Welcome, son," her father finally said, and throwing his huge arms around Cullen, squeezed before releasing him with a hardy slap on the back. He then turned to Sara. "Looks like you finally did good." He turned back to Cullen. "Come, there's food and ale aplenty."

Cullen turned, extending his hand to Sara. "Not without my wife. I want her by my side at all times."

Donald McHern laughed as he slapped Cullen on the back again. "That will change fast enough."

"The four horses are for you," Cullen said with a nod to her father before they reached the door. "In appreciation for your daughter."

Donald McHern nodded slowly at his daughter. "Very good."

The horses were left to a young lad to stable while everyone entered the great hall.

Unlike many keeps, her father kept no special place on a dais for himself. He favored a long table framed by two benches in front of the fire, where his men usually joined him.

Tonight, Sara sat at his favorite table for the very first time, beside her husband, who sat across from her father, and she felt honored by the position.

Cullen placed his hand over hers, resting on the table, every now and again bringing it to his lips for a kiss, and he made certain he sat leaning against her, their shoulders rubbing. To all, they appeared a loving couple, and for the moment she felt a loving wife.

She reminded herself to enjoy it. It wouldn't last forever. But then, nothing did.

Cullen and her father found conversation easy, and Sara barely was able to sneak a word or two in. Cullen handled her father well, playing into his every word while sharing food off her plate or popping a morsel into her mouth, insisting she try the delicious fare.

"Sara, the women will attend you in the second floor chambers," her father said to her. "Go, I wish to talk with your husband."

"They can attend me later," she said, not wanting to leave Cullen and her father alone.

"You will take your leave now," her father said with stern firmness.

Sara braced her arms on the table. "I'm not ready to leave."

Donald McHern shook his head. "You'll lose a good husband soon enough unless you learn to obey a man's order."

"It's my orders she needs to obey, not yours," Cullen said, his strong voice slicing through the air like a sharp knife.

"Then see that she obeys her husband," McHern challenged with a sharp glint.

Cullen turned to Sara and tucked one of her unruly curls behind her ear. "Go and enjoy. I won't be long."

Sara wanted to kiss him, and she did, to the shock of

her father and all those around her. Then she slipped off the bench and walked with her chin high out of the hall. Cullen had managed to have her keep her dignity and show his strength by letting her father know he'd give him only so much time and then join his wife.

Yes, she had chosen a very good husband. She just wished he were hers to keep.

Sara stripped herself bare and almost jumped into the large tin tub the women had generously filled with hot water from the caldrons brewing in the fireplace. There wasn't sufficient room to stretch out her long legs, but she didn't care, she just wanted the heat of the water to soak into every aching muscle of her tired body.

She dunked her head and washed it quickly with the lavender soap kept stocked in the keep. When her hair was rinsed and sweetly scented, she rested her head on the tub rim and closed her eyes to enjoy the heat before the water cooled.

It was good to be home. She had many loving memories here and many sad ones, those starting with her mother's death, when she was twelve. It happened so fast, her mother sick but a couple of days before she died, and along with her, a part of her father.

They had been an inseparable pair, falling in love from when they were young and allowing nothing to stand in the way of that love. She had hoped to find such an enduring love, but time, or luck, hadn't been on her side.

Though that wasn't entirely true, she thought now. She'd met Cullen, a good man and a man she could easily love. He treated her with respect, cared about her safety, and was true to his word.

She sighed softly. What good did it do thinking on what could never be? It only served to upset her, and she didn't have time to feel sorry for herself. She had to attend to her bargain with Cullen and see him and his son reunited and then safely out of here. She would adjust to life once he left. After all, they'd spent only a week together and would probably not know each other more than two months. And yet she felt as if she'd known him her entire life.

There were things she wanted to learn and experience, and she would fill her days with adventure so that at night she would fall exhausted into bed and sleep. Then she would be too busy to think of Cullen and how she missed him beside her.

She was grateful that he'd been wrapped around her the night she suffered her nightmare. His embrace had been like a loving cocoon that she could snuggle within, knowing she was protected from all harm. She had felt safe and secure, and it hurt to know that she would never know that endearing contentment again.

A sprinkle of water dusted her face.

"The water cools. You'll chill."

Sara's eyes sprang open wide and she near popped out of the tub until she remembered that she was completely naked, with Cullen hunched down beside her. Not that her nakedness was concealed, which she tried to rectify with flaying arms and hands and little success.

Cullen chuckled. "I'm your husband," he reminded

her, "and from what I can see between your useless attempts to hide from me, you have a beautiful body."

Sara froze in shock. Either she hadn't heard him correctly or he was simply trying to impress, but then, she hadn't known him to lie.

She hugged herself, concealing her breasts as best she could and crossing her legs while gooseflesh rushed over her body, reminding her the water had cooled considerably.

"We need not be that familiar with each other," she said.

"I beg to differ," he said, and reaching out, took hold of a large towel on a nearby stool. "You could have a mark since birth your father would know of, and what if I don't? Or perhaps a scar or—"

"I possess no such marks or scars you need know of."

He stood draping the large towel in front of him. "Perhaps I should see for myself."

Sara scrambled to her feet, sloshing water out of the tub in her hurry to reach for the towel, not caring that gooseflesh still prickled her chilled skin, being more concerned in concealing her nakedness from her husband.

Cullen didn't relinquish the towel, but he wrapped it around her, encasing her in it and drawing her into his arms. "You need warming."

Her shivering body betrayed the protest that died on her lips.

Cullen rubbed her back, firm yet slow, his fingers kneading every inch all the way down her to backside. Warmth spread throughout her body, slowly at first, then turning to liquid fire and igniting her flesh.

She hadn't realized that Cullen was nuzzling her neck until she felt herself melt against him, lost in his magical touch.

"You smell heavenly," he whispered, burying his nose in her damp hair. "And taste delicious." He nibbled along her ear to her neck, making her shudder and sigh all at once.

Before she could gather her senses, he walked her over to the bed while continually feasting at her neck, his hands meanwhile working their magic along her body, stroking up and down, heating her flesh even more.

He lowered her to the bed, going down with her, gently kissing every inch of her face before landing on her lips, to dance across them in teasing whispers.

Trapped beneath him, cocooned in the towel, her passion rising, her surrender near, she didn't know where she got the courage to say, "Stop."

It was a mewling, pathetic, barely audible *stop*, but she had gotten it out and followed it with a more forcible *stop*, albeit reluctantly and regrettably, but certainly necessary.

"Why?" he asked softly.

Was that disappointment she heard or did she merely want to hear it?

"It's better that way."

"I don't believe so," he said, and tinged her lips with his until they trembled.

"I know so," she insisted, struggling to ignore the ache to taste more of him.

He smiled. "There's time to convince you."

"I wouldn't count on it."

He pushed off the bed and began stripping off his garments. "I would."

She loosened her arms from the towel and secured it around her breasts as she sat up, her eyes steady on him. She warned herself to ignore his actions, his unsubtle challenge, but damned if she could. "Trying to impress me?"

"Would it help?" he asked, dropping his kilt and slipping off his shirt.

Sara studied him, all of him, and had to admit he did impress. He was well-endowed and perfectly crafted all hard muscle and flesh. Damn, but he did impress.

However, she simply shrugged, not trusting the croak in her throat to squeak out, stood and walked away from him.

"I take it I impressed," he said, striding past her to the tub.

He had a good backside, not flat or flabby, but tight and round. His muscles stretched taut when he reached for the caldron, grabbing the handle with a thick towel to avoid burning his hand. He moved with a fluid grace, not doubting a single step or his strength, hefting the caldron to add heated water to the tub.

"My son?" he asked after all was done and he'd settled in the tub.

She took the opportunity to step out of sight and slip on her white linen night shift trimmed at the neck with a pale blue ribbon. Then she sat in the wooden, claw-handled chair next to the fireplace and in clear view of the tub to comb her hair.

"I'll take you to him tomorrow."

She didn't worry that once he had his son he would leave her without so much as a good-bye. Having determined that he was an honorable man, she had no such worry. He would remain as he had promised and make their marriage seem a proper one.

"He's close by?" Cullen asked eagerly, and began scrubbing his head.

Sara chuckled. "You'll be smelling like me."

He winked at her. "Then you won't be able to resist me."

She already couldn't resist him. If he smelled sweet, it just might damage her resolve. She yanked hard on the comb, caught on a knot in her hair, and hoped the pain would erase the passion that still tingled her senses.

"Alexander is less than an hour's ride from here," she said, forcing herself to focus on his son.

Cullen wiped away the soap that dripped from his wet hair into his eyes. "How did he get here, close to your family?"

Sara set the comb on the handle of the chair and drew a pitcher of water from a caldron near the fire, keeping it warm though not hot. She took it over to Cullen and poured it slowly over his head while he rinsed the soap from his hair, face, and upper torso.

"I knew he'd be safest with those close to me, and the only way to get him here, to my home, was to pay a couple a handsome sum with the promise of more once they arrived at the destination."

"How did you know he arrived safely?"

"I received confirmation."

"From whom?" he asked as he scrubbed his legs.

"My sister Teresa."

Cullen stood with a start, water and soap dripping off him. "Your sister has my son?"

She threw him a towel and walked over to the bed to climb beneath the thick coverlet and sit watching him. They would share this bed tonight and many nights to come, and she had to make certain that was all they did—share the bed.

He caught the towel and roughly rubbed his wide chest and thick arms dry as he approached the bed and in turn braced each foot on the edge to dry his legs. She knew he purposely stood there naked in front of her, rubbing every inch of muscled flesh dry, to tempt her, and damned if he didn't. However, she intended to ignore him and the tingling sensation between her legs.

"I knew my sister Teresa would see your son safe."

He tossed the wet towel aside and grabbed another one from a stack on the chest near the bed to quickly rub his hair dry.

"She often looks after strays you send her?" he asked, and climbed over her into bed, though he could have easily slipped beneath the covers from the other side.

Sara ignored his teasing action and her thumping heart and rested her head on the soft pillow before turning to face him. "I've never sent her any strays."

"Then why accept the care of my son?" he asked.

"Teresa thinks Alexander is *my* son."

Chapter 22

Cullen stared at her, speechless. He knew she spoke the truth; she always did, when called for; until then, she wisely kept her counsel. The more he discovered the lengths at which she'd gone to keep his son safe, the more grateful he was to her.

"You let your sister think you gave birth to a babe at the convent?"

Her response also answered his next question. "Only my sister, no one else, for I knew she would treat him as her own and keep him safe without question. Everyone believes the child a stray no one wanted. Teresa has a generous heart, so no one would question her decision."

"That was a great risk you took," he said, reaching out to try and tame an unruly curl at her temple, but the stubborn lock refused to obey so he tucked it behind her ear, where naturally it sprung lose as soon as he moved his hand away.

Her hair was much like her, stubborn and unpredictable, popping up in a direction that was least expected.

"A necessary risk," she said frankly. "What if something would have happened to me? What then of your son? With my sister believing Alexander was mine, she would raise him as her own. I could place him only where I was certain he'd be protected regardless of what happened to me."

"You did right by my son."

"And you've done right by me. We struck a good and honest bargain and honored it. It's done."

He thought to differ with her but knew it was senseless. She had made up her mind and would have it no other way. He, however, had given his word to her, and he would see to honoring the full bargain. Besides, in the short time they had known each other he'd grown comfortable with her, and he found himself attracted to her. He needn't worry about love or commitment. She understood how he felt about loving anyone other than Alaina, and yet . . .

He chased the persistent thought away, though it bounced back again, teasing at the fringes of his mind, annoying him until he couldn't help but pay attention to it. There was a stirring in his soul for Sara, and no matter how much he tried to ignore it; it refused to go away. He had convinced himself it was merely a sexual stirring, but that had proved false, especially when her father ordered her out of the hall. He had taken umbrage to the man dictating to Sara. He was her husband now, and no one told his wife what to do, not even her father.

"What did my father have to say to you?" she asked on a yawn.

"You're tired. We can talk tomorrow."

"Then he had nothing of importance to say or else you would tell me," she said, burrowing under the blanket to turn on her side toward him.

Cullen leaned over and gently kissed her cheek, pleased with the easy trust they shared. "Nothing important."

"I knew you would impress him. I picked a good husband." Her eyes drifted closed.

"Your father's exact words," he confirmed.

He watched her drift off to sleep thinking how natural it seemed being in bed beside her. Neither of them had hesitated in sharing the bed, but then the week's journey had forged a close bond between them that neither expected.

The bond had started well before the journey. It began when Sara decided to save his son. He reached out to brush a stubborn curl away from the corner of her mouth. She was a beautiful woman, and not only to the eyes, but to the heart. She was caring and compassionate and blunt in her efforts to do what she saw was necessary, and more so, what was right.

He hadn't given thought to loving again, but Sara would be easy to love.

He turned on his back with a soft sigh. He couldn't think about her now, he didn't have the right. Tomorrow he would fulfill the promise he'd made to Alaina. He would hold his son in his arms and keep him forever safe.

Cullen had never doubted this day would come. He

would have moved heaven and earth to keep his word to Alaina and find their son. But he'd never imagined he would be doing so with his wife.

He turned at her soft cries and saw that she stirred fitfully in her sleep. Was she dreaming once again of forfeiting her life for him and Alexander? He would never let that happen. He might have failed to protect Alaina, but he wouldn't fail in protecting Sara. He would make certain no harm came to her.

His revenge against the Earl of Balford would serve twofold. He'd avenge Alaina's senseless death, and he would guarantee Sara's safety once he was gone. If he left Scotland without doing so, he'd leave Sara in peril. The earl would certainly track her down, and once he discovered her deception, he would execute her, if torture didn't claim her first.

Sara's fretful moan had him responding instinctively. He reached over and took her in his arms, tucking her in the crook of one arm so her head rested comfortably on his chest. Her arm wound around him and her leg slipped comfortably between his two.

They fitted naturally together, as if carved from the same stone, and the thought pleased yet disturbed him. He had thought he and Alaina a perfect match, that he would fit no other but her. Yet here he slept fitted perfectly with his wife.

How did he make sense of it?

Did he want to or did he just enjoy the time he had with her?

How, then, did he walk away from her?

The questions played havoc with his thoughts until finally he simply surrendered to the comfort he felt with Sara snuggled against him and he fell asleep.

He woke with a stretch, working the sleep from his body, then bolted up in bed when he realized Sara wasn't beside him. He was quick to dress and run her comb through his long hair. He was wrapping the ties of his sandals around his legs when she came prancing proudly through the door, a smile of joy on her face and a platter of food in her hands.

"You are the talk of the village," she said, placing the platter on the table near one of the two windows. "Everyone agrees I've done well for myself, though none believe it will last. Most are sure you will grow tired of my blunt tongue and willful nature soon enough. Some of the women plan to vie for your attention, assured you'll be looking for another wife."

"And this pleases you?" he asked, annoyed.

"It should please us both. No one will be the wiser when we begin to bicker and you take your leave."

Suddenly, he didn't care for the plan. Sara would suffer ridicule once he was gone, and she didn't deserve that.

"Honey bread, eggs, porridge, meats, fruit, eat your fill," she offered, slipping onto one of the two chairs flanking the small table.

Cullen joined her, not very hungry. He didn't like thinking of the fate Sara would suffer because of him. It wasn't right. She was a good woman and deserved so much more.

"I'd prefer to see my son as soon as possible, and I'm not ready to bicker just yet." He leaned down and deposited a kiss on her cheek.

Sara placed a gentle hand to her cheek where he had kissed her. "Neither am I."

"Good, then let's enjoy the day, for it will certainly be a good one. I will finally hold my son in my arms. But first . . . " He took a plaid cloth from one of his satchels and handed it to Sara.

She stood, accepting it, and asked, "What is this?"

"My plaid for my wife to wear."

Sara's eyes grew glassy, as if close to tears, then she broke out in a big grin and worked quickly to secure the red, black, and yellow plaid over and across her blouse and around her waist.

"Thank you for letting me wear this," she said. "It will please my father and impress my clan even more."

He wanted to make it clear that the plaid was meant for her, his wife, not to impress anyone, but held his tongue. It would only cause a debate he wasn't ready to have, and perhaps he would never be. He could, however, let her know how well the colors fit her and how proud he was for her to be wearing them.

"The plaid suits you, and you bring honor to my father's colors."

Her grin vanished in a heartbeat and she stood staring at him as if struck dumb.

It was his turn to grin as he walked over to her, grabbed hold of her chin and planted a solid kiss on her lips, making certain his tongue teased hers for a moment or two before gently brushing her lips with his and sealing their kiss.

"Time to go," he said, and took her hand to tug her speechless out the door.

They entered the great hall with arms around each other, smiling, and Donald McHern greeted them with a wink and grin.

"I can tell it won't be long before I have a grandson."

Most women would have blushed, Cullen thought, but not Sara.

"That's my husband's and my business," she said. "Right now, I wish to take my husband to meet my sister."

"I imagined as much," her father said. "But tomorrow Cullen is mine. He can show me if he is as fine a hunter as he claims to be."

"Make no bones about it, Father, Cullen will best you with a bow," Sara said proudly.

"We'll see about that," McHern said. "And, Sara, I'll have a talk with you when you return."

Cullen wasn't pleased to see the sparkle fade in Sara's eyes. It was a subtle shift that would go undetected by most, but not by someone who knew her well and could almost feel it before seeing it. He felt it, a sharp little jab, and he didn't like it at all.

Sara nodded, and Cullen tugged her to the door while he called out to McHern, "If my wife returns tired, you can speak with her tomorrow."

He gave the large man no time to respond; he shoved

Sara out the door and into the bright sunlight and the balmy warmth of a fine spring day.

"You play your part well," Sara said as they headed to fetch their stabled horses.

"You're my wife, my responsibility, and your father needs to honor that," he said sternly.

"Be prepared for my father to disagree."

"Disagree or not, he'll do it my way."

It was no surprise to Cullen that their horses were ready and waiting for them. Sara knew how anxious he was to see his son, and she had seen that nothing would delay their journey.

Their departure from the village was slower than anticipated, with many villagers calling out congratulations and salutations. Cullen welcomed the quiet of the surrounding countryside once the houses disappeared in the distance. He was eager to see his son, yet apprehensive. He had no experience with babies, and Alexander was a mere babe. Was he walking yet? Could he talk?

"He will need time to get to know you," Sara said, as if she knew his mind. "Unless he is a friendly one and takes to you right away."

Cullen confided his fear. "What if my son doesn't like me?"

She smiled. "Do not worry. I think Alexander and you will get along well. Besides, my sister Teresa will assume that you are the babe's father and see that he spends time with you."

"You're right. She will assume me the father."

"Ironic, isn't it? But a ruse I think we'd be better off sustaining," she suggested.

"Agreed," Cullen said. "I'd prefer no one to know the truth. It could possibly place them in danger."

"I thought the same myself. If the Earl of Balford ever made his way here and questioned my clan—" She shuddered. "We must hurry and be done with this all. You and Alexander must seek the safety of your brother's ship and leave Scotland as soon as possible."

"After I see to the earl," he said solemnly.

Sara snapped her head around at him. "What do you mean?"

"I intend to avenge Alaina's death."

"You can't mean to tell me that you intend to foolishly take the chance of killing the earl?" she asked incredulously.

"He deserves killing."

"I couldn't agree more. He's a vile, evil man, but to place yourself and your son in danger is foolish."

"I will make certain my son is safely on my brother's ship before I carry out my plan," he said confidently.

"And what if your plan doesn't go as planned?"

"My son will be safe in America and raised by my brother."

Sara shook her head. "I cannot believe you would be so selfish and *stupid*!"

Cullen crinkled his brow. "I am not stupid or selfish. I do what is right."

Sara reined her horse to a halt. "Do you think Alaina

would agree with this dumb plan of yours?" She held up her hand while shaking her head. "She wouldn't. She would want you, his father, raising Alexander."

He couldn't get over how beautiful she was when she grew agitated. Her cheeks blossomed a bright red, her eyes glistened like the surface of a sparkling lake, and her rigid posture was one of resolve and courage. She was a remarkable woman who had somehow worked her way into his heart without him even realizing it.

The startling thought angered him and he barked at her, "You don't know what Alaina would want."

Sara stood her ground. "Every woman worth her salt wants to protect her man and her child, and I know Alaina was worth more than her salt."

"She certainly was, and that's why I'll do what is right and avenge her death." Cullen held his hand up. "Not another word. My mind is set and that's all there is to that. We'll speak no more of it."

"Like hell we won't," she said, and with a tug of the reins, she urged her horse forward.

Cullen followed, though he kept a safe distance. He didn't intend to argue with her. It wasn't an issue they'd agree on, therefore it was senseless to discuss it. He would do what he must whether she liked it or not.

He did, however, appreciate her concern, and it made him realize that perhaps Sara thought more of him than she even realized. Or perhaps she did realize it and was wise for having made the choice not to consummate their vows. Intimacy would only draw them closer together, and they had already drawn quite close without it. He could only imagine how intimacy would cause more of a problem for them.

But damned if he didn't want to give a try!

The remainder of the ride was silent, each of them lost in their own thoughts, opinions, and plans, so when they finally approached the cottage tucked in the hillside and surrounded by fields ready for planting, they both were surprised by the sight of the little boy wobbling around on uncertain feet as a woman stood nearby, ready to catch him if he should fall.

The woman snatched the child up when she spied them and shaded her eyes with her hand to see them better. Once she caught sight of Sara waving wildly at her, she returned the enthusiastic wave and even took hold of the boy's little arm for him to welcome them with a wave.

Sara barely stopped her mare before she was sliding off it to run to her sister and hug her and the boy.

Cullen expected a crying fest between the two women, though he hadn't thought he would get choked up himself when he laid eyes on his son. The boy was a miniature copy of him, eyes, nose, and the stubborn set to his small chin. That he was his son was undeniable, and he ached to have Alaina there at that moment to thank her for this beautiful child.

Alexander wiggled out of Teresa's arms as soon as Cullen dismounted, and to his surprise wobbled over to him.

The child tilted his head back, stretched out his pudgy arms and said, "Da."

Chapter 23

With tears damp on her cheeks, Sara's eyes welled up again as she watched Cullen reach down and scoop his son up in his large arms. The little boy giggled and poked at Cullen's nose and cheeks.

Cullen grinned from ear to ear, his excitement palpable, his relief something only Sara could detect. She had gotten to know his nuances in the time they'd spent together and could now read him easily. And, of course, he had been waiting for this moment since they first met. The little bundle of joy in his arms was the fulfillment of his promise to Alaina and the reason for him to live after her death.

"Give him a kiss, Alexander," Teresa called out.

Alexander opened his mouth wide and planted a sloppy kiss against his father's cheek.

Cullen smiled and returned the kiss, though with a closed mouth.

"He certainly can't deny him," Teresa said, turning to Sara. "But I think he's got your stubbornness."

Sara wiped the tears off her cheeks and laughed softly, wishing that were true, wishing she was Alexander's mother and that the three of them truly were family.

Cullen joined the women, his son tucked safely in his arms, Alexander's tiny fingers busy trying to pick the stripes off the plaid that crossed his father's chest while repeatedly saying, "Da!"

"He calls everyone Da," Teresa explained. "It's his first word and he's very proud of it, and it appears he's learned it at the perfect time."

Sara appreciated her sister's acknowledgment of Cullen as Alexander's father before he had even been introduced. It allowed for an easier rapport between them all, especially Cullen, since his smile brightened even more at her sister's remark.

Sara saw to proper introductions. Upon meeting herself and Teresa, most people did not realize that they were sisters. Where she was tall, Teresa was no more than a couple of inches over five feet; slim and simply beautiful with long, honey-blond hair. Now, she introduced her sister with pride. "Teresa, my husband Cullen Longton. Cullen, my sister Teresa."

Cullen offered his hand and Teresa took it with a smile. "I am pleased to meet my sister's husband."

"Pleased I am to be her husband and grateful to you for taking care of our son." He drifted over to Sara and slipped his free arm around her waist, still holding his son in the other arm.

Alexander leaned over, opened his mouth and gave Sara a wet, sloppy kiss on her cheek. She near cried again, and almost did so when Cullen leaned down and followed his son's actions, kissing her cheek.

"Thank you," he whispered.

It was no simple thank-you. It was heartfelt. He was thanking her for saving his son's life, knowing he would not have had this moment of sloppy kisses if not for her courage at sneaking his son out of the abbey and sending him to safety.

Sara smiled at Cullen. "It was all worth it," she said, understanding him.

Teresa laughed. "She can say that now, after the pain is but a faded memory."

Cullen hugged Sara close. "She's a courageous woman; I'm proud of her."

"You've got yourself a good man," Teresa said.

"A very good man," Sara confirmed, smiling while her heart ached. This was all make-believe and she wished it were real.

"I was about to set the outside table," Teresa said. "It's such a fine warm spring day. Shamus will be returning soon. You can join us and we can catch up on things. In the meantime, why don't you and Cullen taken Alexander for a walk. This is the time of day we go to the creek so he can throw pebbles in and laugh at the splashes they make."

Sara hesitated, not having seen her sister in two years and wanting to spend time with her, yet knowing she had little time to spend with Cullen and his son.

"We'll have time to talk," Teresa said with a gentle nudge at her sister. "Alexander needs to get to know the both of you."

* * *

As they walked in the direction Teresa had pointed, Cullen said, "Your sister is an understanding soul. I can see why you sent my son to her."

Sara smiled at Alexander, who giggled as his father bounced him in his arms. "She'll do what she can to make this an easy transition for Alexander. She had planned for this day, for she knew I would return for him."

He was an adorable child, the image of his father, with the same dark brown hair, Teresa having braided the sides to keep the strands out of his face. He wore a blue linen dress that reached to his pudgy knees, with a dark blue sweater atop it that hugged his chubby little belly, while his feet were bare.

"He's a strong one," Cullen said with pride. "Look how he grips my plaid."

"He is like you, strong and determined."

Alexander poked his father in the chest repeatedly while singing, "Da. Da. Da."

"I cannot believe I'm holding him." He shook his head. "And I fear letting him out of my arms."

"The safest place for him is with my sister."

"I know, but—"

"You finally have him and you don't want to let him go," Sara said, anticipating his thought. "I know how you feel." She didn't want to let father or son go, especially now, seeing them together, being here with them, sharing this moment as a family.

"You're right. I don't want to let him go. Not ever."

"You won't have to," Sara said, squeezing his arm reassuringly. Father and son had a right to remain together. Their reunion had been a long time in the making, and a life had been lost in the process. They had lost time to reclaim, starting now.

"Da! Da!" Alexander cried out, his tiny hand waving at the creek then shoving at his father's chest.

Cullen swooped him up and out of his arms, placing a laughing Alexander on the ground. The little boy near tumbled over searching the ground for stones.

Sara joined him in the hunt and followed as he toddled to the creek and flung a stone in. He screeched with joy and clapped his hands when the stone made a splash, then reached his hand out to Sara for another stone.

Cullen plopped down beside him with a handful of stones and joined his son in throwing stones.

Sara fell in love at that moment with father and son. She tried to convince herself that she didn't know either one of them long enough to fall in love, but it didn't work. Her heart was lost to them. Actually, she realized, she had lost her heart to Alexander from the first time she held him in her arms and fought to save his life. He had been such a precious little bundle and so trusting, but then, he was new to the world then. What did he have to fear? That was what a mother and father were for, or a woman who could do what his mother couldn't—save him.

His father, however, had been a different story. There had been no love at first sight. It had grown out of admiration, respect, and, strangely enough, challenge. She had found in him what she'd been looking for—a man worth loving.

She laughed at Alexander's antics and at herself. How foolish was she for thinking herself in love with a man she barely knew? But she did know him, better than she knew most. How and why, she couldn't say for sure, though she could say that he knew her just as well. In their short time together, they had managed to come to know and understand each other as if they had been friends for years.

Friends.

That's what did it. Somewhere along the way they had become friends, and that opened the door for so much more, whether either of them had planned on it or not. She would have liked to believe that Alaina would have approved of her loving Cullen. If Alaina loved him as much as she thought, then Alaina wouldn't want to see Cullen alone. She would want him to love again.

But could he ever love her?

Alexander fell in her lap with a squeal and she hugged him to her, kissing his chubby cheek. He rubbed his eyes and nestled his face against her chest.

"He grows tired," she said, more from instinct than knowledge. She cradled him in her arms and he settled comfortably against her as she rocked him gently. His eyes drifted closed and in no time he was asleep.

Cullen moved closer to Sara and ran a tender hand over his son's forehead. "I am so very grateful to you. I owe you a great deal."

"You owe me nothing. I did what was right."

Cullen shook his head. "No. Most would believe it foolish to take such a dangerous risk. After all, what difference did it make? Why bother to save a babe?"

Sara hugged Alexander close. "A babe is a precious and entrusted gift, not to be taken lightly or discarded at whim. A babe must be protected at all cost."

"I'm glad you believe so strongly—" He smiled gently. "No, I'm glad you know what is right."

Sara smiled and nodded. "I knew you'd understand."

"I do. I truly do understand, though it is strange to find someone who knows what is right and does what is right. Many ignore it, and even more refuse to act on it. You are rare, Sara *Longton*."

Her heart leapt, hearing him emphasize her marriage name. She had not thought of herself as a Longton, but she was a McHern no more. She belonged to Cullen and he to her . . . though not for very long.

Her heart suffered a blow at the discouraging thought, but she had little choice and little time to enjoy father and son, so there was no time to wallow in self-pity.

Cullen stretched out his legs and sighed heavily. "I don't remember when I've felt this content."

It pleased Sara to hear him admit that, for she felt the same, being here with Cullen and Alexander. It was as if her dream had come true and she was happily married with a family of her own.

"It does feel good," she said. "Like a breath of fresh air."

"Like a new life beginning."

How she wished it were true. A new life for the three of them. But it would be a new life for only two, she told herself, and she would have to accept that.

"He took to you right away," Cullen said with a nod to his sleeping son.

"He's a friendly little fellow."

"Or maybe he remembered you and what you did for him."

"That's not possible."

"You never know," Cullen said. "Sometimes I think instinct is stronger than we know. Instincts tell me you'd make a good mother."

"I'd like to think I would."

Cullen stroked her cheek. "I *know* you would."

She liked when he touched her, especially his soft, simple touches. They made her feel so alive, tingled her senses and sparked her passion. She never felt more like a woman, a desirable woman.

"I will see you're taken care of before I take my leave."

This time the blow stunned her heart. She didn't want to think of his leaving, didn't want to think he would never touch her so simply yet so lovingly again, or that she'd never see or hold Alexander in her arms.

The empty ache was like none she had ever experienced. It hurt down to the very core of her and radiated out until every inch of her felt the pain. This parting was going to be so much more difficult than she ever believed possible.

"I think we should get Alexander back so he can nap comfortably in his cradle."

Cullen nodded and stood, then leaned over and,

before assisting her up, kissed her gently. "Thank you again for saving my son."

She almost lost it, but bravely fought the tears that threatened and forced them to remain locked away.

With no difficulty, he hoisted her up without disturbing the sleeping Alexander, and together they returned in a slow stroll to the cottage.

Shamus, Teresa's husband, was hugging his wife as she tried to set food on the table shaded under the branches of a large pine. A gentle breeze stirred the edges of the pale blue linen cloth that covered the table, which was set with pewter dishes, tankards, and goblets.

Sara smiled, the scene a perfect one, and one she wished for herself, though she intended to enjoy what she had this day and worry about tomorrow when it came. She did not want to waste a moment with Cullen and his son, and if she continued her worries, she would waste too much precious time. She would enjoy here and now, and feast on the memories later.

Teresa waved for Sara to follow her, and Shamus released her. The two women then disappeared into the cottage to put Alexander in his cradle.

Teresa's husband held out his hand. "I'm Shamus."

"And I am Cullen," Cullen replied.

By the time the women emerged from the cottage a short time later, the two men who had but just introduced themselves were laughing over tankards of ale.

"You've met the only man my sister will ever love," Sara told Cullen, and got a huge bear hug from her brother-in-law. She loved Shamus like a brother. He was a good man, and though shy of her height by three or four inches, stood tall and proud and was heavy with brawn and intelligence. He also was a good-looking man, with dark hair and eyes and strong, compelling features. But most of all she loved him for treating her sister like a princess. He would do anything for her, even raise his wife's sister's baby as his own.

Shamus grabbed his wife from behind, slipping his arms around her waist and hugging her. "Right you are. I'm the love of her life."

"And what of me?" Teresa teased.

"You . . . " Shamus nuzzled her neck. " . . . are my world."

"You two obviously are a perfect match," Cullen said, and saluted them with his tankard.

Sara joined in raising a goblet she had filled with wine. "To the perfect pair."

"And a delayed thank-you to two generous people with much appreciation," Cullen said.

"Not necessary," Shamus said, and with his arms around his wife, rubbed his hands together. "Let's eat. I'm starving."

They feasted on the hardy fare while relaxed conversation ensued, and when Alexander was heard crying over an hour later, Sara and Teresa went to tend him.

"Why don't you change his diaper?" Teresa said, placing Alexander on the thick towel she had spread out on her bed.

Sara eagerly tackled the chore.

"I won't ask you to tell me the whole story, unless you want to," Teresa said. "What I do want to know, though, is what troubles you. Something isn't right. What is it?"

"You were always perceptive."

"Only when it came to you."

Sara had wanted to confide in her sister, but feared the truth could harm her. Yet she badly needed to unburden her worries.

Teresa placed a gentle hand on her sister's back. "Tell me, Sara. We always shared our secrets because we trusted."

"But our secrets could never hurt either of us."

Teresa smiled. "Now you've sparked my curiosity, so you must tell me."

Sara didn't need any further urging, and with a deep breath told Teresa everything from the beginning, from saving Alexander up to the present and Cullen's inevitable departure without her. She finished with, "Please, don't share this with Shamus. It is safer he doesn't know."

Teresa was silent for a moment, and Sara worried that perhaps she should have kept the truth to herself, but she felt such a relief sharing it, and she was confident that her sister would not say a word to anyone.

She didn't, however, expect Teresa to respond as she did.

"You have no choice. You must go to America with Cullen and his son."

Chapter 24

Cullen stared at his sleeping son in the cradle. He had come into the cottage to kiss him good-bye. He and Sara needed to be on their way, having stayed longer than they planned since he hadn't wanted to leave his son.

He was a beautiful babe, and every now and then when he smiled, Cullen saw Alaina in him. Otherwise there was no denying that Alexander was his son. If it hadn't been for Sara's courage, he would have lost him. There would have been nothing to show that Alaina and he had loved, but there he was, Alexander, a legacy of their love. In him, Alaina would always live, their love would always live.

He leaned over and kissed the boy's cheek lightly, not wanting to wake him, though Teresa had said he would sleep after having run himself ragged, not to mention tiring out his father and Shamus, who had chased playfully after him.

Cullen wanted to stand here and watch him sleep, watch him breathe, watch him wake ready and eager for his da. He pried himself away from the cradle, sneaking one last look before slipping out the door.

"He'll be fine here with us until you're ready to make it known he's yours and Sara's son," Shamus said when Cullen approached the three at the table outside.

"I appreciate all you've done," Cullen said, holding his hand out to Sara. "I'd like to be in the laird's good graces before we even consider telling him of Alexander, though I hope to see my son often."

It was a lie, though a good enough excuse. He didn't plan to tell anyone anything; he'd simply disappear. It troubled him that Sara would be left with the aftermath, but she had repeatedly assured him she had gotten what she wanted—freedom from a forced marriage.

"Good idea, and you're welcome here anytime," Shamus said.

Parting greetings were exchanged, then Cullen and Sara were on their way.

"We need to keep a good pace if we hope to reach the keep before nightfall," Cullen said, and Sara agreed with a nod.

Cullen was glad the hurried pace left no room for them to talk. His mind couldn't focus on anything but his son and the torment it caused him to leave him behind even though he knew he'd be safe.

He had just gotten to hold him, had begun to know him, and then had to leave him. He knew it was right to leave him there, but it didn't make it any easier. He simply wanted his son in his arms for now and always. He had thought the ache from Alaina's loss was painful, but this cut at his gut. His son was so small, so trusting, so vulnerable, and as his father, he was intent on protecting him and keeping him safe.

It was his job, his duty, his promise, but they meant little compared to his love for his son. He had never imagined the depth of love he would feel. It went so deep, felt so strong, tugged so hard at his heart that he feared it might kill him. Then he realized it had the opposite affect. It made him stronger. His son had actually made him more of a man.

He had Sara to thank for it all, and though he'd thanked her throughout the day, he felt his words were inadequate. He owed her and he would repay her; arguing though she would, he would see it done.

Then he'd be on his way to his new home with his son.

They entered the village as night fell over the land, and after seeing to their horses, walked hand in hand into the great hall. Sara's father was waiting.

"We'll have that talk now, lass," he ordered, and a few of his men at the table quickly vacated their seats.

Cullen held her hand firmly. "Not tonight," he said. "Sara's too tired."

"I've waited," McHern said, annoyed, and shot Sara a heated glare. "Why did you linger at Teresa's when I told you I wanted to talk with you?"

Cullen tugged her hand to keep her quiet and answered. "With all respect, Laird McHern, Sara no longer answers to you."

McHern pounded the table once, creaking the wood. "Damn, son, I like you."

"Good, then you'll see Sara tomorrow—"

"At breakfast," McHern said.

"Sara will be sleeping late, she's tired. You'll see her after our hunt. Good night," he said, and scooped Sara up in his arms to walk out of the great hall to the sound of McHern laughing.

"You can put me down," Sara said once they were out of sight and earshot.

"Don't want to. You feel good in my arms."

"I'm too heavy for you to carry all the way up the stairs," she argued.

He laughed. "You wound my pride, wife."

"I'm large for a woman."

"Sweetheart, you're not large, you're just right." He kissed her cheek.

"If I did not know you to be truthful, I would think you say the words just to please me."

He shoved the door to their bedchamber open with his shoulder. "Then it is good that you know me as a man of his word."

He released her to stand, though he drew her into his arms. She, however, splayed her hands over his chest to push away from him.

"A kiss, just a kiss," he urged, reaching out for her.

She shook her head and moved away from him. "Not a good idea."

"Why?" he asked softly, and pursued her with cautious steps.

She moved closer to the fireplace, away from the bed. "You were my champion just now. No one has ever stood for me as you just did." She drew a deep breath and placed a hand to her chest. "You tempt my heart."

"Is that so bad?" he asked, maneuvering closer, though slowly, not wanting her to flee from him.

"In this situation, yes. I can't afford to lose my heart to you, and you of all people should understand."

He knew she spoke of Alaina and his feelings over losing her. Would he wish the same on her? But that would mean she . . .

"You can't mean to say you love me!"

She hesitated. "I can't mean to say I don't or I do for sure, though it would be no chore loving you and your son. I have known you for a short time but I feel as if I have always known you, that somehow you have always been part of my life."

He felt the same, though he couldn't bring himself to say it. How could he? He had loved Alaina with all his heart. He couldn't possibly have feelings for a woman he'd known for just over a week, and yet as she had said, it felt like he'd always been part of her life, and she part of his.

It made no sense, none of it, and yet it seemed perfectly clear.

"It's foolish, I know," Sara admitted with a sad laugh. "I tell myself it's ridiculous, pure nonsense, that I'm lonely and you're convenient and it will pass easy enough when you're gone. I only need to get through this temporary madness and all will be well."

"Madness?" he questioned softly.

She shrugged. "Better I deem myself temporarily mad than temporarily in love."

"There's really no difference between the two. Madness and love are synonymous and not temporary."

Sara caught a quick breath. "Don't tell me that. I thought to suffer this madness, assuming it would end."

Cullen shifted his stance while actually moving closer to her. "It never ends. Love haunts with a never-ending madness."

"I won't have it," Sara said sternly. "I refuse to—"

"Love?" he whispered near her ear.

She turned her face and their cheeks brushed before she murmured, "Yes."

"You can't refuse love. It claims you without consent or invite."

"I'll cast it away," she said bravely.

"It will return with a vengeance and plunge you into the depths of its madness." Their lips were so close that he felt hers quiver, and he was tempted to kiss the tremble away. He didn't, though; he wanted her to submit to him. He wanted it to be her choice.

"I can't love you. I can't, I can't, I can't . . . " Her pleading litany faded as her lips reached out for his.

He let her kiss him lightly, timidly, cautiously, but before she might regret her actions, he took command. His arm went around her waist, his hand grasped the back of her head, and his tongue plunged into her mouth to mate feverishly with her.

It was a kiss born of desperate need, of desire too long ignored and passion not quite understood but impossible to refute.

She returned the kiss with the same desperation, her fingers digging into his muscled arms.

They fought yet surrendered to the kiss, both unsure and certain at the same time. It was a strange feeling for Cullen to surrender to his need since he suspected it was more than an elemental need he'd satisfy. He didn't want to accept the feelings that stirred deep inside him for Sara. He couldn't betray Alaina, and yet Sara filled his soul.

He didn't know how, and presently didn't particularly care. He only knew for the moment that he wanted to be right where he was, holding Sara, kissing her, and damned if he didn't ache like hell to make love to her.

Cullen halted their kiss with a start, his hands rushing to cup her face before pressing his forehead to hers. Between heavy breaths he said, "I want you."

When she didn't answer, he eased his face away from hers, while keeping her face cupped in his hands. Her glaring eyes told him that her desire warred with her pragmatic nature. At this very moment she fought herself, and he feared she would follow her head instead of her heart.

"Don't deny yourself this pleasure, Sara."

She eased away from him, his hands falling away from her face. "Is it pleasure I deny myself or heartache?"

"Only you can decide that, but only if you take the

chance and taste lovemaking from a man who truly wants you."

"But doesn't love me. Will never love me. Will love only Alaina."

"I have been nothing but truthful with you where that is concerned."

She nodded. "That's the saddest part of it all. You've been nothing but honest in that respect, so I cannot fault you. It is only my own foolishness I have to blame."

He tried to approach her but she retreated from him. "This began as a challenging game. If it would make it any easier for you, know that I surrender more than willingly. I surrender without reserve and with great anticipation."

"It's no longer a game," she said, turning away from him, only to turn back again. "And you truly wouldn't surrender. I want a man to surrender to me as much as I surrender to him. I want nothing to stand between us. I want to merge with him and become one. I want to know love, taste love, live love. I refuse to settle for anything less."

Cullen remained silent. He had wanted all of that himself, but with Alaina, and if he couldn't have it with her, he didn't want it with anyone else. How then did he explain this overpowering need for Sara, and not just desire, but a need to protect her, share with her, laugh with her, comfort her?

His anger at himself caused him to be blunt. "But you settled, you married me."

"You served a purpose," she corrected.

"Not entirely," he said, and approached her with a forceful stride. He wasn't surprised that she stood her ground. There was no other place for her to go except toward the bed, and that was an invitation she didn't intend to extend to him.

"Entirely enough," she said, and attempted to step around him.

He reached for her and pulled her into his arms with a smile. "What do I do with you, Sara Longton? You are a stubborn woman."

She placed her hand to his cheek. "You remember me fondly."

He felt a solid jab to his heart. "What if I want to remember more?"

"There is no more to remember," she said sadly.

"I disagree," he whispered, and kissed her gently, lovingly, longingly.

"Don't," she murmured, easing away.

"I want you," he said, refusing to heed her puny attempts to struggle free of him.

"No, you—"

"Don't tell me what I think," he said harshly, yet then kissed her softly. "You have no idea how I feel at this moment."

"Tell me," she urged. "I want to hear."

"I burn with desire for you. It's like a scorching ache I can't douse and it grows more potent when you're near me." He ran his lips over hers. "Kisses quench for the moment, then heat me even more until I want to drink endlessly of you. Only you can satisfy my endless thirst, for I thirst for only you."

"Oh, Cullen, if only I could," she sighed.

"You can." He kissed her again and they melted against each other, lingering in the tenderness they shared.

He eased her steadily toward the bed until together, arms wrapped around each other, they fell on the bed side by side, locked in a kiss. His hand stroked her back, moving down to cup her backside and urge her closer against him.

She submitted willingly, and he pressed into her, wanting her to feel the strength of his desire for her. Her sensuous moans intoxicated and he couldn't get enough of her. He wanted to feel her naked beneath him, to get lost in the depths of her, to capture her cries of release with his lips and to taste love with her.

"I want you naked," he whispered roughly, his breath labored from their ardent kisses. "I want to touch you, all of you."

He heard and felt her breath catch, and he expected her to reach out and help him rid her of her clothes. Instead, she placed her hand to his chest and eased him away from her.

"Don't do this, Sara," he urged, reluctant to let her go. "You'll regret it."

"I already do," she said.

Chapter 25

Sara left her bed and the keep as soon as her husband went off to hunt with her father the next morning. She had feigned sleep so she didn't have to speak with Cullen when he woke. She didn't want to face him, refused to face him, as she had last night when she crawled beneath the coverlet, hugged the edge of the bed, and pretended to fall fast asleep. In truth, she had lain awake for hours, her body throbbing for his touch, for release.

She didn't know where she got the stamina to deny him or herself. She only knew that it was better this way. She was growing ever more accustomed to his presence each day. She could only imagine how she would feel in a month or two, after spending endless time together. How did she say good-bye to him after sleeping beside him every night, waking beside him every morning, sharing meals with him, laughing with him, kissing him, walking hand in hand and living like a wife with him? If those memories would sting, how would she ever deal with more intimate memories?

She kicked angrily at a small stone along the bumpy path to her sister's front door. She had thought it pure genius to wed Cullen and be released from exile at the abbey. Cullen had been the answer to her endless prayers, arriving in the eleventh hour and rescuing her.

Now she felt more trapped than ever, and in a trap of her own making at that.

"Fool," she mumbled.

"You or Cullen?" Teresa asked.

Sara looked over to where her sister sat on a blanket under the shade of a pine tree and walked over to join her. Teresa warned her to be quiet, pressing a finger to her lips and pointing to a sleeping Alexander beside her.

"He just fell asleep, morning nap," she explained softly.

Sara sat beside her sister and kept her voice low. "How long did it take you to realize you loved Shamus?"

"From when I first laid eyes on him."

"Love can happen that fast?"

"Only a strong, sustainable love," Teresa said.

"How do you know if it is sustainable?"

"That's the catch, since only time will tell."

"So you take a chance no matter what when you fall in love?" Sara asked.

"You have to take a chance when you fall in love or you may never find love."

Sara shook her head. "Love confuses me completely."

Her sister laughed gently. "Then love is surely nipping at your heels."

Sara glanced over at Alexander sleeping on his stomach, his rump up in the air, his full cheeks rosy. "I could love him and his father so very easily."

"Shouldn't you be saying you already love him and his father?"

Sara cringed. "Is it obvious?"

"I thought you both in love when I first saw you together, and was surprised when you told me the truth of the situation."

Sara shook her head. "The love you see in Cullen isn't for me. It's for his departed wife. He'll never love another. Would you if you lost Shamus?"

Teresa shivered and rubbed her arms. "The thought chills me to the bone. I don't know what I'd do without Shamus. I love him dearly. I think the real question is, would Shamus want me to wed again, or I him if I departed first?"

"Would you?" Sara asked. "Want him to wed again?"

"I can't say the thought doesn't sting my heart, but then the thought of Shamus being alone for the rest of his life hurts my heart, and it's a hurt I wouldn't want him to suffer. I would want him happy, and that, I believe, is true love."

"I wish I had more time with Cullen before he leaves so I could see if love had a chance between us."

"You haven't given an ounce of thought to what I told you about going to America with Cullen and Alexander?" Teresa asked.

"Not really," Sara admitted. She hadn't wanted to, since Cullen had never once suggested the idea to her, and she certainly wasn't going to ask him. She wouldn't go where she wasn't wanted.

Her sister seemed to have guessed her thoughts. "You're being stubborn," Teresa said. "He hasn't mentioned it to you, so you won't mention it to him."

"He tells me often enough of how he will see me safe before he leaves," Sara replied. "His plans are for him to go off to America with his son and for me to remain behind. He couldn't have made it any clearer. Our marriage was simply a means to an end for us both."

"That was before you both started falling in love," Teresa clarified.

"We barely know each other."

"We've already made it clear that time has no meaning when it comes to love," Teresa reminded her. "Besides, he's not leaving just yet. Use what time remains to you wisely. See what develops between you both, and don't be stubborn about it."

"Cullen wants to be intimate," Sara blurted out with a sense of relief.

"He is your husband, and you should see if you are compatible." Teresa giggled softly. "Shamus and I are very compatible."

"Sex is a good thing then?" Sara asked apprehensively.

"With the right man, it's superb," Teresa said dreamily.

"I don't know," Sara said, shaking her head. "I fear being stuck with memories that will haunt me for the rest of my life."

"Good ones or bad ones?"

Sara grinned at her sister's teasing.

"Seriously," Teresa said, "you need to find out. You need to find out many things these next few weeks and *seriously* consider going to America with Cullen, whether he wants you to or not. I fear for your safety once the truth is learned."

"Cullen plans to eliminate any threat to me."

Teresa took her sister's hand. "There's always someone left who seeks revenge. You will not be safe here once it is known what you've done. And while the prospect of never seeing you again tears at my heart, the prospect of your death pains me even more. At least in America you have a chance, and who knows . . . " She shrugged. " . . . Shamus and I may come to visit you one day."

Alexander stirred.

"He'll wake soon, hungry. You feed him while I get us something to eat, and promise me," Teresa said, squeezing Sara's hand, "you will not dismiss, but at least consider what I've suggested."

Sara nodded. "Do you know how glad I am to have you for my sister?"

Teresa grinned. "You're *lucky* to have me as a sister. I got you out of enough trouble through the years."

"Wait just a minute," Sara said, smiling and was interrupted by a loud—

"Da!"

The next few hours were a carefree, thought-free time for Sara. She and Teresa talked and talked some more while enjoying playful moments with Alexander.

The little boy took an instant like to Sara and managed to win her heart even more than he already had. They had taken him to the creek to throw stones and dunk his feet in the water. He delighted himself with splashes and tumbled around on the grass in sheer joy. He was a happy and content little boy.

"I should get back to the keep," Sara said a few hours later. "Father wanted to speak with me, and Cullen will want to see Alexander again."

"Then why leave? Wait until he arrives and return later with him. Father must realize you have a husband now and he comes first."

"You would think, but Father treats me like a constant thorn in his side that he refuses to remove. He seems to enjoy the pain he insists I bring him."

"That's only because you are so much like him and he truly admires you, though refuses to acknowledge the fact."

"He acknowledged that he liked my husband, though I wonder how he will feel when my husband deserts me, never to return."

"Perhaps that won't be the case," Teresa said, scooping up a yawning Alexander. "Nap time."

"Do you mind if I remain here awhile? I could use a solitary moment or two," Sara said.

"Not at all. I'll be at the cottage."

Sara sat near the edge of the creek. The last few hours had been so enjoyable, free of worry and thoughts that haunted her much too often. Now, however, they returned to plague her, and though she much preferred to ignore them, she had no choice but to address them.

She still didn't understand how a simple plan could have gotten so complicated, but then she hadn't expected love to be thrown into the mix. Sharing her concerns with her sister had helped a great deal, but it now meant making choices she wasn't certain she was ready to make.

She also couldn't comprehend her indecisiveness. Practical problems demanded practical solutions, or so she always believed and practiced with direct bluntness. And while the whole situation seemed a practical one, she couldn't bring herself to make a reasonable decision. Clearly, her heart was interfering.

A sudden familiar stench filled her nostrils, and she got quickly to her feet and turned around. "What do you want, Harken?"

He smiled, a sad mistake since Sara found it hard not to cringe at the sight of his rotten, yellowed teeth, what ones he had left.

"I've come to welcome you home," he said, walking toward her.

Sara backed away, his sweat-stained shirt and grubby plaid adding to the stomach-rolling odor. "I'm married, Harken."

He nodded. "I heard."

Sara didn't trust him. He had a glint in his dark eyes that didn't bode well. However, he did not appear to be angry with her, and Harken had a temper, especially when things didn't go his way. Not that she felt threatened by him. She had handled him once before and could do it again if necessary, but she much preferred not to touch him.

"Happily wed?" he asked.

His question disturbed her and warned her that something wasn't right. "Why would you ask me that?"

He shrugged, his soiled fingers toying with a stick he discarded carelessly. "Something I heard made me wonder."

What could he have heard? She and Cullen only spoke of their situation when they were alone.

"Your father wanted you wed good and proper, he did, and to wed a man who would remain by your side, though difficult that may be, you being so bold and unattractive."

Sara had to laugh. "At least I don't smell like a horse's ass."

"Think you're better than me, don't you?" he snapped. "If you're so much better, why couldn't your father find a single man who would wed you? Even with a generous dowry, no man wanted you. I was the only one with the courage to take on a harping wife like you."

She couldn't say that his words or the memory of that time didn't hurt. They dug deep into her, reminding her of the mockery she had suffered. But that was all behind her and she need not suffer it any longer. She had a good husband and needn't worry about being forced to wed the likes of Harken McWilliams.

"Perhaps, but I wasn't willing to wed a filthy, smelly, ignorant man like you."

"Scorn me all you like, but when that husband of yours leaves you and your father learns the truth, you'll be suffering for sure." He grinned, and Sara cringed. "Unless of course you take a new husband."

It finally dawned on Sara. "You weasel, you've been lurking in the bushes listening to me and Teresa talk here by the creek."

"What does it matter?" Harken shrugged. "I'm sure your father would like to hear what I know, unless of course—"

"He won't believe you," Sara said.

"He will when it comes to pass," Harken boasted. "And I'm a patient man, I can wait."

Sara had been caught off guard. She'd never expected something like this to happen, hadn't even known Harken was around, nor had she considered him a threat in any way. Now here he was, threatening to spoil her plan. How did she handle him?

Killing him would be preferable and solve the problem, she thought, but she had only killed that once, in self-defense; this was a different matter.

Then she realized she wasn't alone in handling this, and folding her arms across her chest, smiled. "Why don't we discuss this with my husband and see what he has to say?"

"I'm not afraid of your husband," Harken boasted with a tremble.

"You should be," Sara warned. "He won't take kindly to you threatening his wife."

"False wife," he accused with a sneer.

"And you'll be proving that how?" she said on a laugh.

Harken raised a shaking fist at her. "Mock me, woman, and you'll be sorry."

Sara took a couple of quick steps toward him and he stumbled away from her. "You remember the last time you thought to threaten me or do you need a reminder?"

"You were promised to me and I'll see that I get what is mine," he said defiantly.

"Sara is mine!"

Harken paled a deathly white and his eyes near popped from his head, while Sara's heart leapt and her legs quivered beneath her dark blue skirt at her husband's thunderous proclamation.

Cullen's arms were soon around her, having approached from behind, and she hugged the strong arms that embraced her waist. He pressed his body hard against hers, letting her know he was there for her, would protect her, keep her from harm, and that knowing filled her with an indefinable pleasure.

"Explain yourself," Cullen ordered with a shout at Harken.

The man looked ready to run, inching slowly away like a crawling bug.

"I'm a patient man," Harken said, staring directly at Sara, then he turned and ran.

"What was that all about?" Cullen asked, turning Sara around in his arms.

She almost sighed at the sight of him, so handsome

and clean and fresh smelling. She wanted to hug him close and never let him go. Instead, she kissed him, nothing passionate, simply generous.

She eased away from him, though took his hand. She would not have him think her upset. She would not have him know how she truly felt.

"It's nothing. Let's go see your son."

He halted her with a tug. "Alexander is sleeping and we go nowhere until you tell me what this is about."

Did she tell him or did she deal with it herself? The way Harken had paled and trembled at the sight of her husband probably guaranteed that he wouldn't show himself again until after Cullen left, though she couldn't be certain of that. If it were the case, would she be able to handle him herself?

She had been handling her problems alone well before she'd wed Cullen, she thought. She would do so again.

"He's disgruntled, having lost his chance at joining the McHern clan," she said, speaking the truth though not all of it.

"Before I leave, I will make certain he will not bother you."

"Not necessary," she advised, her tone light, her heart aching.

Then they walked hand in hand, the sun a bright yellow globe in a clear sky and the air warm for spring. It was a perfect day, a perfect moment; if only it were real, she thought.

Chapter 26

Cullen woke alone the next morning and turned to bury his face in Sara's warm pillow, the scent of her still fresh on the white linens. Hints of lavender and pine mixed with her unique womanly aroma and he inhaled deeply of it.

He threw the coverlet off and rushed out of bed, perturbed by the fact that he favored Sara's scent while unable to remember Alaina's. He'd come to realize that Alaina had been fading from his memory little by little each day. Where once he could picture her so clearly in his mind, it was now more of a faded view, as if obscured by a mist.

He blamed this failing memory on Sara. Since entering his life, his mind had been consumed with thoughts of her, and not all good, at least at first. Then she began to grow on him, and now she invaded his thoughts and senses nonstop. She wouldn't leave him alone, or was it that he wouldn't stop thinking about her?

Cullen dressed in a tan shirt and plaid, and after slipping on his sandals, reached for Sara's comb. He stared at the tangled hairs nestled in the teeth. If only their bodies could tangle like that.

He shook his head and mumbled a few oaths as he dragged the comb through his hair with pulls and tugs before replacing it on the table. He spied Sara's night-dress draped over the chair, reached out for it, then stopped.

"Fool," he mumbled, turning to leave, then turning back and grabbing the nightdress and doing what his reflex had first bade him to do—bury his face in it. Her scent was strong and alluring, and damn if he didn't get a rise from it.

He tossed the garment back on the chair and stomped out of the room. It was clear that he wanted his wife in the worst way, and as clear that he was failing miserably at accomplishing the simple task.

The conflicting thoughts were driving him crazy, while his guilt over betraying Alaina's memory ate at his heart. He had no idea how to settle his torment, and could only wish, pray, and beg that it would end. Yet he knew that only he could end it, however that might be. He wasn't sure.

He wished he were leaving today with his son, yet glad that he wasn't—more conflicting musings that made no sense. In a few days, Sara and he would have known each other for only two weeks, and he was act-ing, feeling, as if she'd been in his life forever.

He near cursed aloud, but his wife beat him to it.

"Like hell I will!"

Cullen entered the great hall to see Sara sitting rigidly

at the table while her father paced in front of the fireplace, his hands hooked behind his back.

The man had a gruff manner about him, but Cullen had come to realize that McHern actually had a soft heart where his daughters were concerned, especially for Sara. She was without a doubt her father's daughter, stubborn and bold, yet kind and honest. And because of this, he expected from her what he expected from himself—strength, courage and a do-what-was-necessary nature.

Sara, however, wasn't complying.

"It's a good cottage," McHern said sternly.

"It is too close to the keep," Sara argued.

McHern caught sight of Cullen, stopped pacing and smiled, and Cullen knew that the old man saw him as an ally. He looked to his wife, wanting to reassure her of his support, and wasn't surprised to see that she didn't require it. She sat self-assured, positive, while her pacing father sweated.

McHern waved for him to join them. "Cullen, we need your help."

"No we don't," Sara corrected.

Cullen walked over to his wife, placed a hand on her shoulder and a kiss on her cheek. "What's the problem?"

"I'm offering Sara and you a nice cottage—"

"Too near the keep," Sara finished.

"What's wrong with that?" McHern barked.

"I want privacy," Sara snapped. "I want the land and cottage that sits between here and Teresa's place. Katie's old place."

"That's too far, and what about your husband?" McHern demanded. "What about what he wants?"

"I want what Sara wants," Cullen assured him.

"I thought to keep you closer," her father grumbled.

Cullen understood Sara's tactics. Once he was gone, her father would most likely have a different opinion of her, and a home a bit of a distance from the keep would serve her well.

Sara's eyes softened just as her father's did, and Cullen couldn't help but smile at how alike father and daughter were.

"The cottage you suggest is too small," she explained.

McHern grinned. "It's a brew you'll be having then?"

Cullen answered for Sara, knowing it would disturb her to lie even more to her father. "As many as we're blessed with."

McHern grinned at his daughter and rubbed his hands together. "I knew you'd do right by the clan." And with a pound to his chest he declared, "I'm proud of that."

Cullen could feel the weight of her father's praise descend on Sara's shoulders, and he watched them slowly droop. He knew this deception upset her, but she had little choice, and after seeing Harken, he realized the necessity of the ruse.

"You have a fine man there, Sara," McHern said. "Do right by him."

Her head snapped up. "What about me? Do you tell him to do right by me?"

McHern cringed. "Don't go getting your nettle up. You don't want to go chasing a good man away."

Sara slammed her hands on the table and stood, the bench near toppling over if Cullen hadn't saved it.

"Me? Chase him away?" she asked, affronted. "He'd do well to keep me happy or it'll be me leaving."

"Don't threaten your husband, daughter," McHern warned.

Cullen remained silent, sensing that Sara was setting their plan into action, but when he caught the hurt in her eyes, it stung his heart and the need to shield her overwhelmed him and propelled him into action.

"Don't raise your voice to my wife," Cullen ordered, stepping around the table to stand face-to-face with McHern.

The older man shook his head, his eyes more weary than angry. "You'll need a firm hand with her or she'll drive you away."

"Sara can't drive me away. I love her." His own declaration startled him, especially since it came so easily, without a shred of hesitation.

"Good, good, my son." McHern smiled and encouraged him with a firm nod. "Remember that, always remember that, and it will serve you well and save you trouble in the years to come."

Cullen heard his advice, but was more concerned with the astonished look in Sara's rounded eyes. She didn't believe his words, did she? He merely was adhering to their plan, wasn't he? He hadn't planned on announcing he loved her, had thought demonstrating it by holding hands, a kiss now and again while in the village, a protective arm around her waist, would be sufficient to give the impression that they were in love.

"Sara, feed your husband then take him to see your new home," her father said with a satisfied smile. "And move in when it pleases you."

"Thank you, Father," Sara said stiffly.

It was as hard for McHern to accept his daughter's gratitude as it was for Sara to give it, and the old man simply shrugged and walked off.

"You don't make it easy for your father to love you," Cullen said, sitting beside her and helping himself to a thick slice of honey bread.

"You declare your love easily enough," Sara snipped.

"Isn't that part of our bargain?" Cullen asked.

Sara stood, though kept her voice to a murmur. "I respect honesty above all things. You didn't have to tell such a blatant lie. You could have phrased it differently."

She walked off in an anxious flourish and was out the door before Cullen could blink. The woman could be frustrating at times, while other times impossible, and in between lovable. She was a riddle of sorts, which intrigued him, and had since he first met her.

He feared solving that riddle would take years, and he wondered if even then he'd ever find the answer. But he wouldn't mind trying. If only he had the time. Time, however, wasn't his friend. He had little of it, and what was left to him he'd dedicate to Sara's safety.

He reached for another slice of honey bread and stretched to a stand. He'd best go be the good husband with the limited time allotted him, though honestly it was no chore, even when Sara bristled. He had yet not to enjoy her company, or ever found conversation with her boring. She possessed a quick mind, and though her tongue matched, he'd never seen her abrasive or malicious to anyone.

She was a good soul with good intentions, and a far more beautiful woman than anyone noticed, and he believed that was because she intimidated most people she met. Her tall height, her overpowering nature, and that bright red mane of hers captured the attention before the gentleness of her eyes was seen or the smoothness of her flawless skin was noticed . . . or how perfect her rosy lips were for kissing.

He shook his head and his reverie away and went to join his wife, reminding himself that this was all a ruse and he would soon be gone. He needed to do what needed doing and be done with it, as he had advised her from the start.

Cullen hadn't been surprised to learn that Sara had left for the cottage without him, and after mounting his horse, it didn't take him long to find his way there, the women of the village graciously offering help with directions.

He arrived just as a broken chair came flying out the front door of a good-sized cottage. It had a fine thatched roof, and two windows with broken shutters flanked the open door. A large garden overrun with weeds ran along the left side of the cottage, while a well-worn path cut its way to the front door.

Cullen dismounted and left his horse to wander over by Sara's mare, who was busy drinking from a trough near a grove of oaks. He made his way carefully to the door, ready to step out of the way if any more furnishings should take flight.

"Sara," he called out when near.

She appeared in a flash at the open door, her hands hugging her hips, and he smiled. A smudge of dirt ran across her nose and dotted her cheek and chin. Her bright red hair was piled atop her head, and her eyes glared a little too brightly.

Had she been crying?

Impossible. He had rarely seen Sara cry, at least a hard cry. He didn't think her capable of it.

"What do you want?" she asked, near snapping his head off.

"To help."

"I don't need your help. I do just fine on my own." She turned and entered the cottage.

He followed her into a large room, light spilling in from the open windows and filling the space with iridescent sunshine. A fireplace with a fine oak mantel occupied the wall opposite the door, and the only furnishings were a spindle-backed rocker, a small table, and a bed, the mattress in need of fresh stuffing.

"Have I upset you?" he asked, reaching out for her hand.

She moved out of reach. "Whatever gave you that idea?"

"You've been snarling and snapping at me since I first greeted you this morning." He walked over to the table, reached for the cloth draped over the rim of the bucket of water and wet it.

Sara stood staunchly, arms crossed over her chest, in front of the fireplace. "I suppose I'm feeling cross today."

Cullen nodded and approached her slowly. She didn't move, and he didn't expect her to. She would show him no weakness or fear. He knew that was how she hid her deepest hurts—with a false bravado.

"Your face is smudged with dirt," he said, and wiped at the spot on her chin.

She kept silent and moved not a muscle.

Cullen cleaned each smudge off her face, slowly and methodically until her skin sparkled a rosy pink and her blue-green eyes softened. Then he kissed her.

It was a simple kiss, or meant to be. A mere brush of his lips to let her know he was there for her even if she were angry with him. But when he tasted her, he couldn't stop.

She was lusciously delicious, like a favorite treat you simply couldn't refuse.

He tossed the cloth aside and cupped her face to feast on her, as she did on him. It felt as if he'd been hungry for her forever and that if he didn't quench this relentless hunger he'd die from starvation.

He nibbled along the silky column of her neck, and

she dropped her head back to give him full rein. He took it, nipping and nibbling until she shuddered in his arms.

"I want you," he growled, then nipped at her ear and moved to her mouth to claim any objection.

She shook her head and pushed him away, but he didn't give in so easily.

"Don't deny us," he demanded.

"This will serve no purpose."

He couldn't take his eyes off her lips, ripe from his kisses. "The hell with purpose. I want you and you want me. Don't deny it."

"I won't deny I want you. But I can't deny I fear falling in love with you," she said, and pushing him off her, ran to the door.

Cullen got there first, slamming it shut and grabbing her arm to swing her around and pin her against the closed door. He anchored her there with his body while he planted his hands on either side of her head, encasing her.

"Don't so this," she warned.

He had to smile. "Only you would warn. Most women would plead with want."

"I'm not most women."

"And grateful I am for it." He leaned in to kiss her, and she turned her head.

"Why are you grateful?" she asked challengingly.

"You are a woman of great passion in everything that you do," he replied, meeting her challenge. "You seize the moment, you take a chance, you defy the common, you defend the helpless, you fight for life on your terms, and . . . you are so very beautiful."

"You believe me beautiful?" she asked doubtfully.

He brought his mouth slowly to hers. "More beautiful than you can ever imagine."

She ducked and squeezed out from against him. "I can't."

"You can," he urged, frustrated, and reached out for her.

She skirted away from him anxiously, yet he saw the ache of unfulfilled passion in her misty eyes, and in response his own passion soared like a mighty warrior prepared for battle.

Then he descended on her so quickly that she didn't have a chance to slip out of his reach. He grabbed hold of her arms and held her firm as she attempted to wiggle free.

"I'll not let you go this time," he warned.

"I'll not submit to you," she argued.

He shook his head. "I see the desire raging in your eyes. You have denied yourself too long."

"I will not—"

"You will," he snapped.

"I won't."

"You want me."

"I don—" She clamped her mouth shut.

"I want you," he declared, and captured her mouth in a searing kiss that soon had their blood on fire.

He yanked her against him so she would feel the strength of his desire, and groaned into her mouth when she ground her body against his. He quickly lifted her up, her legs locking around his hips and his groin near ready to explode as the heat of her nestled against him.

"I'm going to take you, Sara, here and now, unless you say otherwise," he said with labored breath.

She rested her forehead to his. "I want you, Cullen. God help me, I want you."

He smiled and was about to rush them to the bed when they heard: "Sara, it's me and Alexander. We've come to help you."

Chapter 27

Sara sat crossed-legged on a blanket with her sister, the bright sun shining down upon them while Cullen scooped up a squealing Alexander time and again in a playful game of chase and catch.

Her thoughts were in turmoil and she didn't know what to do with them. She wanted Cullen, but did she truly love him? How could she want him so badly if she didn't truly love him? Why then did her heart ache every time she thought about him leaving?

Was she simply a foolish woman desperate to be loved?

Why worry about love? Why not just satisfy both their needs and be done with it? Why be so stubborn? She waited for answers but none came, only more haunting questions. She had almost surrendered to Cullen before her sister appeared. Was it the right thing to do? Would she ever know if it was the right choice?

"You'll be sorry if you don't go with them, Sara," her sister urged.

"Cullen doesn't want me." It hurt to know, but hurt much more to admit aloud.

Teresa smiled. "Cullen doesn't know what he wants. He's as confused as you are, which makes for too much confusion and disappointing choices."

"Foolish choices," Sara corrected.

Teresa shook her head. "It takes a fool to take that leap of faith and know that all will go well."

"I don't know," Sara said with a laugh. "I've been leaping like a fool for years now and things haven't gone well."

Teresa nodded toward Cullen. "I'd say you leapt and landed exactly where God meant for you to land."

"What of Alaina? He can never forget her."

"She will always be a memory, but you are here now with him and that makes all the difference," Teresa said. "He needs you and his son needs you. The seeds of love have already been planted. Give them time to take root, blossom, and grow strong."

She stared at Cullen tickling Alexander's neck with kisses while the little boy giggled and squirmed in his arms. "We don't have time."

"He is your husband and Alexander now your son," Teresa said softly. "You have your whole lives together."

"Our bargain was made out of desperation. I don't wish a marriage made from the same."

"Then make love with him," Teresa whispered. "And see for yourself if love is there."

Sara had no time to digest her sister's remark since

Cullen and Alexander joined them, the lad reaching for the crumbled bits of cheese on her lap. She scooped him up and into her lap, while Cullen plopped down beside her. He reached as greedily as his son for food and yawned along with his son.

"You'll need a nap along with Alexander," Teresa teased.

"He's a handful," Cullen admitted with pride.

"That he is, but a child is no chore to a mother," Teresa said.

Sara wanted to reach out and pinch her sister, just as she had so often when needed, and this especially was a when-needed time. Teresa had no business pointing out the fact that Alexander needed a mother.

Her remark caused Cullen to glance over at his son sitting so cozily and comfortably in her lap, which made Sara wonder over his thoughts. Did they mirror her own? She favored the moment, feeling much like a mother and a wife, her husband residing not only comfortably beside her, but resting against her.

Her first thought was that he played their game well, but the game wasn't necessary in front of her sister. Teresa knew the truth so there was no reason for him to appear so familiar and loving with her.

Did that mean he simply wanted to be this close to her?

He had wanted to be much closer just before Teresa arrived, and perhaps wanted to let her know now that he continued to desire her, in hopes of finishing what they had started.

Alexander yawned and rubbed his eyes.

"Nap time," Teresa said.

Cullen stretched out on the blanket and held his hands out to the lad. Alexander crawled off Sara's lap and into his father's arms, snuggling against his broad chest.

Tears glistened in Teresa's eyes. "There's no denying he instinctively knows who you are."

Cullen hugged his son close. "He's mine and I will always protect him."

Sara stood with a jerk. "Nap with your son, Teresa and I have work to do in the cottage." Then she walked off, stubbornly refusing to shed any tears that threatened to spill. Her heart should be familiar with that empty ache by now, she told herself, and would have to get used to it. No one, not a soul, would ever say such loving words to her.

This was all a ruse of her own making, and she had to see it through to the end. She had to keep her wits about her and protect her heart from further hurt. She was thrilled that she could reunite father and son, and that Cullen loved his son as much as he did, but knew he would never love her and that she wasted her time on such nonsense. She would ready her cottage so that when Cullen left she would be set to live her life with the freedom it had cost her so dearly to achieve.

The next couple of hours she worked herself senseless sweeping, scrubbing, and repairing her cottage. When she was done for the day, she could barely raise her arm to wave good-bye to her sister and Alexander.

She was glad that Cullen insisted on seeing the pair

home. She intended to return to the keep and bathe her soreness away, maybe even crawl into bed for a nap before supper.

Her plans changed fast enough, however, when she turned to see her father and Harken McWilliams approaching on horses.

She near sighed aloud, but instead jutted her chin up and her shoulders back and approached the men as they dismounted. If Harken thought to intimidate her, he was in for a surprise and maybe even a punch or two. Lord, how she wanted to give the sniveling weasel one good fist to the jaw.

Her father offered no greeting but asked, "Is Cullen here?"

"No, he's seeing that Teresa and Alexander get home safely."

"Good," her father said with a firm nod. "Since I want to talk with you in private."

"Then what's he doing here?" Sara asked caustically with a jab of her finger toward Harken.

"He's told me some disturbing news and I want to know the truth of it," her father said, and pointed to the cottage.

Sara blocked the path. "I'll not have the likes of him sullying my home. Say what you have to say here."

Her father did just that. "Harken says he overheard you tell Teresa that your marriage is a ruse and that your husband will be leaving you. I want to know the truth of it, daughter. Have you played Cullen for a fool with intentions of sending him packing?"

So much for patience on Harken's part, and so much for her father thinking it all her idea, though it actually had been, but not without Cullen's consent.

"You would believe a man who's been jilted twice now over your own daughter?"

"A stubborn daughter who refuses to obey her father or any man for that reason," Harken snarled like an angry dog.

"Answer me," her father said, barking the order.

Sara felt herself hounded by nasty dogs about to attack, so she struck first. "How dare you even suggest I would do such a thing, and how dare you believe the likes of a sniveling coward over your daughter."

"I'm no coward!" Harken yelled.

"Then why didn't you face me instead of going behind my back to my wife?"

Sara swerved around along with her father and Harken to see Cullen walking toward them. He went straight to Sara's side, slipping his arm around her waist and giving her a kiss.

"We met up with Shamus," he said, explaining his quick return.

McHern answered for Harken. "Harken told me you knew nothing about her deception."

"Did he now," Cullen said, his heated glare making Harken tremble. "Did he also tell you that he approached my wife when she was alone and threatened her?"

McHern turned on the man with a scowl. "Is that true?"

Harken sputtered. "I—I—I heard—"

Cullen's sharp laugh abruptly silenced him. "You heard nothing. Your tongue lies, and if I hear you speak another lie about my wife, I will cut it from your mouth."

Harken's actions condemned him. He clamped his mouth shut and took a step away from Cullen.

"Get out of my sight," McHern shouted at him. "And don't show yourself around here again or I will run you through with my sword for speaking false of my daughter."

Sara smiled as she watched Harken mount his horse and flee in fright. That was one problem disposed of, and more easily than she had imagined, thanks to Cullen. She rested her head on his shoulder in appreciation and to whisper her gratitude.

He hugged her close and tweaked her nose with his. "Anything for you, love."

"My apologies," her father said, looking directly at her. "But you must understand that through the years you've stubbornly seen to getting things your way, one way or another. So it was easy to believe the fool when he suggested your marriage was a ruse."

"You could have spoken to *us* first," Cullen said.

McHern shook his head. "Harken convinced me that Sara was using you to get her way."

Cullen burst out laughing, and when he calmed, asked, "You believe I'm fool enough to be deceived by your daughter?"

Sara wasn't certain if she should be insulted or proud

and chose to accept the latter. She was proud of the husband she had chosen for he was truly no one's fool.

"My husband has a good point, Father."

"You're right—"

Sara stepped away from Cullen. "What did you say?"

McHern grinned. "Don't think I'll repeat it just to please you. It's about time you did something right for the clan and for your father." He mounted his horse. "I'll see you back at the keep."

Cullen stepped up beside her. "My time grows limited here. One more week at most and then we best begin to show strain on our marriage or your father will surely question my disappearance."

Her heart thudded in her chest, though she outwardly remained calm. "When do you plan on leaving?"

"We talked about two months but I think six weeks would be a safer departure time. I don't want to give Balford too much time to find me."

Sara had to agree with his sound reasoning. The longer he waited, the more dangerous it became for him and Alexander, and she didn't wish to place them in any more jeopardy than they were already in.

In less than four weeks he'd be gone, out of her life forever, never to see him or his son again. The pain stabbed at her and wrenched her insides. She would miss him. Lord, how she would miss him.

She did what she did best to hide her pain; she masked it with a smile. "By then I'll be tucked safely and soundly in my cottage."

Cullen went to reach for her and she moved away and hurried toward her mare. "Let's get back to the keep. I'm tired and need a bathe."

"I thought we'd linger here awhile, by ourselves," he called out.

Sara shook her head, refusing to turn and glance at him, fearing she might just do something she'd regret, like jump all over him and beg him to make love to her every night left to them.

"No, it's best we get back to the keep."

"Afraid, Sara?"

She turned swiftly, sending a cloud of dust swirling around her. "Not of you."

"Of who then? Yourself?"

Sara stared at him, so strong and handsome and defying her to deny him. They both knew she wanted him as much as he wanted her. Did he believe she would argue the point?

"I want you," she said bluntly. "Does that make you feel better? Does that make the situation any different?"

"Let me love you," he urged.

"We've been through this before. You don't love me, whereas I believe myself falling in love with you. Do you want to complicate this situation even more?"

He rubbed his chin, giving pause to her question, and she watched the way his long fingers stroked his flesh, and damn, if she didn't want him to stroke her naked flesh as well.

"It's a chance I'd take," he admitted with a nod.

She recalled her sister's words—that she had leapt and landed where God wanted her to be. The rest was up to her.

"What will it be?" Cullen asked.

She stared a moment before answering, "I'm going to take a dip in the stream. Then I'll meet you in the cottage."

Chapter 28

Sara lingered at the stream as long at she could. She had scrubbed herself from head to toe, her pale skin sparkling pink. She had made a commitment. Actually, she had surrendered. Was she giving into her own desires or surrendering to love?

She wasn't sure and didn't know if she wanted to look any deeper into her decision to finally make love with Cullen.

A cloud drifted overhead, causing the sunny, warm day to suddenly turn gray and chilled. Early spring weather was often unpredictable, though she couldn't help but wonder if the sudden change had something to do with her decision.

She shook her head at the nonsensical thought and marched to the cottage, determined not to hesitate or show trepidation. This was her choice and she would see it through no matter how apprehensive she felt.

Sara reached out for the door latch and hesitated. Would he be in bed naked, waiting for her? Would she need to disrobe in front of him? What did he expect of her? She shook off her concerns and silently scolded herself.

"Be done with it," she murmured aloud and quickly opened the door.

She breathed a sigh of relief when she saw Cullen standing near the burning hearth. He had taken the time to light a fire and chase the damp chill from the large room.

He turned with a smile and held his hand out to her.

She went to him, and when she slipped her hand in his, he grasped hold and swung her back against him, wrapping his arm around her waist and leaning down to nibble at her neck.

"You smell of fresh spring, like flowers at first bloom or berries ripe with sweetness."

She smiled and tilted her head back, exposing her neck to his nibbles.

"Lord, how I've wanted to taste you." He nuzzled near her ear. "All of you."

She shivered at the thought, and he turned her around in his arms as the first roll of thunder sounded in the distance.

"The horses need securing before this storm hits," he said. "You have a choice. I'd be more than delighted to disrobe you, or you can be waiting in bed naked when I return. I leave it up to you." He kissed her then and headed to the door. "Be quick in your choice for I won't be long."

As soon as the door closed behind him, Sara rushed out of her clothes. She wanted him, but self-doubt still invaded her senses. She might smell sweet to him, but how would he view her body? She wasn't exactly petite, though she curved quite nicely at her waist and hips, or at least thought she did. Would he think so too?

She blessed her sister for having brought fresh bed linens and climbed beneath the pale blue coverlet, pulling it up to her chin. Then, realizing how foolish she must appear, she settled the blanket just above her breasts.

The door opened, and her breath caught when her husband entered and shook raindrops off after latching it behind him. He was such a handsome man, broad in shoulders, thick in chest, his dark eyes smoldering with passion.

Cullen stripped as he approached the bed, dropping his garments as he went, not caring that by the time he reached her, he stood completely naked.

His nakedness didn't startle her. He had stripped before in front of her. Besides, it was as if he announced proudly that he had nothing to hide from her. He was willing to bare all, show all, give all, and in a strange way, it eased her trepidations.

She pulled the blanket back, inviting him in.

He smiled, slipped beneath the cover and stretched out on his side next to her. He tugged the blanket from her firm grip to rest lightly at their waists.

"We have nothing to hide from each other, and I ache to see your beauty."

Sara almost protested his compliment, but he pressed a finger to her lips, preventing a single word from escaping.

"You are beautiful, Sara Longton," he said, a kiss replacing his finger while his hand stroked her full breasts and along her curved waist.

It took only mere moments for her body to flare to life and for her hands to reach out and eagerly explore him.

They were soon teasing each other and laughing softly. She moaned as they became intimately familiar with each other. It was as if they had been reunited after a long absence. Nothing seemed strange or unfamiliar, but as it should be and once was, as though they had been together many times before.

His hands traced over every line and curve of her body, settling in intimate places and causing her to gasp, smile, and moan with pleasure, and then she did the same to him. Their lovemaking was a synchronicity of long-shared partners who knew each other on the most intimate levels.

When his mouth settled at her breast, she knew he belonged there, that she had been waiting for him and him alone to bring her pleasure.

He raised his head and stared at her with bewildered yet passionate eyes. "This feels so right, so very right."

She understood, for she felt the same. She had hoped to enjoy their lovemaking; she had never expected it to feel as if they were destined to be together, that they were meant for each other.

The thought served to heighten her pleasure and passion, and she reached out, needing him to fill her and fulfill her. She couldn't wait another minute, did not want to, needed him now, right now.

Her hand cupped him gently then stroked him, her fingers enjoying the velvet feel of him. "I can't wait any longer."

"I haven't tasted all of you yet," he whispered on a moan.

"Another time," she begged.

"Is that a promise?"

"You have my word," she said with a kiss.

He eased over her, nudging her legs farther apart with his knee. "I'll hold you to that."

"I'll honor it."

"I'll see that you do," he murmured before kissing her with a hungry need that she returned with equal fervor.

She moaned when she felt him slip gently into her, and before she knew it, she felt the length of him settle inside her and begin to move. She moved along with him until she felt herself riding a crest of a wave that grew larger and larger, soaring higher and higher.

Her fingers dug into his back as she held onto him, matching his rhythm, feeling herself soar higher than she ever thought possible, feeling the sheer joy of being one with him and finally cresting and slamming to shore in a breathtaking climax that left her gasping for breath.

Cullen didn't move off her immediately, and she didn't want him to. She held onto him, not wanting to let him go, not wanting him to slip out of her just yet. She wanted to feel the very last pulse of him ease away inside her.

When he finally slipped off her, he took her with him,

his arm firm around her, her head on his shoulder and their breathing calming little by little.

Sara heard the roll of thunder then and the rain that pelted the cottage. She hadn't heard the rain start or the thunder draw near, having been too engrossed in making love, and now she smiled at the thought and snuggled her face to Cullen's chest.

"That was beautiful," she said.

"More beautiful than I ever expected," he said with surprise.

She looked up at him. "Had you expected to be disappointed?"

"No, not at all," he said quickly. "I just never thought . . . "

Sara waited for him to finish, but he seemed reluctant and she wasn't certain if she was prepared to hear . . .

" . . . it would feel so—" He hesitated again before quickly finishing. " —perfect."

She grinned happily. "I never thought of making love as perfect, but that's how it felt, so *very* perfect."

His agreement came in a tight hug, and she swung her leg over his and draped her arm across his middle, content with the familiar security and safety she felt beside him.

"It's as if I've always known you," she said honestly. She had picked a complete stranger to wed, one dropped on her doorstep, and found herself familiar with him. How did that happen?

You leapt and landed where God wanted you.

Her sister's words resonated in her head. She had

asked God for a husband, and he had delivered. Was she where she was supposed to be—in Cullen's arms?

Had she found what she'd always been looking for—love?

The thought frightened her. And why wouldn't it? If she found love, how was she ever going to let it slip out of her hands?

A clap of sharp thunder jolted the lovers, and they hugged each other, laughing.

"Are the Heavens angry with us?" Sara asked.

"Or perhaps they warn us," Cullen suggested.

The thought sent a shiver through Sara, and Cullen held her firm.

"I won't let anything happen to you," he said.

No, he wouldn't, Sara thought, but then he could only protect her while he was here with her. What would happen when he left?

"As soon as the rain stops we should get back to the keep," she said, feeling a sudden need for her home. But then, this was her home now, she thought, and she needed to believe it so, to make it so.

"I thought we'd stay the night here."

"We have no food—"

"If you hadn't noticed, your sister left the overstocked basket. We have all we need." He grew quiet though he uttered a bare whisper.

Sara didn't think he was aware that she'd heard him. He'd said, "We have each other." It startled her, though she made no comment. She needed time to think on it.

"No one will miss us," Cullen said.

"My father—"

"Will assume, and be pleased, that we're busy giving him the grandchildren he expects."

Sara had to laugh. "You're right about that."

"We need this time, Sara."

"Why?" she asked anxiously, uncertain what she wanted to hear him say. What did she truly wish from him?

He turned her on her back, leaning over her, his fingers stroking her cheek, his dark eyes intent on her face. "I'm not sure. I only know that this time is important to us. The next few weeks are important to us."

She turned her face to kiss the palm of his hand. "My thoughts as well, though I don't know why."

"It's so strange," Cullen said, kissing her lips gently and brushing his cheek across hers.

"How so?" she asked.

"You and me, and how we came together."

"Perhaps the Heavens decreed it," she said with a hint of uncertainty.

"We were meant to be?" he asked, unsure as well.

"I don't know what to think anymore. We needed each other and found each other. We are familiar with each other, though we know each other barely a month. None of it makes sense, and yet it seems to make sense." She shook her head.

"Perhaps we'd be best not to question it and just simply enjoy the time we have together."

His words struck at her heart. *Time we have together*. Once again it disturbed her to know that they would eventually part. She wasn't one given to tears easily, but now, feeling the swell of them building, she buried her face in his chest.

"Sara?" Cullen said, and tugged at her until she had no choice but to look at him.

Tears glistened in her eyes, intensifying their blue-green color.

Cullen stared at her, bewildered. "I've rarely seen a tear in your eye."

"And you needn't have now, if you had let me be," she accused bluntly.

He wiped the tear stuck in the corner of her eye with his thumb. "Tell me what bothers you, Sara."

She was quick to respond. "Nothing bothers me."

"Nonsense, you cry," he said, and kissed the corner of her eye. "It hurts me to see you cry."

"Why?"

He looked at her awkwardly, as if fighting to find a reason.

Sara answered for him. "You don't know why, do you?"

"I care for you," he said quickly.

"Why?" she repeated, though not accusingly.

"You saved my son's life. I owe you."

Sara refused to let her disappointment show. She had hoped that perhaps there was more to his feelings. She had discovered that her own feelings were growing day by day, actually soaring, particularly since they had made love.

Their lovemaking had only proven to her that something special existed between them, and try as he might to deny it, she certainly couldn't, nor did she want to.

Her feelings were a gift from the Heavens. Hadn't she asked for a husband, and hadn't she been immediately presented with one?

"Let's make the most of this time, Sara," he said, cupping her face with one hand.

It sounded as if he were pleading with her, or did he plead with himself?

She smiled to hide her ache and poked at his bare chest. "You are a great lover, Cullen Longton."

"Glad I am to please you, Sara Longton."

"How about pleasing me again, husband?"

"I knew you wouldn't be a shy one," he said with a smug grin.

"Do you want shy?" she asked with another teasing poke.

He shook his head as his mouth descended over hers. "I want you just the way you are, unafraid and eager to love."

"That I am, Cullen, that I am," she whispered before his mouth claimed hers.

Chapter 29

Cullen watched his wife from his perch on a log near the keep. Sara was speaking with a couple of women in the village. They all wore smiles and laughed now and again. It hadn't taken long for him to see why she felt an outsider in her clan. It wasn't that the villagers didn't like her; it was because they revered her, just as they did her father.

She carried herself with distinction and confidence, and didn't hesitate to offer a sound solution to problems. Sara was a born leader, and it was obvious to all who knew her, even her father.

While her blunt, honest comments rarely offended, they did often startle, and that left many villagers leery of approaching her. Sara might not tell them what they wanted to hear, but they would hear the truth from her, and the truth, Cullen knew, wasn't always easy to accept.

He'd been dealing with that realization for the last couple of days, ever since he and Sara had made love.

He wiped the smile off his face, though it would reappear soon enough. It always did when he glanced at his wife. Her natural beauty was apparent, and even more so when she stood among other women. Her unique height, her blazing red hair, her confident posture, her flawless skin, her shapely body, her keen mind, her courage, her unabashed passion, all pronounced her a woman worth loving.

And damned if he didn't think he was falling in love with her.

He kicked at a pebble in the dirt, thinking the kick would have been more appropriate to his bottom. He was torn by the unexpected feelings of love for Sara and wasn't sure what to do with them. And what of when it was time for him and his son to take their leave? How did he walk away from her?

The thought ripped at his heart. But was this love true, or was Sara simply a convenient replacement for his Alaina?

Cullen laughed at the thought. Sara and Alaina were nothing alike, which made him wonder if what he felt for Sara could actually be real, and did he have enough time to find out or would he need to make a decision he might regret for the rest of his life?

He looked over at her again, her fiery red hair tossed back as she laughed, her cheeks flushed red from the slight chill in the air, spring having yet to fully claim each day with its gorgeous weather.

Her cheeks had been flushed like that early this morning, he recalled, when she woke him with an exploring hand. Their mating was slow and lazy, as it had been since the night they first made love. They couldn't keep their hands off each other. One touch and passion was sparked.

Sara could be a tempest or an angel when it came to passion, and he liked the vast opposites in her. It made for never-ending pleasure and satisfaction more potent than he'd ever imagined.

He bent his head with a shake. Another thought that irritated him. Making love with Alaina had been beautiful. Making love with Sara was memorable. How did he rationalize both, or did he need to?

"That scowl tells me something troubles you," Sara said, stopping in front of him.

He reached out and tugged her between his legs, his arms snaking around her bottom. "I forgot to tell you how beautiful you were today."

She shoved away from him. "That certainly isn't going to help us."

He stared at her, empty arms extended.

"Play dumb," she snapped. "And don't talk to me until you apologize." She stomped off mumbling to herself.

He stared after her, confused, and then it dawned on him. She had reminded him just this morning that they best begin the demise of their marriage. Their agreement had been fulfilled and it was time.

He, however, wanted more time, though he knew that wasn't possible. The longer he remained, the more dangerous it could be for him and his son and the McHern clan if he were found with them.

The thought annoyed him, and he stood and went after his wife.

"I want to talk with you," he said, grabbing her arm.

She yanked it out of his grasp. "Not now."

Cullen grinned, and in one swoop he lifted her off her feet and tossed her over his shoulder. He whacked her backside once and said, "Now we talk."

He wasn't surprised when her only retaliation was to spew some venomous words his way. She probably was pleased with the attention-getting scene, and sure enough when he deposited her a safe distance in the woods away from curious eyes, she was smiling.

"That was perfect." She adjusted her dark blue shawl and pushed ringlets of hair away from her eyes. "A few more like that and the villagers will be gossiping up a storm."

"I don't like fighting with you," he said honestly.

She reached out, her fingers lightly stroking his palm before her fingers locked around his. "It is necessary."

"Is it?"

"What else are we to do?" she asked as if she looked to him for a different solution.

He brought their entwined hands to his mouth and kissed each of her fingers before answering. "I don't know, but I don't feel comfortable with it this way. I don't wish to fight with you whether real or merely play. It doesn't feel right. It doesn't feel like something *we* would do."

"It does feel strange," she admitted. "But you need to leave soon."

He slipped his arm around her waist. "I could go away due to a family matter, and you could receive a message a week or so later that I perished in an accident."

She shook her head. "That would leave me a widow, able to wed again, which my father would expect of me eventually."

He couldn't bring himself to suggest that it would give her more time to find a good husband. The thought of another man touching her angered him and made him pause to think of the quandary he was in, and with little time to do much about it.

"I could just disappear," he snapped.

"For what reason? My father would search for you and could very well discover the truth. If he merely believes my actions sent you running, he'd leave it alone, not wanting to embarrass the clan."

She made sense; she always made sense, which didn't make things any easier. But who had made the situation more difficult? He had, he thought, with his confused feelings. Had he remained firm to their agreement and simply done it without involving himself with her, none of this would be an issue.

That, however, hadn't happened. He was very much involved with her, and wanted to remain involved with her. Even now he wanted to rush her to the cottage and make love with her and forget their problems, just feed their passion.

"We must stay the course and see it through," she said softly and not at all convincingly.

"Let's go see my son," he said. It was the one place they could be themselves, and right now he wanted them to be themselves. No fights. No talk of separating. Just Sara, Alexander, and him. Her sister more often than not left them alone.

Sara smiled. "He's such a joyful lad and has grown attached to you, but then you spend much time with him. He will go easily with you when the time comes."

He almost asked if she would go easily with him, but held his tongue, while admonishing his foolish thoughts. He had given his word to find his son and keep him safe, and that should be his only priority. He had no business thinking of anything but getting Alexander safely to his brother's ship and sailing to America, where he could give his son a rich, fulfilling life.

"Let's go," Sara said, tugging him along. "This is actually good. We can enter the village arguing and ride off separately. That will give the villagers more fodder for gossip."

"No," he said, yanking her to a stop and wrapping her in his arms, to rain kisses over her face. "No more fighting today."

"But—"

He captured her protest with a kiss, finishing with a deep hungry thrust that stole both their breaths. He rested his forehead to hers, his fingers stroking her neck. "No more fights, not today. Today we love."

She lifted her head away from his and said sadly, "*Just today*. Just today we love."

Was one day enough?

The thought startled him, and he shook it from his head, grabbing her hand and tugging her along after him. "Let's go and enjoy the day."

He didn't bother to tell her he feared it might be their last, their only time to love without thought or consequence. He didn't know why he thought as much, and it troubled him that he did, but it also made him seize the day.

Alexander ran to greet them, his father scooping him up before his short little wobbling legs toppled him over. He squealed in delight and gave his father a big, wet, open-mouthed kiss.

"He'll learn," Teresa assured Cullen, having kept pace behind the lad and stopping with a smile once the babe was safe.

"You'll miss him, won't you?" Cullen said, struggling playfully with a wiggling son.

Teresa's smile was brilliant as she looked from Cullen to her sister. "More than ever, but he has taught me much and I am ever so grateful, especially since—" She stopped, her eyes sparkling with tears and her hand going to her stomach.

Sara screeched with joy. "You're with child!"

Teresa nodded, and the two sisters hugged and laughed and grew teary-eyed and hugged some more.

Cullen forced a smile. Though he was happy for Teresa, it made him realize that Sara could very well be with child. What would he do then? He didn't know why he hadn't given it thought before now. Perhaps he hadn't wanted to.

With Cullen's arms and hands a makeshift swing, Alexander enjoyed the ride while his father listened to the two women blather about babies, names, and sewing garments for the little one.

Teresa finally ended it by saying to her sister, "I'm glad you've come to visit. I'm feeling tired and could use a nap."

"Go," Sara said with a gentle shove. "Our plan was to spend time with Alexander. We'll take him to the creek."

"I'll get you a basket for lunch and an extra blanket so Alexander can take his nap. It's a bit chilly today."

Sara hurried after her sister. "I'll help."

Cullen watched them disappear into the cottage. He looked down at Alexander on the makeshift swing. "Women, my son, are something men will never understand," he said.

The little boy giggled, squealed, and kicked his feet.

Alexander spent much of his energy throwing stones and bouncing up and down, his little chubby hands clapping with delight at every splash. He ate in between rubbing his eyes, his father folding back the sleeves of his beige knit sweater to keep them out of his busy mouth. It didn't take long for the child to cuddle in the extra blanket and fall sound asleep.

With time finally theirs, Cullen whispered to Sara, "What if you're with child?"

Her startled eyes met his and he saw in them a flash of joy that faded all too soon as her hand drifted to rest on her flat stomach.

She turned the question on him. "What if I am?"

"You would go with me," he responded without reservation. He'd have no child of his growing up fatherless.

He watched her breath catch, and then she took a deep breath as if fortifying her courage.

"Perhaps it is best we no longer—"

"Make love, be intimate, lose ourselves in each other," he said, shaking his head. "I don't think so."

"We consummated our vows, so it isn't necessary—"

"The hell with necessary, I want you," Cullen said bluntly.

He was glad he made her smile. He loved when she smiled, her eyes sparkled, her cheeks flushed pink and her rosy lips grew dewy and just ripe for kissing.

"We should be practical," she advised.

"The hell with practical." He leaned closer to her. "I want to be wicked."

Sara reached out and toyed with the ties on his shirt. "I love when you're wicked."

"You can be wicked yourself," he teased, unable to keep himself from running his finger over her plump juicy lips. They were warm and wet, just right for a nibble or to suck and kiss. and damn if he wasn't growing hard with the thought.

"I know that look," Sara said, sinfully soft.

"Tell me about it," he urged, his finger stroking down along her neck to the mounds of her breasts peeking from her blouse.

Sara's grin was as blunt as her words. "You grow hard for me."

He laughed quietly, definitely not wanting to wake his son. "How can you be sure?"

Sara slipped closer, their shoulders touching, and she slipped her hand beneath his kilt to rest faintly over him. Her laughter was more a smug murmur. "I don't even have to touch you to feel your strength."

"I insist," he breathed across her moist lips, though never connected with them, and felt her shiver.

Her eyes closed slowly and opened just as slowly as she ran her tongue in a wicked tease over her lips. And when she squeezed him, all of him, he nearly jumped in tortuous pleasure.

"Mmm," she whispered. "I can almost feel you filling me."

He kissed along the edge of her ear. "I can almost feel your tight sweetness wrapping around me."

He groaned when she squeezed him more firmly.

"I want you," he whispered, nibbling at her earlobe.

"And I you," she murmured, and stroked the hard length of him.

"Keep that up and—"

"We'll soon be mating on this blanket, where your son sleeps," she reminded with a gentle kiss to his cheek.

"'Sleeps' is the opportune word," Cullen reminded.

Sara giggled. "We'll have to be quick, lest he wake, and discreet, if prying eyes should be watching."

Cullen grabbed hold of her and tumbled her back on the blanket, coming to rest on top of her. "We'll simply look like—"

"Playful lovers?" she asked, reaching down to release him from his kilt.

He groaned, his forehead resting on hers. "And quick it will be, I assure you."

Sara wiggled beneath him. "I couldn't agree more. I am so very ready for you."

He smiled and kissed her quick, his eager hand roaming down to hike up her skirt.

"Da!"

Cullen and Sara turned to see a smiling Alexander roll to his knees, then stand and toddle over to them.

Chapter 30

A few hours later, Sara saw that Cullen's passion continued to lurk in his dark eyes. It was faint, barely distinguishable and certainly not noticeable to anyone but her, and it kept her own desire edgy.

They rejoined her sister in the cottage, the day having grown cloudy with a cool wind. Cullen sat on the floor before the burning hearth, he and his son playing with the wooden whittled horse he had brought him, while Sara and Teresa brewed hot cider to chase away the chill.

If she thought her passion would subside easily, she learned fast enough that her husband did not intend to let that happen. Each time she brushed past him and he was certain no one saw, he'd run his hand beneath her skirt to stroke her leg. One time he managed to reach and brush intimately between her legs.

She near gasped but caught herself and merely smiled and hurried away from him. When she failed to slip past him again, he mouthed *coward* at her and she nodded to let him know she fully agreed.

A short time later a rough wind arrived along with Shamus, who shut the door firmly against it. "It looks like a storm is brewing and it won't settle easily."

"I agree," Cullen said, standing with his son in his arms and casting Sara a look that warned of a far different storm, one of passion too long delayed.

Sara reached out for Alexander, and the lad went to her eagerly, his pudgy arms going around her neck. She hugged him close knowing that any minute his father would announce their departure, and he did.

"We should leave before the weather worsens."

"Or you could stay the night," Shamus offered.

Sara knew his answer for it would have been her own.

"We need to return tonight," Cullen said, though he offered no explanation.

"Then you best be on your way," Teresa urged, and took Alexander from Sara, handing him to Shamus. She then grabbed a small cloth-wrapped parcel and shoved it at Sara with wink. "Something for later."

Sara hugged her sister, so very grateful for her understanding.

With quick good-byes, they were out the door and to their horses.

"The cottage," Cullen ordered once mounted.

Sara nodded, knowing the rapidly darkening sky would allow them to go no farther, nor would their passion.

It was a chase against nature's fury and human desire, both raging strong and both needing release. They raced against time, against desire, against the wind, aching and wanting with a need so deep that it grew with the barest of thoughts and the mightiest of tingles.

Sara knew her breath was lost to more than the persistent wind, her rising passion claiming most of it, as did the thunderous beating of her heart. Lord, but she wanted to love Cullen and have him love her and never have it end.

The rain pelted the ground just as they rushed into the cottage after sheltering the horses against the storm.

Sara turned from hitching the door latch, to be grabbed swiftly around her waist with a firm hand claiming the back of her neck, and then Cullen's mouth descended on hers. He gave her no room to breathe, to think, to react, only to surrender to the passion that had lingered and tormented them throughout the day.

Their kisses were urgent, born of a need so strong neither of them could fight it, but only surrender to it.

Cullen hooked her around the waist and hefted her up. She locked her legs around him and threw her arms around his neck to grab hold of his mouth again. She didn't want him to stop kissing her, and she damn well didn't want to stop kissing him.

He tasted too good, felt too good, and oh good Lord, she wanted to feel more, so much more, and knew from experience that he could make her feel like she had never felt or thought she'd ever feel before.

"I want you," he said, pulling away from her hungry mouth only long enough to rush his words out, then reclaimed her mouth.

His hands worked their way under her skirt as he walked to the bed with her, and she groaned when he grabbed tight hold of her bottom and squeezed a squeal of delight out of her.

He tossed her on the bed. "No time to undress."

She laughed and yanked up her skirt as he shoved his kilt aside and dropped over her.

"Damn, but I love your unselfish passion," he said as she reached out to guide him between her legs.

"And you, husband, are the best lover—"

He rushed his mouth over hers and finished for her. "The best and only lover you've ever known."

"Aren't I lucky to get the best the first time out?" she said, laughed and wiggled his stiff erection inside her with a joyful squeal.

He took over from there, driving deeper into her, forcing her to grab hold of him and hold tight while he took them on a ride she would long remember and never ever want to forget.

He made her climax in seconds, her screams alarmingly satisfying, but he wasn't done. He drove deeper and deeper into her until she felt the passion well up inside again and build until she exploded with an agonizing cry. And then he started again, and later the only thing she could remember was screaming out his name over and over until he finally took her in his arms and held her while she collected her senses, found her breath, and waited for her heartbeat to calm.

"This isn't enough, you know," he said, their garments sticking to their sweat-drenched bodies.

She laughed, though it was brief. "I do get a chance to rest, right?"

"Not for long," he teased with a hug.

They laughed, though remained as they were beside each other, both still recovering from their anxious love-making.

Cullen turned on his side and kissed her. "This is still our day. We have the whole night ahead of us, just you and me . . . not the present, not the past, not the future to think about, just here and now, you and me."

"And tomorrow—"

He hushed her with a single finger to her lips. "There's no tomorrow, only now, this moment, you and me."

They stared at each other, dark eyes holding to soft blue-green, and she wondered if his thoughts mirrored her own. Did he feel as she did? Did he believe that tonight just wasn't enough for them? They needed a life-time to satisfy their hungry need, and she wondered if even that was enough time.

But if this day, this night, were all she had, she would take it gratefully, though with an ounce of regret for more. She rested her hand to his cool, smooth cheek, damp from their sweaty encounter.

"I'll not let you sleep a wink," she teased.

He grinned, his dark eyes glinting with a wickedness that tingled her intimately, though she wondered how, when she had thought herself spent.

"Is that a challenge, my love?"

"A promise," she whispered on a sigh.

"Then it is best I get you naked," he said, and proceeded to do just that.

He refused to let Sara lend a hand. He did it all, removed every stitch of clothing she wore with a slow methodical touch that had her soon on the edge of complete surrender, especially since he kissed every inch of her naked flesh along the way.

She couldn't believe she wanted him so soon, but then, she always wanted him. A simple touch, an innocent kiss, and she was ready for him. It wasn't right, but it felt so perfectly right.

"I want you all the time," she breathed on a sigh.

"I like that thought," he confessed before teasing her nipple with his mouth.

They lingered in touches, kisses, and an intimacy born of an indefinable need they both equally surrendered to.

It wasn't until night claimed the sky that they halted their lovemaking and sat on the bed wrapped in a shared blanket, nibbling on the sweet bread and cheese that Teresa had packed for them.

"Bless your sister," Cullen said, eating the food with a ravenous hunger.

"Teresa has been a godsend," Sara agreed. "I am so happy that she is with child. It will make Alexander's absence that less painful."

"She has been good and generous with my son. I will never forget her kindness."

"Or mine?" she asked bluntly.

He tweaked her nose with his finger. "At the rate

we're enjoying each other, it's a good chance you'll be with child and will have to join my son and me."

"And if not?" she snapped.

Cullen stammered. "I—I—"

"Don't know what to say?" Sara accused sharply. "You can't love me, can you? That just wouldn't be possible. You loved Alaina, God forbid you should love anyone else."

"You've known how I've felt from the start," Cullen shot back.

"Of course, you refuse to live. Better to die with Alaina than to ever chance loving again."

"She's been gone only—"

"Alaina's gone for good," Sara spat. "You're not."

"Love doesn't disappear with death."

"It also doesn't die with it," Sara said boldly.

"What would you know?" he accused.

Sara threw her hands up, the blanket falling down around them, leaving them naked to the waist, though she didn't care. "You're right. I don't know. I only know how I feel about you, and even that seems crazy. How do you fall in love with someone you barely know?"

Cullen stared at her. "I've wondered the same myself."

Sara couldn't dare hope he meant her. She couldn't stand the disappointment, and besides they were talking about Alaina.

"Alaina was easy to love?" she asked.

"Easy, gentle, predictable," he confirmed.

"As it should be," Sara proclaimed with a bravado she didn't feel.

"I would have agreed at one time."

"You don't any longer?" she asked anxiously.

He asked instead of answering. "How do you feel about me and why is it crazy?"

"I love you." The words surprised her, but then she couldn't have stopped them from spewing from her mouth if she wanted to. She had contained her feelings long enough, and with such a short time left, she would have her feelings known and be done with it. The consequences would fall where they may.

"How?" He shrugged. "We barely—"

"Know each other," she finished, the nagging thought too often on her mind. She shrugged. "I have no explanation for you or for myself, though I've searched hard for it. Can't say when or where it is that I realized my love for you. It sort of popped up one day right in my face, and try as I might, I couldn't make it go away."

"You wanted it to?" Cullen asked.

She laughed gently. "It would have been so much easier if it had, but I knew it wasn't going anywhere. Love had embedded itself in my heart and it was there to stay, whether I wanted it or not didn't matter."

"So you accept it willingly?"

"What else is there for me to do? Deny it? Ignore it?" She shook her head. "None work."

"You've tried?"

"I surely did, and for my own sanity, but I learned quick enough that love borders on madness, which means there is no sane thought where love is concerned. Nothing makes sense, and to try to reason it is committing yourself to abject failure, thus plunging you into madness, though more accurately into the very depths of love. Does any of that make sense?"

Cullen shook his head. "Nothing has made sense since I met you. But tell me, why do you love me?"

"Do I need a reason?"

He smiled. "There is usually at least one, maybe two or three."

"Let me think," she said, tapping her finger to her chin.

"You need to think?"

"It's an important question," she said seriously.

His smile sobered. "You don't know why you love me?"

"I could give you the usual—that you're a good man, a good father, courageous, and so forth."

"That sounds good," he admitted.

Her slow nod turned to a quick shake. "Something's missing."

"What?"

He sounded anxious for an answer, but how did she explain? She wasn't certain how to put it into words or even if it would make sense.

"Tell me," he urged, gently nudging her shoulder with his.

She placed a hand over her heart. "I feel the love. It's there when I glance at you, when you smile at me, when you touch me." She patted her chest. "I can feel it each and every time, and sometimes it's just there for no particular reason at all."

Cullen remained silent.

"It makes no sense, I know—"

"No," he said. "It makes sense, though—"

She pressed her fingers to his mouth, not ready to hear that he couldn't love her. "You told me this day was ours. Let's keep it that way. Make love to me until the sun comes up. Tomorrow will bring what it may, but today is ours."

They drifted into each other's arms then, and began a night to remember.

Chapter 31

Cullen wasn't sure what to make of the situation with Sara. He only knew it had become more complicated than he'd ever expected. When he agreed to their bargain, the thought of leaving her behind wasn't a concern. Now, however, he wasn't sure if he could just simply walk away from her without missing her.

And if he would miss her, could he possibly be falling in love with her?

They rode quietly into the village, neither of them having said much since they woke. It was as if something had changed or perhaps was about to change. Cullen couldn't quite grasp the feeling, he only knew he felt it. It nagged at him, disturbed him, and he didn't know what to do about it.

Clouds followed them overhead, though the sun peeked through on occasion and the chill from the day before was gone, replaced by a breath of spring. It promised to turn into a pleasant day, or so it appeared until they entered the village.

Whispers and stares followed them, and Cullen saw

315

one of McHern's warriors hurry into the keep before they reached it. He wasn't surprised to see Donald McHern rush out, his face bright red, his eyes bulging with anger.

Cullen dismounted and went directly to his wife, reaching up to grasp her around the waist and whisper as he lowered her to the ground. "Something is very wrong."

"Agreed," she murmured before they turned to face her father.

"How dare you bring the Earl of Balford's wrath down upon the clan," McHern spat out, pointing an accusing finger at his daughter. "You knew he was a wanted man when you wed him, didn't you?"

Sara stood tall and confident. "Aye, Cullen's wanted by me. I love him."

McHern shook his fist at her. "Then you'll join him when the earl's soldiers arrive to take him away."

Cullen stepped forward. "When do they arrive?"

"From the message I received from a neighboring clan, two days at the latest, and I sent word promising the soldiers your presence, so do not think to run," McHern said with a nasty glint.

"You would turn us over to them?" Sara asked incredulously.

Her father's face glowed like a hot cinder. "You would have me place the clan at risk for you and him?" He shook his head. "The McHern clan has survived because I fight battles I know I can win. No one wins against the Earl of Balford. He has strong ties to the king. You put the clan in danger, now you'll rid us of that danger."

Cullen grabbed hold of Sara's arm when she moved to protest. "We'll do what's right for the clan," he said.

"You damn well will," McHern said with a shake of a fist, then turned and stomped off into the keep.

Cullen and Sara made their way to their bedchamber, with far too many accusing stares following them. Even with the door safely latched against curious ears and eyes, Cullen still spoke in a whisper. "We leave tonight. We can carry little since we'll have Alexander to consider."

Sara nodded. "Teresa will see that you have food to last, and I'll not let Father know of Alexander's absence until much later, so the earl doesn't make the connection."

Cullen grabbed hold of her arms and squeezed tight, as if he feared she would escape him. "You're coming with us."

Sara shook her head. "Why?"

"If the Earl of Balford gets to you before I get to him, he will see you tortured for information and then executed. And even if I can eliminate him as a threat, his cohorts may seek revenge in his name. There is no way I will allow that to happen. You're going with Alexander and me to America."

"And if I don't want to?" she said defiantly.

He grinned and yanked her up against him. "You have no choice, wife. You're going with us. Start getting

317

your things together, but remember we must travel light. I'm going to see that the horses are looked after and made ready for us tonight. There's no time to warn your sister of our plans. Your father won't let us leave here."

"Teresa will help us," Sara said with certainty.

"I don't doubt that, but it's best she know as little as possible. We will stay to ourselves today. The villagers will assume we're repentant of our actions, and it is best they think that. They will not suspect us of attempting an escape."

Sara agreed with a nod. "We will need to be careful if the soldiers are only two days from here."

"We'll skirt the border of McHern land and keep away from nearby villages. We can't be seen. The soldiers have probably already made the surrounding villages aware of who they're searching for and made certain the consequences if they help us."

"We're on our own," Sara confirmed.

He hugged her, holding her close, letting the warmth of her seep into him and aching to touch her more intimately, yet knowing there was no time. "We have each other, wife."

Sara leaned back against the closed door after Cullen left and placed a hand to her rolling stomach. She was glad she hadn't eaten this morning for she would have never kept the meal down. She had hoped, though never thought it possible, of going to America with Cullen and his son, but that hope was born of a love she prayed would be returned.

Her prayers had been answered in a strange manner, and while she was glad she was going with father and son, she couldn't help speculate over the future.

She shook her head and pushed away from the door. There was no time to waste. She had to gather her things and be ready; ready to leave her home and family, probably never to see them again.

It was a double-edged sword she faced, leaving the only way of life she knew and a sister she loved dearly, and while her father would deliver her into the hands of Balford, she was aware he did it for the benefit of the clan and not because he didn't love or care about her.

She would have no chance to speak with him before she left, to speak the truth to him and let him know she never intended the clan harm. She would tell Teresa and have her tell her father.

Her heart ached when she thought of saying good-bye to her sister, so she pushed the painful thought from her mind and got busy sorting through her garments and personal belongings. Night came fast enough when you didn't want it to, and soon enough her time here would be finished.

As much as she ached to cry, Sara contained her tears and did what was necessary. She'd be ready to leave, though her heart would be hurting in more ways than one.

Cullen rubbed the horses down, fed them, and looked over the saddles. He purposely took his time, not rushing, appearing withdrawn in troubled thought, so that curious eyes assumed his repetitive actions were born out of worry.

"Preparing to go somewhere?" McHern asked, entering the stable.

"Needed my hands active to calm my concerns," Cullen said, prepared to play his part in this charade.

"And concerned you should be," McHern bellowed, and sat on an upturned barrel, gave a gruff cough and lowered his voice. "I don't like that Balford fellow, a devious and mean man, takes pleasure in hurting people."

Cullen glanced at him suspiciously.

"A leader's duty is to protect his clan, *all* of his clan."

Cullen nodded slowly, waiting for him to explain further.

"Protecting the clan sometimes means keeping them unaware of the truth for their own safety. So that when torture is threatened by a mean bastard of a man, the people have nothing to hide."

"That takes a wise and courageous leader."

"It takes—" McHern sniffed and rubbed at his nose with his sleeve. "It takes a coldhearted man."

Cullen smiled. "No, it takes a man with a brave heart."

McHern stood and held out his hand.

Cullen took it and McHern grasped tight hold while placing a firm hand on his back. "You take good care of my little girl. She's a lot like me, God help her."

"I—"

McHern threw his hands in the air and walked away. "Don't want to hear anything. Know anything. You best be ready for Balford's arrival."

"I'll be ready," Cullen said.

McHern turned before walking out the door. "Don't disappoint me."

"You can count on me, sir."

"Good, I'll remember that—always."

Cullen wasn't surprised by the man's actions. McHern admired his daughter more than he let anyone know. He knew how difficult it was for her, since she was so much like him—only she was a woman. And that made things more difficult, since women didn't have the same rights as men.

McHern had purposely made it known in front of the clan that his daughter and her husband where to remain and face their fate at Balford's hands to keep the clan from danger, thus protecting his clan from the truth—that he expected Sara and Cullen to escape.

Cullen was pleased that he'd be able to tell Sara how much her father truly loved her and in the end protected her even at the risk of having her think otherwise.

While Cullen looked a burdened man, his footfalls heavy, his shoulders slumped, his head down as he returned to the keep, he actually felt relieved. Though he would take precautions when he and Sara took their leave tonight, he knew no extra guards would be posted or extra measures taken to prevent their escape.

And once on the road, he would have only the soldiers to contend with, since McHern would send no warriors in search of them.

Cullen entered the bedchamber to find Sara sitting in a chair by the hearth, staring at the fire. He went to her, kneeling and placing a hand on her knee as he knelt before her.

"Are you all right?"

She nodded. "I'm ready." She placed her hand over his. "Father sent word that he preferred we didn't join him for supper this evening. He must truly hate me."

"That's not so," Cullen said, and proceeded to tell her of his encounter with her father in the stable.

Tears glistened in Sara's eyes. "He said I was like him?"

"Proud of it too."

She hugged her husband. "You don't know how wonderful that is to hear. I always thought I disappointed him."

"No, if anything, I believe your father wished he could have done more for you, though he was limited because you were a daughter, not a son."

"I always believed he wished I was born male."

"Only because he could have provided more easily what you needed," Cullen confirmed.

"I'm happy I can leave with good memories of him and knowing he loved me." She sighed. "There's only one thing."

"What's that?"

"What are we to do until we leave late tonight?"

"We'll rest," he said.

"But I'm not tired."

Cullen laughed and scooped her up into his arms. "I promise you will be."

They stole quietly out of the keep hours after everyone retired. Not a soul stirred or a sound was heard. They walked the horses into the woods before mounting and riding off, Cullen halting beside his wife as she gave one last glance back at her home.

"I'll never see it again, will I?" she asked sadly.

"I'm afraid not. You'll have a new home now with Alexander and me."

"Because it's necessary," she confirmed.

Cullen nodded, relieved it was necessary. He hadn't wanted to leave her behind, hadn't wanted to bid her good-bye, never to see her again. He had feelings for her, confused as they were, or perhaps clear as they were and he just refused to acknowledge them. Whatever the reason, he was glad she had been forced to join him.

They woke Teresa and Shamus and explained that it was time to take Alexander and that for their own safety it was best they didn't ask any questions.

Teresa quickly got Alexander's things together and advised Sara of his care, though Sara had become familiar with it, having spent much time with her sister since her arrival.

It was a heart-wrenching good-bye for all, Teresa hugging a sleeping Alexander tightly before Shamus took him, did the same, and then handed him to Cullen, who was already mounted on his horse.

"No sense in warning you to keep him safe, I know you will," Shamus said, and the two men shook hands.

Sara and Teresa hugged tight.

"I am glad you go with them," Teresa said, wiping a tear off her cheek. "Cullen will keep you from harm."

"I will miss you so much," Sara said, her own tears too difficult to hide.

The sisters hugged tight again, and Teresa shoved her away. "Go, it's time."

Shamus helped Sara to mount.

Cullen looked at the couple who had cared so lovingly for his son. "Words can't express my gratitude for what you've done for Alexander," he told them. "I will be forever grateful. If you ever wish to visit or leave Scotland for America, go to St. Andrew Harbor and inquire about a Longton ship. You will be provided with free passage and brought to our home in the Dakota Territory."

"Thank you," Shamus said, hugging his weeping wife.

Cullen led the way, knowing Sara would wave to her sister until they were out of sight. He hugged his sleeping son snuggled contently in the crook of his arm.

I have our son, Alaina, he's safe and I will keep him that way. And forgive me, my dear Alaina, but I believe I have fallen in love. I didn't mean to. I wasn't looking for it and never expected it. But I cannot fight it and I know Sara will make a good mother to Alexander.

Forgive me, and know that I will always love you.

All was good now. They would reach the ship and set sail for America, but first he had one last thing to see to. He would kill the Earl of Balford.

Chapter 32

Night was not made for travel, and if it wasn't for the near full moon, Sara was certain they would not have gotten very far. Distance was necessary in their situation; however, so was sleep.

Sara was relieved when Cullen decided to settle down for a few hours sleep, especially with Alexander's schedule of waking shortly after dawn. They couldn't remain exhausted, continue to travel, and at the same time look after the lad.

Remarkably, or perhaps it was a babe's lot to sleep soundly, Alexander hadn't stirred and remained asleep when she and Cullen cuddled around him to keep him warm, since a campfire was prohibited in their situation.

Sara cherished the feel of her husband's arm draped across her waist and Alexander nestled comfortably between them. She felt they were a family, even though she had been forced upon them. They belonged to her, and just as Cullen intended to keep his wife and son safe, she would do anything to keep her husband and son safe.

She expected sleep to claim her soon enough, and it did, but not for long. Anytime the lad stirred, she woke, which created a fitful slumber. But it wasn't only the babe that disturbed her sleep. She also worried over the immediate future.

They had a rough road to travel, though the terrain didn't bother her. It was the Earl of Balford's compelling need to see this child dead, along with his father, that concerned her, and that powerful men usually got what they wanted. The soldiers' orders were clear, and if not obeyed explicitly, they would face punishment, and so they would be determined to find father and son at all costs.

Sara didn't believe the earl considered her important, and that could prove beneficial. But she also wouldn't underestimate the earl. He was a sly one. She had seen that firsthand with what he had done to his daughter. The man was pure evil.

"You should sleep."

Her husband's whisper made her smile, and she looked over to see that he too lay awake. "I have."

"But not enough."

"It will do," she murmured.

He reached out and stroked her cheek gently. "I would have missed you."

Her voice failed her.

He grinned, tracing her lips slowly with his thumb. "A miracle, I silenced you."

She nipped playfully at his finger. "You're not that lucky."

"Yes," he said quietly. "Yes, I am that lucky."

Sara felt her heart slam against her chest and thump wildly. Was he attempting in his own way to tell her that he cared for her, could even possibly love her? He had admitted he would have missed her, and what of him claiming he was lucky? What was he truly saying?

"I'm married to a good woman who will make a wonderful mother for my son."

This time her heart dropped and her stomach tumbled. Her hope had been short-lived. To him, she simply was a good mother for his son, and she had no doubt she would be. She had fallen in love with Alexander as fast as with his father.

"Have no doubt about that," she confirmed.

"I want so badly to kiss you right now."

Her heart softened again and she silently admonished herself. This time wasn't for wondering if Cullen would ever love her. This time was for making certain father and son were kept safe. Time enough later to work on love or to accept what she had—a good husband and a fine son.

"I could do with a kiss—and more," she teased with a hushed whisper.

He squeezed her chin. "Be careful what you ask for."

"I know exactly what I want from my husband." She sighed gently. "Pleasure beyond reason."

"You truly enjoy our lovemaking?"

"You need to ask?"

"I had assumed, though I'd prefer to hear it from you," he murmured.

Sara obliged. "I love your gentle touch, your considerate actions, your eagerness to bring me to pleasure, and I love when you're impatient and take me fast and furious and how we're both drenched in sweat afterward. And . . . " She smiled wickedly. "I love the taste of you."

"As much as I love knowing that, now was not the time to tell me."

She grinned along with him and they locked hands, resting them across Alexander.

"Sleep," he ordered.

She gave a whispered laugh. "Do you think that is possible?"

"You mean you suffer the need for me as I do for you right now?"

"A *powerful* need," she emphasized.

"Soon," he whispered. "I promise soon I will pleasure you."

"I'll hold you to that promise."

"You won't have to."

They drifted off to sleep, their eyes closing simultaneously.

Sara had worried that Alexander might be upset when he woke to find her and Cullen in place of the only parents he had known. Fortunately, all the time she and Cullen had spent with him was their saving grace.

Cullen scooped his son up in his arms as soon as he woke, and while Alexander looked around, he spoke to the lad, explaining that Da was taking him on a trip. His little lower lip quivered but Cullen was quick to distract him with food and the wooden horse that had fast become a great distraction.

"He'll adjust," Sara said.

"I know, but it hurts me to have to hurt him like this."

Sara placed a comforting hand to his arm. "He won't even remember this time."

"Thank the Lord for that."

Once on their horses, Alexander tucked safely in his father's arms, they took off, their tempered pace allowing a good distance to be covered. There was no time to converse or dwell on worries. Attention had to be kept to the road, ears had to listen for unexpected company and minds to remain focused.

It would take over a week to reach St. Andrew Harbor, and anything could happen in that time. They had to remain cautious, take no chances, and always be alert and aware that at any moment the earl's soldiers could pounce on them.

Alexander's presence made that all the more difficult. They had to stop more frequently, and the worry that he would cry out or make noise when silence was imperative was an ever-present concern. That was why they continued to remain off the main roadway and chose the less frequently traveled path.

Two days of travel passed without incident, and they knew they would soon reach the market where they had once spent a pleasant day together. This time, however, they would need to be cautious while replenishing some supplies.

"You'll stay here with Alexander while I go collect what we need," Cullen ordered.

"That's a foolish decision," Sara said, though she kept a smile on her face as she and Alexander piled stones on one another on a blanket.

"And I suppose you think it would be better if you went?"

"You know it would be," Sara challenged. "The soldiers look for you, not for me. I'm just another woman going to market. I have a far better chance of slipping in and out unnoticed than you do."

"Damn, I hate when you're right," Cullen said, joining her and Alexander on the blanket. "I don't like sending you into harm's way. What if you should need help?"

"Unless I'm foolish, which I'm not, I should have no problem," Sara insisted.

"You'll not dally?"

Sara rolled her eyes. "That question wasn't necessary."

"With you it is necessary," he teased.

She jumped up. "For that I will not bring you back any sweet cakes."

"Da!" Alexander said, pointing to his father and nodding.

"You tell her, son. Da needs sweet cakes."

Alexander laughed and patted his chest.

Sara laughed. "It looks like your son wants a sweet cake too."

Cullen glanced up at her. "You be careful, wife. I don't want to lose you."

Her heartbeat skipped twice before settling back to its normal rhythm. Lately he kept catching her off guard, making her think that he truly cared for her, perhaps even loved her in his own way.

"I'm not going anywhere," she said, and her smile confirmed it.

"Yes you are," Cullen boasted. "You're going to America with Alexander and me."

Alexander looked to his father at the sound of his name, his full red cheeks puffed with a grin, and nodded along with his father.

Sara leaned over and kissed father and son on the cheeks. "Love you both."

Before she reached her horse, Cullen called out, "You come back to me safe, wife."

She grinned. "As you wish, husband."

Cullen winced. "Promise me you'll hold your tongue while at market."

Sara mounted her horse and took hold of the reins. "Now you're asking for the impossible." She laughed and took off in a trot, ignoring her husband's shouts to behave.

The busy market provided perfect cover for her to move about without detection. She was just another peasant woman among many searching for bargains. All she had to do was keep to herself, purchase the few items they needed, and not forget the sweet cakes.

She stabled her horse with the farmer that had looked

after their horses the last time they were there. More soldiers roamed about than usual and kept suspicious eyes on any man or couple who entered the market, though not single women, unless they fancied them. Sara didn't have that problem and did not draw a notable glance.

She was quick to make her purchases with the money Cullen had provided, and even found another whittled animal for Alexander, this one a dog. She neared the sweet cake stand happy to be near done when chaos broke loose.

A soldier had grabbed a young lass and was dragging her off, screaming. Those who tried to help found themselves threatened by soldiers protecting their own.

Sara couldn't ignore the young woman's agonizing screams for help. It wasn't right, and brawn would not help in this matter. She knew it would take a quick mind and mouth to outwit these fools, and she was glad she hadn't promised her husband that she'd hold her tongue.

She hurried over to the sweet cake table, the soldier having dragged the young woman behind it.

"Four sweet cakes," she said, placing a coin on the worn wooden planks supported by four barrels. She stretched her neck, staring outrageously at the soldier, who laughed at the woman's struggles.

"What are you looking at?" the soldier demanded when he caught her stare.

Sara took her bundle of sweet cakes. "You do know who you've got there, don't you?"

"She's a peasant," the soldier barked.

"True, but a favored one," Sara said, and turned to leave.

"Who favors you?" he asked the girl, and when she didn't answer, he called out. "You! Wait there."

Sara turned.

"Who favors her?" the soldier asked.

Sara shrugged. "It's not for me to say."

The soldier moved off the lass and stood yanking her to her feet, to drag her around in front of Sara. The lass trembled and her terror-filled eyes pleaded for help.

Sara did not fear the soldier, a runt of a man she was sure she could send flying with one good blow to his soft gut. But she knew his lingering comrades might object.

"Tell me," he ordered with a raised fist.

She almost laughed at his puny threat, but that wouldn't help her cause, and besides, she had to make him think the lass was favored by someone he would fear enough to release her.

"I really shouldn't say, and she certainly won't," Sara said, shaking a downcast head.

"One of you will tell me now," he shouted.

"We'd rather face your wrath than his," Sara said with a quiver.

She didn't expect to be backhanded across the mouth, and the taste of blood from her split lip sent her temper soaring. But it would do her no good to lose it now, she told herself. She had the woman's safety to consider, and then there was Cullen and Alexander. She could not jeopardize their safety any more than she already had.

She slowly gathered the packages that had been knocked from her arms and stood to face the soldier once again.

"Need I tell you again, woman?" the soldier demanded.

Sara performed courageously, shaking her head and shuddering. "I will not speak his name. Do what you may to me but I will not speak his name."

The young woman finally realized what Sara was about and joined her charade.

"She is right. His name should not be spoken, not even whispered."

The soldier hastily shoved the lass aside as if she had the pox. "Be gone with you."

The lass retreated quickly, though not before sending Sara a slight nod of gratitude.

The soldier brazenly approached Sara. "Perhaps I should take you in her place."

Sara smiled. "If you don't mind the pox."

He stumbled backward. "Be gone with you and don't show your face around here again or I'll see you imprisoned."

Sara hung her head and with repeated whispers of gratitude rushed off. She was quick to get her horse and make her escape, not wanting to be around when or if the soldier discovered the truth and saw himself for the fool he was.

She enjoyed a battle of wits rather than a battle of brawn. It was so much more challenging and satisfying when victorious. However, she wasn't foolish enough to believe herself superior, and took precautions on her return trip to make certain she was not followed.

Her split lip swelled and refused to stop bleeding, and she had to spit the blood from her mouth as she rode along. Cullen wasn't going to be pleased with her actions, but how could she have left that woman to such a horrendous fate and do nothing?

It wasn't her way to ignore the defenseless, and Cullen would surely realize that, since she had done the same for his son. She walked with pride and bowed to none, believing all people were the same, none holier or greater than others. From what she had heard of America, she might just fit in nicely.

Clouds gathered overhead and thunder rumbled in the distance, promising rain soon enough. She hurried her pace, keeping a keen eye for possible shelter from the impending storm.

She took a moment to slip the hood of her cloak over her head to keep the chill off her cheeks and to hide, if only briefly, her wound from Cullen. Then she entered camp, to find Cullen mounting his horse, Alexander in his arms.

"I've found a cave not far from here," he said. "We'll be safe from the storm."

"Good," she called out, keeping her face from his view, and turned her horse, ready to follow him.

"Sara?" he questioned.

She pranced her horse away from him. "We should be on our way."

He came up beside her quickly, and just as quickly slipped her hood from her head.

Sara had no time to keep him from seeing her wounded lip, which had stopped bleeding but swelled considerably.

Her breath caught in a gasp at the fierce glare in his dark eyes, which was pure murderous.

Chapter 33

Cullen sucked in his anger and held it deep in his chest as his horse, sensing his master's fury, pranced nervously.

"I got us sweet cakes," Sara said holding up the bundle.

He gritted his teeth. "They cost you dearly."

Alexander cried out when fat raindrops began to fall in earnest.

"You'll explain after we take refuge in the cave," Cullen growled like an animal ready to attack. He could barely contain his rage as he sped to the cave, the vision of Sara's badly wounded lip burning vividly in his mind.

It did not help his mood that Sara had responded to his evident anger with an offer of sweet cakes. Though her thoughtful gesture touched him, it also annoyed him. He hoped she hadn't suffered a wounded lip for those sweet cakes.

Knowing her, he imagined there was more to it, and he was determined to find out what it was. He settled

Sara and Alexander in the cave, then tethered the horses to a tree, gathered their things and rushed out of the rain to join them in the enclosure.

Sara sat with Alexander on a blanket. His smile was wide, his little mouth sticky from the sweet cake Sara shared with him, though she tore even tinier bites off for herself.

Cullen's anger bubbled up again, though he kept it from spewing over.

Sara pulled a wooden dog from one of the bundles and Alexander squealed with delight.

"Da! Da!" he yelled, waving the animal in the air.

Cullen joined them, putting aside his anger in order to make a fuss over his son's new toy.

"I didn't think you'd mind," Sara said.

"You thought right," he said and nodded. "That lip needs tending."

"I'll see to it." She moved to stand.

"You'll stay put," he ordered curtly.

Sara froze for a moment, then bristled. "I can tend myself."

His tone eased though remained determined. "I know you can, but I want to tend you."

She stared at him.

"What happened?" he asked, then raised his hand. "Wait, before you tell me . . . "

Cullen searched through the bundles, grabbed a piece of cloth, stepped to the mouth of the cave and held the cloth out to be soaked by the rain. He returned squeezing some of the rainwater out of it.

He sat beside Sara, Alexander occupied with his wooden animals and feeding himself from the bits of sweet cake Sara had torn apart for him.

"Now tell me," he said as he gently began to clean the dry blood from her chin.

Sara told her story, and as she did, Cullen's hand slowed to a halt. He envisioned the whole scene, seeing clearly what she had faced and how she'd placed herself in a difficult situation to protect another.

"I couldn't just leave her to such a horrible fate," Sara finished.

Cullen leaned closer and patted at her swollen lip with the wet cloth. She winced, and he felt her pain. He wanted badly to race out of the cave, mount his horse, and go after the bastard who had hurt his Sara, but that wasn't possible. Such rash reaction would satisfy his need for revenge but only endanger them more.

"No, you couldn't and you wouldn't," he said, understanding she was not a passive woman, but a woman of action. He admired that quality, so how could he not respect and accept her actions?

He could, however, voice his opinion and concern. "I could have lost you."

She smiled wide, which caused her to wince and her eyes to tear. "Never. You're stuck with me."

Cullen patted her lip, trying to cleanse the crusty blood, when Alexander crawled between them, his head popping up, his little hands grabbing at his father's shirt to help him stand. When he finally wobbled to his feet, he pointed a finger at Sara's wound.

"Ow."

Sara hugged him, and he giggled, then she rolled on the blanket with him in her arms.

"What about Da?" Cullen said, joining the duo, hugging them both with a growling laugh as they rolled around. This was his family, Alexander and Sara. He either accepted this new joy in his life or would forever pine for a woman who was gone from him, never to return.

And damn if Sara wasn't a good, fine woman with qualities he admired and respected. A woman he had somehow fallen in love with. How, where, when, the Lord only knew. He had tried to make sense of it, but nothing had made sense to him since he met Sara.

What did finally make sense was that he had found his son, fallen in love, and was about to start a new life in America. Now he had one more thing to look after, and though it put their future in jeopardy, he knew it was something that had to be done.

Alexander retired earlier than usual, exhausted from their travels, playing with his wooden animals, and content with a full tummy. That left time for Cullen and Sara to be alone, and after tucking a blanket around his sleeping son, he moved to the opposite side of the small campfire he had started to chase the chill from the cave and snuggled beside Sara, who sat crossed-legged munching on aged cheese.

She popped a piece into his mouth and he nipped at the tip of her finger.

"You taste better than the cheese," he teased.

She placed a hand to his cheek. "I want to taste you, but my lip . . . "

He touched her wound ever so lightly. "Let me taste you."

She shivered and rested her cheek to his. "I would love that."

He eased her down onto the blanket, the fire's flickering light dancing across their faces, their passion as heated as the fire itself.

Cullen started at her neck, and as he drifted down over her body, he slowly moved her garments out of his way, exposing intimate areas he wanted to explore to bring her to pleasure.

His lips claimed her nipples, enjoying the taste as much as she enjoyed his feasting on her. He loved the feel of her hands digging into his head, urging him to enjoy. Her unbridled passion never failed to excite him and want her even more.

He moved down over her, pushing garments out of his way, tasting her, a salty taste here, a sweet taste there, until he descended between her legs and went to the very core of her.

He knew her well enough to know that she contained her moans, keeping them soft and quiet, not wanting to wake Alexander. Her hands digging into his head, however, told him he was driving her insane, and that thought spiked his own passion beyond control.

He moved over her, and as much as he wanted to kiss her, knew he'd only hurt her bruised lip. He buried his face next to hers so he could whisper in her ear how he ached for her, wanted her, needed her, and then he slipped into her.

They rode together on a wave of passion that consumed and devoured them into oblivion, and crashed together, exploding in lights and sounds and feelings that had them holding tight and refusing to let go.

"I love you," she whispered on a labored breath.

Cullen wanted to speak but wasn't sure how to say what he intended and have her believe it—that he had fallen in love with her.

She held him close, and he sank into her embrace, wanting it, needing it, and accepting it.

Later, settled in each other's arms for the night, Cullen broached the subject he had avoided. "There were extra soldiers at the market?"

"Too many," Sara said, spooned against him.

"Balford has covered the area well."

"Which means he's determined to catch you and your son."

"He'll not want his daughter's bastard alive to one day lay claim to Balford land," Cullen said.

"Then he will hunt until he finds you."

"And you?"

Sara glanced over her shoulder at him. "I pose no threat to him."

"You saved his bastard grandson. You are his enemy and he will want you to suffer. He enjoys making people suffer."

"He made you suffer," Sara said sorrowfully.

Cullen hugged her tight against him. "I knew the

consequences of falling in love with his daughter and I paid them."

"Without regret?" she asked softly.

"Without an ounce of regret," he answered, and squeezed her tight. "But that time has past and it is here and now we must consider."

"Alexander is what matters," Sara said, glancing over at him.

Cullen snuggled with a nibble to her neck. "He's ours, and hopefully we'll give him a slew of siblings to grow with."

Sara grasped hold of his hand resting at her stomach. "You want more children?"

"Don't you?" he asked, hoping she wished to build a home and family as much as he did. He wanted to leave his old life behind and start anew, and they could do that in America.

"I always wanted as many children as possible," she said eagerly.

He continued to nibble at her neck, and now patted her stomach. "Then I will give them to you. Our child could already be growing inside you."

She sighed and joined her hand with his. "That would be wonderful. Alexander would have a sibling to play and grow with."

"And more to follow."

She laughed softly. "You intend to keep me busy."

"All the time," he growled as he nuzzled her neck and moved to her mouth, abruptly stopping. "It pains me to see your lip swollen."

"It was worth it," she assured him.

"I would argue it was foolish, but I know better. You keep your wits about you even in the most difficult of circumstances and speak boldly when needed."

"That worries you?" she asked.

"I have concerns, but it's more for what we may face in the next week or more. We need to work together to make sure that you and Alexander are deposited safely on my brother's ship."

"Along with you," Sara said firmly, casting a questionable glance at him.

"I will join you after I see to Balford."

"Is that absolutely necessary?" she asked.

He didn't intend to argue with her. This was his decision and he would see it through, and he knew it was now more necessary than ever.

"Balford is an unforgiving man," Cullen informed her.

"We will be gone from Scotland—"

"But your family won't be," he finished.

Sara turned in his arms. "He would hurt them?"

"He will need to take his anger out on someone whether he or she is guilty or not. Revenge is simply his way. He will want someone to suffer, and if we're not here, he will choose someone close to either of us. And being I have no family left here—"

"He will go after my family."

"I would count on it," Cullen confirmed.

Sara stroked his face with a single finger. "I understand when something is necessary, though it doesn't mean I like it, and it doesn't mean I don't fear for your safety. I will help make sure you remain safe."

He tapped her nose. "I will do this on my own."

"You will not," Sara said, poking his chest.

"I won't argue this with you, Sara."

"You're right. You won't. I will help you."

There was no point in debating the matter with her; she was a stubborn one and determined to have it her way. However, as far as he was concerned, though he would not argue it with her, he would see to it that would happen as he wished. He would not take even the smallest of chances that Balford would get his hands on Sara.

Balford was for him and him alone to face. She would have no part in it.

"Your silence warns me that I will need to keep a good eye on you, lest you sneak away and do something foolish," Sara said.

"I'm not the one with the swollen lip," he reminded.

"And you will remain without wounds if I have anything to say about it."

His laughter rippled around them. "I doubt anyone could stop you from saying what you wish."

"Make fun all you want, husband," she said sternly. "I'll still have it my way."

"We'll see," he said, kissing her cheek.

"Don't think to distract me," she warned with a pointed finger.

"Never," he said with feigned shock, and kissed the tip of her nose.

"I will have it my way," she cautioned, though on a softer note.

The gentle kisses he planted over her face did the trick. She grew silent while her body grew limp in his arms, and with her guard down, yawns attacked her one after the other until she drifted off to sleep, her face snuggled against his chest.

Exhaustion was fast overtaking him as well, and as he drifted off her words resonated in his head and raised concern. She was stubborn enough to try to have it her way, and that could prove fatal for her.

He couldn't lose another love.

He couldn't lose Sara.

She proved more special to him than he had ever thought possible, and besides, he was waiting for just the right moment to tell her how he felt about her. It had to be a perfect moment so she would believe him and know without a doubt how very much he loved her.

Chapter 34

Sara followed quietly behind her husband. It had been a tiresome and worrisome week reaching St. Andrew Harbor, and now, though they were finally here, it was still not over. Soldiers filled the harbor town, hassling almost everyone in search of Cullen and the babe.

Not a man, woman, or a couple with a child was safe from accusations or from being detained until the soldiers could ascertain their identity. It had taken considerable effort for them to sneak past the soldiers and reach the outskirts of the harbor, and even more fancy maneuverings to finally make it to within yards of the ship.

They presently took shelter behind a building amidst stacks of crates and barrels and discussed the quagmire they faced.

"Everyone with a child is being questioned," Cullen said, hugging his napping son in his arms.

Sara was bluntly honest. "The one relatively safe way to reach the ship is through a huge distraction."

"Agreed, and I must be that distraction."

Sara near punched him, she was so angry. "Are you truly a fool?"

"No," Cullen said sternly. "But it is the only way."

"We haven't even discussed other possibilities," Sara accused, and glared at her husband, fear grabbing a firm hold of her stomach. He looked so worn and yet remained so determined. He'd fight to the bitter end to protect her and Alexander.

However, he failed to understand that she would risk her life as well in order to see father and son safe—she loved them that much.

"There are no other possibilities," he said, "and besides, I have unfinished business with Balford."

"We get Alexander on the ship and then we both go take care of Balford," Sara said, as if it was done and he need not argue with her.

"You know I will not allow that," Cullen said confidently.

"I was afraid you'd say that," Sara replied, and sighed heavily.

"It's the way it must be. It's the most sensible solution to our situation. The soldiers will be so busy with my capture that you and Alexander can sneak easily on board and no one will be the wiser."

"What if the soldiers decide to search the ship?" Sara asked.

"I imagine they already have, but even if they did so again, I have no doubt that my brother keeps a hiding place where you and Alexander can remain undetected until they leave."

"You've had this all worked out," she said, annoyed that he'd been scheming to have things his way without regard to her concerns or opinions. His journey to find his son hadn't been an easy one, but he had succeeded, and it was important that he not jeopardize his life now that he was so close to freedom for himself and his son.

"This is my fight, not yours."

"Wrong!" she snapped. "We are husband and wife and therefore the fight is ours."

Cullen tried to reason. "It was mine before you came along."

"It was made mine when I became your wife."

"We can't waste time arguing over this," Cullen said. "Alexander will wake soon, hungry, and draw attention. We must get him on the ship now."

"You're absolutely right."

Cullen smiled. "I knew you'd see reason and accept what must be done."

"I do see reason." She grinned. "That was why I married you. It was a reasonable solution to my problem, though I didn't count on falling in love with you."

"I'm glad you did and I'm glad my son will have a strong loving mother to protect him."

She didn't like the sound of that. He was all but telling her that Alexander would be hers to look after and that he trusted her to keep him safe. That would explain the true reason he brought her along. If anything happened to Cullen, he'd know that Alexander was much loved and fiercely protected.

He loved Alaina and he always would, she thought.

There was no room in his broken heart for her, which helped her know what she now had to do.

Sara kissed her husband's cheek. "I love you and I thank you for letting me sample what it was like to have my own family. I will always remember our time together fondly and lovingly."

She stepped away from him.

"Sara!" he shouted.

"Take care of Alexander and have a good life," she said, and rushed from behind the building, away from him, her heart breaking, though she refused to shed a tear of regret. This choice was hers, as it had been her choice to wed Cullen and to love him. She did this not only for them, but for herself, for love.

She ran screaming to a soldier, who grabbed firm hold of her. "I know where you will find Cullen Longton, the man you seek," she said to him. "I am his wife. Hurry, hurry, you must follow me or he will get away. He has many men with him." She tugged at him to follow.

The soldier called out to the others as Sara continued to urge him to follow her.

"How do I know you speak the truth?" the one who had taken hold of her asked as the other soldiers gathered around.

"You should be asking what the earl will do if I speak the truth and you let Cullen Longton escape."

The soldiers grumbled among themselves as more of them gathered around her.

"I tell you, you must hurry," she urged. "He'll get away."

The lead soldier's sneer displayed rotted teeth, and his fetid breath washed over her face when he warned, "You be wrong and the earl will make you pay."

"Then I must be telling you the truth or why else would I do this, you fool?"

The soldier took umbrage and smacked her in the head before shoving her in front of him. "Show me where he is!"

Sara stumbled, her knees near touching the ground before she righted herself and hurried along, leading the soldiers farther from the ship. In that brief instant, with her head down and her hands stretched out for balance so as not to fall, she had seen Cullen, Alexander tucked safely in his arms, racing up the gangplank and disappearing into the bowels of the ship.

The cabin door slammed shut and locked behind Cullen, and with a whimpering Alexander in his arms, he turned and stood, shocked.

"Burke? Storm? I thought you both in America by now."

Storm reached out for the babe. "Let me see your son."

He handed the boy to his pint-sized sister-in-law, who was dressed in outlaw garments that made her appear more a young lad than a beautiful young woman. Then he looked to his half brother Burke for an explanation.

"We made it to France," Burke explained, "where Storm insisted we disembark, nab another ship of mine, and sail back here to wait for you in case you needed help."

Cullen held his hand out to a man he barely knew, though resembled him, his height not reaching his own. But Burke was his equal in strength and courage, and very relieved to see him again.

"I do need your help," Cullen told him. "My wife surrendered herself to Balford so my son and I could make it safely to the ship."

"Wife?" Burke and Storm cried out in unison.

"Da!" Alexander cried, holding his arms out to his father.

Cullen took him and wasn't surprised to see his little head turning and his wide teary eyes searching the room. "He looks for Sara. They play with his animals and she feeds him sweet cakes and—" He choked on the memories, unable to continue. "We'll get her back, son. I promise we'll get her back."

"You need food and drink," Storm said. "Then you can tell us how you came by a wife and how we can help you rescue her."

Cullen smiled with relief. "It is good to have family to help me."

"And it's good that I have a chance to pay back Balford for all the pain and suffering he's inflicted on the innocent," Storm said with a pat to the sword handle that hung at her waist.

"Did you hear the word help?" Burke asked his wife. "He's not expecting you to do his fighting for him."

"One woman taking matters into her own hands is enough. I don't need another," Cullen said.

Burke grinned. "Your wife is like my own, stubborn,

wanting her own way, not listening to reason? Finally, someone to commiserate with."

"I like her already," Storm said, smiling, and playfully poked her husband in the ribs. "Tell us about her."

"No time, I must go after her," Cullen said.

"Not without food, rest, and a plan," Burke cautioned.

Cullen almost argued, but knew his brother was right. Rushing out to help her with no plan of action would only place them both in danger. Not to mention that he was exhausted from the strenuous journey, and hungry as well, he and Sara not having eaten much in the last day.

"We'll work a plan out together," Burke said, "hire what help we need, and see your wife safe on the ship so we can all sail to America together this time."

The table was soon spread with food, and while Alexander sat on his father's lap happily eating, Cullen explained all that had happened to him since they had last seen him.

"I must rescue her and see her safe. She has done so much for me." Cullen ruffled his son's brown hair. "If it wasn't for her courage, my son would not be here now. She endangered herself to save him, and she does so again."

"You admire her," Burke said. "Do you love her?"

"It's apparent," Storm said, reaching for an oatcake. "His eyes beam bright and his face lights with joy when he speaks of her." She poked at her husband. "You do the same with me. For half brothers, you are much alike."

"Storm is right. I love Sara, but I've yet to tell her."

"Feeling guilty about Alaina?" Storm asked.

Cullen smiled. "You are blunt like my Sara."

"I know how you feel for I felt the guilt myself when I fell in love with your brother. I felt as if I was betraying my deceased husband, Daniel. It took a while to understand that I would always love Daniel, but that I also was allowed to love again, that my new love in no way diminished my love for Daniel."

"It is good to hear another speak of what I'm feeling. It took me by surprise. I never expected to love again, especially so soon."

"We have no control over love," Burke said. "And personally, I think that's for the best. I never expected to fall in love with a pint-sized Scottish outlaw, and damned if I'm not glad I did."

"I must get Sara back and I must . . . " He hugged his son. " . . . make sure the earl never hurts anyone again."

"The earl wants you, and Sara will be the bait," Storm said. "He will want to make sure you can get to her easily, though his guards will be in wait."

"I must go after her as soon as possible or Sara will suffer his wrath," Cullen said, knowing the earl all too well from his time in the earl's dungeon. "The man likes to inflict pain, and knowing my Sara, she will not keep her mouth shut, which leaves us little time."

Burke began to lay out a plan. "We need to find out where she was taken," he said, "then scout the area, hire men to help—"

"That will take too long," Cullen interrupted.

"I'll have it all done when you wake," Burke insisted. "By morning we'll be ready to go and rescue your wife, and we'll be sailing to America by nightfall."

"It's good to have a brother like you," Cullen said. "I wish I could help you with the plan, but it wouldn't be wise to take a chance and be seen before we attempt the rescue."

"Soldiers will return to the harbor soon enough. I will show you where to hide if they should decide to board ship again, though I doubt they will. They searched extensively when we first arrived and found nothing, not even Storm and me."

"How will you roam the harbor safely?" Cullen asked.

"As one of my sailors. The soldiers can't remember every one of them, and as long as I act the part, there'll be no reason for them to bother me. We'll also have to come up with a way to get you and Storm off the ship and then all of us back on. Busy yourself with that if you want but make certain to get rest. You'll need it."

"What of Alexander when we're gone?"

"The captain will see to his care and safety," Burke said. "And worry not, he'll not let any harm befall him."

Burke took off to set their plan in motion, while Storm kept Alexander busy playing with his wooden animals and whatever else she could find to occupy him.

Cullen roamed the innards of the ship, needing time alone. He couldn't get the image of Sara's good-bye out of his mind. She all but told him she was doing this for him and Alexander so they would be safe. She sacrificed herself for them, and all because she loved them.

What hurt him the most was that he'd never told her how much he loved her, and he wanted her to know, needed her to know, for then she wouldn't doubt that he would come and rescue her.

Now, at this moment, she could be thinking her fate sealed, he thought, that no one would come for her. She'd be alone, and perhaps think to face death alone.

The thought chilled and infuriated him, and he punched an overhead beam then slouched down on an overturned barrel. It killed him to sit there and do nothing, and yet he knew it was the best course of action for the moment.

He raised his head with a frustrated growl and threw his shoulders back and his chest out. "Hear me, Sara, I love you. Know it in your heart and soul. Know that I love you and I'm coming for you."

Chapter 35

Sara tasted the blood in her mouth. Her lip had been split open again, her arms and ribs were bruised, and the rest of her was scuffed up, the soldiers having dragged and tormented her with kicks and punches when they discovered that she had duped them.

But while the blood left a bitter taste in her mouth, her victory hadn't. She had succeeded in drawing the soldiers' attentions and securing her husband and son's safety. It had all been worth it, and while she would like to believe Cullen would rescue her, she knew better.

She was on her own, and if she gave it careful consideration, she might just find a way out of her predicament. Where she would go afterward was another matter, since returning home and possibly placing her family in danger was not an option.

Of course, Cullen ached for revenge against Balford, but he had his son to consider. She knew they were both safely aboard his brother's ship and could set sail for America without a problem. Why take the chance of leaving his son fatherless?

The metal door of her cramped cell squeaked open and torchlight startled her eyes, now too familiar with the dark. She squinted against the glare until her eyes finally adjusted to the bright light. She didn't move, her chains and metal cuffs tight and rubbing her skin raw with the slightest of movements.

The soldiers roughly disengaged her chains from the wall. They didn't wait for her to stand but dragged her out of the cell along the dirt floor. Try as she might she couldn't grab hold of the chains to ease her skin from being rubbed raw by the metal cuffs. Her body twisted about like a fish too long out of water as the soldiers yanked her along, gleeful in their torment.

She shut her eyes and mouth against the dust that was stirred up but could not shield her body from being battered as the soldiers moved her quickly through the narrow halls. She winced, though held her tongue as she was dragged up stone stairs, her ribs, hips, and legs taking a beating.

Once outside the dungeon, the warm breath of spring burst across her face, and she realized that morning had claimed the land. Her dark cell had kept her oblivious of time, and she hadn't known whether it were night or day. She had yet to meet with the Earl of Balford, but had a feeling that was about to change.

She had heard the soldiers whispering that the earl was due back the next day following her capture. They were excited and pleased with their prize and were certain the earl would reward them.

While they dragged her to the manor house, onlookers gawked at her, no doubt reminded of the consequences of the earl's wrath. She ignored the fearful and sympathetic stares and thought only of Cullen and Alexander.

They were safe, and she hoped they would remain so. She would not betray them no matter what tortures the earl inflicted on her. He would only kill her in the end anyway, and what purpose would her death serve if she didn't protect those she loved?

She was pulled to her feet, forced up the steps and into a room in the manor house. She felt awkward amidst the fancy furnishings, so polished and proper, and she so grimy and bruised and in chains. But she stood tall, her head high, her chin thrust out and her pride intact.

A man fancy in dress, with a cunning glare, entered the room and waved a laced-trimmed handkerchief in front of his turned-up nose as he passed by her.

"I forget how offensive the dungeon can be to the senses," he said with distaste.

Sara shrugged. "It is what you make of it."

His brows arched, and she knew she'd surprised him. He expected her to cower and beg for mercy.

She'd spit in his face first. She was the wife of a true warrior, after all, and would not sully his name. She would stand with pride and honor against this evil man and fight to the end.

"I am surprised he chose you as a wife," the earl said. "My daughter was much more beautiful and much more a lady."

"He didn't choose me, I chose him, so you waste your time if you think he will come for me. Our marriage was nothing more than a bargain, which he fulfilled. He's now free to do as he chooses."

The earl sat down in a yellow silk-covered chair and crossed his legs. He fit the room, pretentious and extravagant, not real or solid, like a truly strong man. This man, she thought, allowed others to fight his battles and had powerful alliances to protect him. He was false in appearance and manner and could never be trusted as friend or foe.

"It doesn't matter," the earl said. "He will come for you."

Sara laughed. "You have a long wait if you believe that. I was nothing more than a thorn in his side, and he will not risk his life for me."

Her own words hurt to hear, but they were the truth. Cullen had no room in his heart for any woman but Alaina. She wished it were different, but it wasn't, and she couldn't change how he felt—or how she felt. She loved him, whether he loved her or not, and she would protect those she loved

It wasn't a matter of choice. It was a matter of the heart.

"Cullen is an honorable man, though a fool. He will come for his wife," the earl argued.

"You're the fool if you believe that."

A deep flush started at the earl's neck and crept up his face, and thinking that he might just burst into flames made her smile.

"I will enjoy having your tongue cut from your mouth, though not before I hear you beg for mercy."

"You'll have a long wait," she quipped, refusing to let him think his threats frightened her.

"Not really. If he doesn't see fit to come for you, he will come for me. A warrior can be counted on to seek revenge. It is a matter of honor, and Cullen is an honorable man."

"From what I know of Alaina, she was an honorable woman. Why then," she asked, "are you such a devious devil?"

Balford sprang forward in the chair. "You're nothing more than an ignorant peasant!"

Sara held her head high. "This ignorant peasant managed to foil your attempt to have your grandson killed."

The earl sneered. "And all those involved will pay dearly for it."

"All?" Sara laughed. "It was I and only I. How does it feel to be defeated by a single woman?"

He rushed out of the chair and backhanded her across the cheek, his heavy gold ring nicking the flesh near the corner of her eye. She stumbled but managed to remain on her feet, a trickle of blood dripping down her cheek.

"I have never been defeated!" the earl shouted in fury.

She challenged his claim. "Alaina defeated you. She loved freely and birthed the son of her lover, a Highland warrior."

"She was a whore who was defeated," the earl spat.

"Not so," Sara argued. "Her son bears proof of her victory."

The earl's guttural laugh shivered her skin cold.

"He will meet his mother in Hell along with his father."

"The only one to go to hell will be you," Sara said, near spitting her words in his face.

The earl grinned with pleasure. "I will enjoy seeing you whipped and beaten, and perhaps I will lay between your legs to show you the power it takes to be victorious."

Sara sneered. "I imagine your prowess is as puny as those skinny legs of yours. You did, after all, produce only one child, and who knows if Alaina was even your true daughter? Perhaps you weren't man enough for your wife and she found pleasure and satisfaction in another man's bed."

She purposely wanted to make him angry, cause him to lose his temper, and thus lose sound reasoning, which could possibly alter his plans and provide her with more time. She quickly braced for the anticipated blow.

His hand was drawn back in a flash, arcing high and wide, and Sara knew it would more than sting; it could possibly take her to her knees.

"Touch *my wife* and you die!"

Balford's hand froze in midair, and Sara wished she could rub her eyes, for she was surely seeing a mirage. Cullen stood a few feet behind the earl, his handsome face awash with anger, though his dark eyes softened when they rested on her, and for a moment, though it was brief, barely detectable, she thought or perhaps imagined that she had seen love there.

Had she seen it, or did she simply want to believe he had come to rescue her because he loved her? Or had he come not for her, but for revenge?

The earl turned and rushed away from Cullen's fast approach, stumbling to the side.

"I'm going to make you pay, Balford, for what you've done to my wife," Cullen said angrily, while gently wiping the blood from her cheek.

"You shouldn't have come," Sara said softly. "You and your son were free."

"There is no freedom without you, Sara. Haven't you realized by now how very much I love you? I haven't been able to stop loving you. Wanting to love you. Needing to love you. Loving you like I never thought possible."

"How touching," Balford mocked.

Sara heard nothing but her husband's profound declaration of love, and still she found it hard to believe. He loved her? Truly loved her? Was it possible? Could her dreams, her wishes, her prayers, have actually come true?

"You look doubtful," he said. "I guess I'll have to spend the rest of our lives convincing you how much I love you."

"That will be about a week," Balford said confidently, "since I intend to make the both of you suffer before I kill each one of you myself."

Tears slipped down Sara's cheeks.

"Don't cry, my love," Cullen cautioned. "I won't let him hurt you."

Sara shook her head, her tears continuing to fall softly. "I don't weep out of fear, I cry for joy. You love me. You truly love me." She laughed. "You don't think I'm going to let a vile man prevent us from sharing a life together, do you?"

Cullen laughed loud and strong. "That's *my Sara*, confident and courageous."

"And as much a fool as you," Balford spat.

"I'll just see to the vile man and then we'll be on our way," Cullen said with a gentle kiss to her cheek.

"Make certain he suffers," Sara said firmly. "He deserves to suffer for all he's done, especially for what he did to Alaina."

"You are both fools," Balford shouted. "You will be the ones who suffer, and as for my daughter? She deserved what she got for giving herself to a commoner, a simple man—"

"He is a warrior!" Sara shouted back. "Courage, integrity, loyalty, something you know nothing of!"

"Power and influence bring far more rewards than what you speak of," Balford said. "If my daughter had done her duty and obeyed me, she would not have died. Her death was of her own doing, sheer stupidity. As your deaths will be."

"And your death?" Sara asked calmly. "Will it not be out of your own doing?"

"My dear, you are in chains, and while Cullen may

have slipped past a guard or two, there are many more who will make certain that neither of you leave here."

"You said yourself that my husband is an honorable man. He tells me he will not let you hurt me, and I believe him."

"What makes you think he can do for you what he couldn't do for Alaina?"

Sara grinned. "He's already done it."

"Such foolish confidence," Balford said, shaking his head.

"It is good that you finally realize that instead of continuing with this folly," Sara said.

Balford glared at her. "I am eager and impatient to see that tongue of yours cut out of your mouth."

"Not even an hour with him, and he wants to rid you of your tongue? That's my Sara," Cullen said, grinning proudly.

"Enough!" Balford shouted.

"My exact sentiments to her at times," Cullen teased.

"I've had enough. Guards!" Balford yelled.

Cullen slipped his arm around her waist and she released her full weight against him. Exhaustion was fast claiming her, along with the burden of the heavy chains.

"You'll be free soon enough," he whispered, and kissed her cheek.

"Guards!" Balford bellowed again, and retreated several steps into the room.

"You overestimate your guards' abilities, or perhaps you underestimate mine. Your guards are presently occupied and will be for some time."

Sara smiled at the pint-sized woman who had entered the room and spoken. She wielded a sword and was garbed in men's garments. She had heard tales of the infamous outlaw Storm.

Balford sputtered and shook a fist and sputtered some more before finally spitting out one word: "You!"

Storm gave a pretentious bow. "That it is. You didn't think that I would slink away and not see you get your due, did you? And while I would so love to be the one to wreak retribution on you, I'll leave that to one who deserves the privilege more."

"I'll see you dead!" Balford screamed.

"That is not going to happen."

Sara wasn't surprised to see Cullen's brother Burke enter the room. Though Cullen was taller and wider, both were handsome men, and she could see the resemblance there between them.

"He really needs to die," Burke said when his glance rested on Sara.

"Cullen will see to it," she said proudly.

Burke nodded with a grin. "Good, you do love my brother. It's there in your eyes for all to see." He hugged Sara gently. "We will all make a fine family and live a good long life in America."

"Hear that, Balford?" Storm asked. "We'll all live, and you will die."

"You know, Cullen, I was thinking," Burke said.

"With the earl's death, your son will be sole inheritor of his grandfather's estate and holdings."

"Never," Balford warned. "Never will a bastard inherit my wealth."

Cullen grinned and drew his sword. "You won't be around to object."

Chapter 36

"**I** love you, husband," Sara said as Storm helped her from the room.

"And I love you, wife," Cullen said echoing her sentiments, his heart in pain for what she had suffered to see him and his son safe.

"We'll be waiting," Burke said, and was gone.

Cullen knew they remained close by, along with a score of hired men, if he should require assistance, but this was a chore he had chosen for himself. He did this for Alaina. But first he had something to tell the Earl of Balford.

"I am unarmed. I thought you an honorable man," Balford said.

Cullen grabbed a second sword from the sheath strapped to his back and rested the weapon against a chair, stepping away from it.

Balford went for it, and once it was in his grip, he laughed. "You truly are foolish. Don't you know I'm an expert with a sword?"

"I'll take my chances," Cullen said, keeping a distance until he delivered his news.

The earl had other plans, and charged Cullen before he could speak.

Cullen deflected his sword, though stunned by the strength of the earl's thrust.

The earl proved a worthy opponent, and it wasn't long before they were locked in a raging battle that left them both with minor wounds, sweating profusely.

The battle stimulated Balford, and Cullen realized the danger in that. The earl's strength grew with every thrust and slice and smashed piece of furniture, as the two of them wreaked carnage. He was in his glory, believing himself more powerful, therefore believing he could deliver the final blow and defeat Cullen.

Cullen, however, had a different plan, and began to position himself for the final blow.

"Did I tell you of a man I met who was rescued along with me from Weighton?" Cullen asked as he and Balford unlocked swords and pushed off each other.

"It is of no importance to me," Balford said with a lunge.

Cullen sidestepped his thrust. "It should be."

"Why is that?" Balford said, annoyed as he attacked with a strong blow.

They engaged swords until once again they pushed away from each other.

"He told me a story of a woman he fell in love with. A woman whose husband was harsh and vile and demanded she bear him children."

"A woman's duty," Balford snapped, and lunged again.

Their bodies slammed into each other, hitting the ground, rolling off, and then, on their feet again, they stood a distance from each other.

"Yes, but this husband was cruel and could not impregnate his wife."

"It isn't a man's fault; it's the woman's, and she should be punished for it," Balford spat.

"Like you punished Alaina's mother, beating her every night until she got pregnant?" Cullen asked, and lunged with fury at Balford. The sound of clashing steel echoed in the high-ceilinged room.

Balford suddenly withdrew and stood, his face bathed in sweat. "The punishment worked, she gave me a child."

Cullen laughed. "Not really. Her lover gave her a child."

Balford's face turned a fiery red. "What lies do you tell?"

"Alaina wasn't your daughter. Your wife had a lover."

"Lies!" Balford bellowed.

"They had plans to leave with their child, but you put Alaina's mother in an institution before they could make their escape."

"The woman was crazy."

"You wanted rid of her, and when a stranger began to question and delve into your wife's whereabouts, you had him imprisoned."

Balford stood still, his face flaming red, sweat pouring off him soaking his disheveled clothes.

"You remember the man," Cullen said. "Remember him well for he is Alaina's father and he waits on a ship to set sail for America, where he will watch his grandson grow, and when the time is right, he will help him claim your land and all your holdings."

"No bastard shall claim my land," Balford shouted, and charged at Cullen, enraged.

Cullen smiled, for at that moment, he knew he'd be victorious and have his revenge for Alaina and her mother and his son.

Cullen welcomed him head on, and with two swift clashes of swords, it was done. The earl kneeled on the floor grasping the handle of the sword Cullen had run through his stomach.

"This can't be," Balford said, blood dripping from the corner of his mouth.

"You've been defeated," Cullen said, ripping his sword out of the man. "Alaina is the victor here."

The Earl of Balford fell over, eyes wide in shock, his mouth hanging open, his life slipping away, with the knowledge that in the end his power and influence failed to serve him.

Cullen waited, wanting to be certain there wasn't a breath left in the evil man, and before leaving the room he gave one last look behind him. "It is done, Alaina. Our son is free."

"You're not getting out of this bed," Cullen ordered, shaking his finger at his wife in frustration.

"If it was because you intended to make love to me

all night, I wouldn't argue with you, but everyone is on deck watching the shores of our homeland fade away. I wish to do the same."

"You are bruised and battered, exhausted and—"

"Aching to see Scotland one last time," she insisted, throwing the blanket off her.

Cullen tucked the blanket back. "You need to rest."

"I have the whole sea voyage to rest," she said, exasperated.

Cullen sat on the bed, nudging her legs over to make room. "You've been beaten and dragged, kicked and punched—"

Sara placed a finger to his lips. "It's over. I'm safe."

Cullen pressed his cheek to hers and spoke of his fears, wanting her to hear, to know how he truly felt about her. "I was afraid I'd lose you. I was afraid you thought I wouldn't come for you. I was afraid I'd be too late. I was afraid you'd never hear me say I love you."

Sara rubbed her cheek against his. "I admit I didn't think you'd rescue me, and I never expected to hear you declare that you love me."

"I would rescue you from the depths of Hell." He kissed her cheek, wishing he could taste her lips, but her wound was too tender to disturb.

"Why? Do you think you'll have to?" she teased.

"Come to think of it," he grinned, "I doubt the devil would welcome you."

She poked his chest. "I'd set him straight."

"Like you did me," he said softly.

"You didn't need to be set straight. You're a good man."

"I was a blind man, blind of the heart, and you taught me how to see again, how to feel, how to love without guilt."

Sara grew teary-eyed and shook her head. "You taught yourself. I simply gave you the impetus to do so."

He felt the overwhelming need to hear himself claim his love for his beautiful wife. "I love you, Sara," he stated. "I love you so very much."

She beamed with joy. "I'll never grow tired of hearing you tell me so, and I'll never grow tired of saying it myself. I love you, Cullen, more than you will ever know. I love you."

He hugged her gently, not wanting to disturb her bruises and cause her pain.

"Now can we go on deck?" she whispered in his ear.

He pulled away from her. "You are persistent."

"Which is why we married in the first place," she reminded him with a grin. "You know I was relieved when you agreed to my proposal but surprised that you did."

He stood and reached for the dark green velvet robe at the foot of the bed. "Why?"

"I thought you'd protest more and I'd have to convince you."

"You convinced me well enough from the start," he said, holding the robe for her to slip into.

Sara hurried out of bed and into the robe, Cullen fastening the belt around her waist. She turned around in his arms. "I was determined."

Cullen laughed. "You're always determined, and glad I am of it. Thanks to you, I have a wonderful, beautiful wife and a loving mother for my son."

Sara hugged her husband tight, though winced loudly.

"Damn, you should be in bed," he scolded, stepping away from her. "One touch and you're in pain."

"First we go topside," she insisted, linking her arm with his.

He walked with her to the door.

"Then we return to the cabin and you make me forget all about my pain."

Cullen grinned and shook his head. "You'll not feel an ounce of pain by the time I'm through with you."

"Promise?" she whispered

He nuzzled her ear and whispered, "I promise."

"Then let's hurry," she said with a tug. "I just realized there's something I cherish much more than bidding Scotland farewell."

Next month, don't miss these exciting new love stories only from Avon Books

Bewitching the Highlander by Lois Greiman

An Avon Romantic Treasure

When Highlander Keelan awakens after a century of magical slumber, his only goal is to recover the Treasure that caused his family's downfall. But Charity is also seeking treasure and when they cross paths, sparks are sure to fly.

The Forever Summer by Suzanne Macpherson

An Avon Contemporary Romance

Lila Abbott is used to the unexpected, but she couldn't have predicted that a woman would drop dead in the supermarket aisle . . . or that her ghost would decide to stick around! Now she has to soothe a cranky spirit, while trying to deny her attraction to said ghost's very sexy—and very alive—ex-husband.

What Isabella Desires by Anne Mallory

An Avon Romance

Marcus, Lord Roth, lives a daring life and knows that love has no place in his future. But when Isabella Willoughby throws herself in the path of danger, Marcus will do anything to protect her life . . . and his heart.

Tempted at Every Turn by Robyn DeHart

An Avon Romance

Willow Mabson is the height of propriety, but all her rules are thrown out when she becomes involved in a murder investigation. Determined to assist Inspector James Sterling, Willow didn't count on this impossible attraction. But how can she develop tender feelings for a man who's doing his best to throw her parents in jail?